Last Night

ON

Union Station

EarthCent Ambassador Series:

Date Night on Union Station

Alien Night on Union Station

High Priest on Union Station

Spy Night on Union Station

Carnival on Union Station

Wanderers on Union Station

Vacation on Union Station

Guest Night on Union Station

Word Night on Union Station

Party Night on Union Station

Review Night on Union Station

Family Night on Union Station

Book Night on Union Station

LARP Night on Union Station

Book Sixteen of EarthCent Ambassador

Last Night on Union Station

Foner Books

ISBN 978-1-948691-18-5

Copyright 2019 by E. M. Foner

Northampton, Massachusetts

One

"In conclusion, it is the view of Union Station Embassy that by inviting alien observers to our upcoming Conference of Sovereign Human Communities convention, we will not only put to rest any lingering fears on the part of the advanced species about CoSHC's mission, but will also increase the profile of and participation in this year's associated trade fair, making it the biggest business event on humanity's calendar."

"Which calendar are you referring to?" the Stryx librarian asked the ambassador.

"It's an expression, Libby," Kelly replied. "I meant to express that it's really important for us."

"Would you like me to dub that in?"

"No need, thank you. Just go ahead and send the report." Kelly glanced down at the replacement for her alien knock-off of a Swiss wristwatch. "Funny to think that it's almost midnight at the president's office on Earth. Life will be much simpler when we implement Universal Human Time on the stations, but I don't look forward to losing seven hours in one go. Couldn't we set the clock back instead of forward so everybody can sleep in?"

"We've been through this already, Ambassador. You would end up a full day behind the other locations adopting Universal Human Time. Moving your clock forward is the only logical solution."

"Since when do humans have to be logical?"

1

"I can't do anything about the fact that you're going to lose seven hours, but if you'd like, I could start cheating the time forward a few minutes a day on the implants of our residents who live by your clock. By the date the change officially takes place, you'd be all caught up."

"That would be great, but we're up to nearly a half million humans on Union Station at last count. If we can't get them all to go along with the gradual change, I'll have to keep coming into the office on their schedules and I'll end up stuck here fifteen hours a day."

"I've done this in the past for other species who needed to adjust their clocks and the key to success is to synchronize entertainment offerings. When their favorite show is on the line, most sentients adapt in a hurry."

"But how will that affect Aisha's broadcasts?" Kelly asked. "I don't want to be responsible for millions of little sentients around the galaxy missing her program."

"The galactic viewership for 'Let's Make Friends' is in the hundreds of billions, and none of the alien children live on your clock, much less a twenty-four-hour day. While the broadcasts do go out live over our Stryxnet, the vast majority of the audience watches it with a planned delay or on-demand."

"You're serious about this? All I have to do is say 'Yes' and you'll start moving the time forward? What about all of the people who use your Stryxnet communication services for business conferences or to call family?"

"When you need to contact another ambassador or the president's office, how do you figure out what time it is where they are?"

"I ask you," Kelly admitted. "Do you mean I'm not the only one?"

"EarthCent Intelligence keeps a row of clocks on the wall that display the times in large human communities and key alien capitals all over the galaxy, but it's strictly for the aesthetic. Everybody who uses our real-time communications services makes sure to ask what time it is where they're calling first. The fees are too high to make mistakes."

"I guess I'm spoiled by being a diplomat. Is Donna still here? I'd like to get her opinion, and Daniel's too."

"As it happens, your embassy manager is conferring with the associate ambassador about vendor invitations for the CoSHC trade show as we speak. I'll let them know you want to talk as soon as she finishes explaining to him how the load-in scheduling works at the Empire Convention Center."

"Dorothy is going to run the booth for SBJ Fashions at the trade show. She's displayed much more patience about returning to work after delivering the baby than I ever expected. I thought she'd rush back, but little Margie just turned six months old."

"Dorothy's alien friends would have been scandalized if she tried to return to work sooner," Libby said. "Frunge and Vergallian mothers take a minimum leave of several years after having a baby, but your daughter talked them into prorating based on your abbreviated lifespans."

"Abbreviated. That's a nice way of putting it. Did you know that Jeeves actually gave Dorothy a raise went she went out on maternity leave?"

"I handle all of the back office work for SBJ Fashions. And it wasn't so much a raise as an incentive to stay home with the baby."

"Really? I didn't know Jeeves was so sensitive to family issues."

"I suspect you're not aware of how much company money your daughter spends on developing new products while she's working. The last six months have been more profitable for SBJ Fashions than all of the prior reporting periods combined."

"That's not a fair comparison. Dorothy told me that the markup on Baa's Bags for role players is enormous, and it's been the fastest growing part of the business the last year."

"Magic sells," Libby acknowledged.

"So, is there any chance you could find Margie with your security imaging while I'm waiting?"

A hologram of the baby asleep in a bassinet appeared floating over the display desk. The ambassador watched her granddaughter's regular breathing before letting out a long sigh of her own.

"Daniel and Donna are finished," Libby announced. "Will you meet them in here or in the conference room?"

"The conference room, of course." Kelly removed her purse from the desk and reluctantly turned away from the hologram that she didn't have the heart to wave out of existence. On exiting her office, she glanced toward the reception desk to see if Donna was still there, but the embassy manager had already entered the conference room, where the ambassador found her waiting with Daniel.

"Was there a problem with your weekly report?" Donna inquired.

"No, more of an opportunity. I was chatting with Libby about Universal Human Time and she offered to start creeping all of the clocks and schedules she controls forward so we don't lose seven hours all at once. Since it will affect all of the humans on the station, I wanted to get your input first."

"Makes sense to me," Daniel said. "Do you realize that the only places on Earth that share the same time as us are a couple of uninhabited islands in the middle of the Pacific?"

"Are you sure?" Kelly asked, looking up at the beach-ball sized lacquer-on-copper globe suspended over the conference table.

"I was curious myself and I checked with Libby," Donna confirmed, standing up and pointing at some tiny dots surrounded by blue on the globe's surface. "She said that Dring exaggerated the size of the islands a little when he made the globe because they wouldn't have been visible otherwise."

"I miss Dring. He said he'd be back soon, but he left right after Dorothy had the baby, so it's been almost six months."

"Maybe he lost track of the time. The Makers are immortal, and I imagine their meetings can drag on for quite a while."

"And he has plenty to report to his brothers," Daniel pointed out. "Joe said that it's Dring's first real trip off of Union Station since revealing himself to the Stryx."

"So both of you are sure about asking Libby to start creeping our clocks forward?" Kelly asked.

"The only problem I see is for visitors to my convention, and I'll just make an announcement at the opening session to remind people using dumb watches to move their own time forward," Daniel said. "I'm sure that the Stryx can finagle the clock on anything that connects to the station networks."

"Is that right, Libby?"

"It doesn't even require intervention on my part," the station librarian replied. "All of the tabs and other wireless devices used by your people automatically update their time from the network because it's considered a trusted source."

"And we're going to lie to them."

"It's just an arbitrary number," Donna pointed out. "That's why being so far out of sync with Earth only matters to diplomats and businessmen who can afford real-time conferencing. And it's only the human populations on Stryx stations and a few orbitals that are making the switch to Universal Human Time."

"That's right," Daniel added. "The majority of delegates coming to the convention live on open worlds with suns, and all of them adopt the local alien clocks."

"Alright, Libby," the ambassador said. "Go ahead and start. How much time a day are we going to lose?"

"Just over seven minutes, you won't even notice," the Stryx librarian assured her. "I'll tell Jeeves to come in and change the rotation speed on Dring's globe to keep it from going out of sync."

"Did you finish filling out our application for the Open University's cooperative education program, Donna?"

"I sent it in this afternoon," the embassy manager replied.

"This wouldn't have anything to do with your son changing majors, would it?" Daniel asked the ambassador while struggling to maintain a straight face. "I'd hate to have to report you for nepotism."

"That's the great thing about it," Kelly said. "Because the Open University selects the co-op students to fill available positions, there's no ethical dilemma."

"If you need me to step in and interview the candidates, just say the word. I'm looking forward to having Samuel help me out with CoSHC."

"There is no interview process," Donna informed them. "The school administration, meaning you-know-who, assigns the students to their jobs. Vivian signed up for the program at the same time as Samuel. She's hoping to work for her father at EarthCent Intelligence, but it's not her decision. She could just as easily end up here."

"How long has EarthCent Intelligence been offering co-op jobs?" Kelly asked.

"They just started after I told them about it," Donna said with a grin. "Vivian originally planned to take an internship there, but the cooperative program pays the students."

"The Open University funds it?"

"They handle the payroll, but we have to reimburse them. Didn't you read the application?"

"I have you for that," the ambassador replied. "Before I forget, do either of you want a credenza?"

"Is that what the Frunge currency is called?" Daniel asked.

"No, it's a sideboard." Kelly noted her associate ambassador's lack of comprehension and added, "A piece of furniture, for your dining room."

"You'd have to ask my wife. Shaina gets mad if I bring anything like that home without checking with her first."

"Stanley and I have too much of our own junk to start taking yours," Donna said bluntly. "We're thinking of downsizing ourselves."

"Tell Shaina it's the one that Mike hid in the time that he and Fenna played hide and seek at our place and we had to have the dogs sniff them out," Kelly said to Daniel. "Joe traded somebody for it before we got married, but we just don't have the room anymore."

"Because you keep adding bookshelves," Daniel observed. "If Shaina doesn't want it, should I ask around if anybody else I know does?"

"Would you? We have lots of stuff we're trying to get rid of, I mean, place in a good home."

"You should have a tag sale," Donna suggested. "You have plenty of room."

"That's not a bad idea," Kelly mused. "I haven't seen a tag sale since I was a little girl, but our book sale to raise money for Flower a few years ago was a great success."

"Hey, could Stanley and I bring some of our stuff?"

"I'm trying to get rid of junk, not add to it."

"But you need to achieve critical mass to get people interested," Donna argued. "It's not like mobs of shoppers are going to show up at Mac's Bones because you list a credenza and an old sink for sale on one of the station boards."

"Let me talk to Joe first," the ambassador said. "He's the one who will be stuck getting rid of everything if it doesn't sell."

"Don't be surprised if it adds fuel to the rumor," Daniel said.

"What rumor?" both women asked simultaneously.

"You know, the one about Gryph selling Union Station."

"What? That's the dumbest thing I've ever heard," Kelly said. "The Stryx haven't sold a station since they began building them tens of millions of years ago. Why would they start now?"

"I've heard it from more than one person," the associate ambassador said. "I know it sounds unlikely, but—"

"Union Station is Gryph's home. I don't know if you can even separate the two."

"Libby?" Donna asked. "Is your parent really thinking about selling Union Station?"

"Certainly not," the station librarian replied.

"Then where is the rumor coming from?"

"That's competitive information."

"You realize by saying that, you're only giving the rumor mongers something to talk about," Kelly said. "People will think that Gryph is shopping it around quietly to prevent a panic that could drive down the price."

"That's ridiculous," Libby said. "Don't you trust me?"

"We trust you, but we aren't the ones spreading the rumors. You know that humans aren't the only species that believes where there's smoke there's fire."

"I just don't want this interfering with my convention," Daniel said. "It won't have any impact on attendance from CoSHC members, but some of the alien businessmen I've invited to the trade show implied that they were taking a wait-and-see approach with everything on Union Station in case the ownership changes hands."

"See what I mean about aliens and rumors, Libby?" the ambassador said. "They're worse than we are."

"I heard a rumor that you'll be giving the keynote address," Donna said to her friend. "Are you going to write a speech or wing it as usual?"

"I believe the word you're looking for is 'extemporize' and I already have a rough draft," Kelly fibbed.

The conference room door opening directly onto the corridor slid open of its own accord and Jeeves came rolling through on his rarely used treads.

"Am I interrupting anything important?" he asked.

"Trick question," Kelly warned Daniel and Donna. "He's looking for an opening to debate whether anything humans do can possibly be important."

"Actually, I'm here to adjust Earth's rotational speed." The young Stryx floated up from the floor and approached Dring's globe. Then he extended his pincer to grip the motorized ceiling mount, flashed a few lights on his metallic casing, and declared, "All set."

"You just gave me the chills," Donna said. "Blythe loaned me one of her translated Dollnick romance novels in which the villain did some sort of high-tech voodoo with whole planets using globes he'd made to represent them. He could flick a drop of water at one of them and there would be a terrible flood, or hold a candle below it and cause a giant inferno."

"What happened in the end?" Daniel asked.

"The hero killed the villain and got the girl. You wouldn't like it. The Dollnick authors write really steamy sex scenes."

"I heard mention that you're planning a tag sale," Jeeves said. "I might have a few things that I'd be willing to bring by on consignment."

"We were just talking about how rumors get started," Kelly told him. "Don't you think it would look funny if people knew that you were dumping possessions like you were preparing to move?"

"Are you trying to get rid of me?"

"I'm talking about the rumor that Gryph is selling Union Station."

"That's the dumbest thing I've heard today, and given the amount of eavesdropping I do, that's saying something."

"I have to get going, Kelly," Donna said, rising from her chair. "We're having the girls and their husbands over for dinner, adults only for a change."

"That reminds me, it's been forever since we had a get-together at Mac's Bones," Kelly said. "Why don't we plan one for as soon as the conference is over. I'll have Joe fire up the bar-b-que and everybody can dress casual."

"How casual?" Daniel asked suspiciously. "Work-clothes-casual to help you set up for a tag sale?"

"All right already. You guys can bring the stuff you want to get rid of too."

"I'll ask Shaina," the associate ambassador gave his stock answer. "The kids have grown out of a lot of their toys and it's surprisingly hard to find somebody who wants them. Maybe adding a price tag will do the trick."

"See you both on Monday," Kelly called after her co-workers as they left the conference room. Then she turned to Jeeves, who showed no signs of moving. "Is there something you needed to talk about?"

"I'll get right to the point. Dorothy is officially returning to work next week to start preparing for the CoSHC convention and I want to know if you think she's ready to leave the baby at home."

"You want me to get into the middle of an argument between you and my daughter? I don't think so."

"Great. See you later."

"Hold on a second," Kelly said, surprising herself with the speed at which she got between Jeeves and the door. "Did you just record our conversation to play to Dorothy?"

"I'm not aware of any law against it."

"And will you present it to her unaltered, or are you going to edit what I said."

"I would never change your words," Jeeves hedged. "Some editing for brevity, perhaps."

"Erase it," Kelly demanded. "I know what you're up to and you're wasting your time in any case. Dorothy isn't planning on leaving the baby at home. They're portable, you know, and she has the full line of transportation accessories."

"Is that what they're calling perambulators these days?"

"Just swear to me that you aren't going to edit our conversation so that Dorothy hears you asking if she's ready to go back to work and me saying, 'I don't think so.' Libby, make him promise."

"You're requesting my help in an argument between you and my offspring?" the station librarian asked. "Very well. Jeeves, don't edit the ambassador's words in a misguided attempt to influence Dorothy against coming back to work and spending your money."

"You haven't heard the last of me," Jeeves uttered in a villainous voice and floated out of the conference room.

Two

"Next, please," the Dollnick clerk behind the counter called out.

"Hi. I'm Samuel McAllister and—"

"I remember you," the four-armed alien interrupted the ambassador's son. "You were in here last year changing your major from space engineering to diplomacy. Let me guess," the Dolly continued, whistling louder as he went to draw the attention of his fellow clerks. "You've decided you want to drop out of the cooperative education program before you even begin."

"What did I ever do to you?" Samuel demanded. "No, don't even tell me. How about you do your job without the commentary and give me my co-op assignment."

"Can't handle a little joke and he thinks he has the right stuff to be a diplomat," the Dolly commented loudly. Then he activated a holographic controller and with a few quick gestures, brought up Samuel's file. "Report to the Vergallian embassy after the Queen's Day holiday. Next, please."

"Wait," Samuel said, trying to make sense of the hologram from the wrong side but getting nowhere with the backward Dollnick characters. "There must be some sort of mistake."

"A mistake?" the clerk whistled in disbelief. All conversations in the Open University's administrative office came to an abrupt halt and every head pivoted to see who had blasphemed. The Dollnick did some manipulation with his hands to rotate the hologram one-hundred and eighty degrees, and at the same time, the alien text morphed into English. "I'm prevented by the school's privacy laws from defending myself by reading out your record, but I'm sure a future diplomat such as yourself will be happy to correct that deficiency and acknowledge that the mistake is yours."

"Samuel McAllister, currently enrolled in Diplomatic Studies," the ambassador's son read out loud. "Report to the Vergallian embassy after Queen's Day holiday." He looked up in disbelief. "But I can't work for the Vergallians. My mother is the EarthCent ambassador. I have a conflict of interest."

The Dollnick exploded in a volley of untranslatable whistling and the other clerks joined in the laughter according to the forms of their own species. Even the students waiting in line couldn't help chuckling at Samuel's discomfort. The ambassador's son realized that arguing with the clerk would accomplish nothing and decided that the only diplomatic option was to beat a hasty retreat. Out in the corridor, he considered contacting the station librarian over his implant, but decided to wait until he had a chance to talk with his family and friends. He almost ran into a Horten student at the entrance to the cafeteria and mumbled an apology.

"Samuel," the Horten girl said. "What's wrong?"

"Marilla? I'm sorry, I didn't recognize you. You're, uh…"

"My skin is bright blue," she said for him, not in the least bit embarrassed. "I know it's unusual, but it's no big deal. I'll explain while we're eating."

The two students took trays and entered the fast-moving cafeteria line. Samuel passed by the pre-wrapped Vergallian vegan salads that most of the humanoid species could digest, if not enjoy, and stopped in front of the human-safe selection.

"Pssst," a Drazen working behind the counter whispered, hiding his mouth with his hand as he spoke. "I've got Earth wedges today."

"How many?" Samuel asked.

"Four left. It's two creds for one wedge or three creds for a pair."

"I'll take two." The ambassador's son handed over the coins, received the slices, and artfully concealed them on his tray with a napkin.

"Any meat on those?" Marilla asked the Drazen.

"Naw, but there's lots of other stuff. My connection said that they're Mediterranean, whatever that means."

"I'll take the other two," the Horten girl said. Samuel waited for her to be served, and the friends continued down the counter to pick up coffees and dessert. They paid at the register and began looking for seats in the packed cafeteria.

"Hey, Blue Girl," a loud voice called. "Over here."

Enough of the students turned in the direction of the disturbance to make locating the voice easy, and Samuel spotted the Drazen student who ran the dojo waving his tentacle in the air just to make sure they saw him.

"I suppose you want to sit there," Marilla said, affecting a long-suffering tone.

"It looks like he saved us the last two empty seats in the place," Samuel replied, heading towards the back corner of the cafeteria. "Besides, Vivian will kill me if I don't sit with her."

"Where is your girlfriend?"

"Across from Jorb. She must have ducked out of sight when he yelled."

"Hey, guys," Vivian greeted the newcomers. "You got the pizza too? We could reassemble the whole pie—at least, we could have before Jorb inhaled his slices."

"They make a great appetizer," the Drazen said. "If the cafeteria put Earth wedges on the menu, they'd be a hot seller."

"What I don't get is that everybody is in on it," Samuel said. "The workers who sell outside food for cash have to be paying off the cashiers to look the other way."

"And the Open University no doubt figures it all into the compensation package for cafeteria help. The only way the school loses out is if students bring their own food to the cafeteria."

"I thought that was banned," Vivian said.

"You can bring homemade food," Marilla told her. "The ban only applies to take-out."

"Meaning we can't save money by bringing in a whole pizza and splitting it up between us," Samuel concluded. "So, why are you blue?" he asked the Horten.

"Mornich asked me," the girl said, and her skin tone grew even brighter.

"You're engaged?"

Marilla's skin briefly turned purple before fading into pink.

"Nice going, Sam," the Drazen commented. "You triggered her blush response."

The ambassador's son found himself apologizing to the Horten for the second time in five minutes. "I'm sorry if I embarrassed you. I seem to be having a bad diplomacy day."

"It's all good," Marilla told him. "I should thank you. Our skin color gets stuck sometimes with a strong emotion and I've been waiting for something to get the pigments moving again. And no, Mornich and I aren't engaged. He asked me to make a doily for his grandmother."

"Huh?"

"We already have permission from our families to see each other on a provisional basis, so now we have to convince the elders that it's worth their time to start negotiations."

"By making a doily?" Vivian asked.

"It's basically a test of how my aesthetic sensibility and attention to detail matches with his family's," Marilla explained. "I tend to turn a little blue when I use that part of my brain and I guess I overloaded thinking about geometric patterns. Now I'm waiting for my grandparents to give me a task to assign to Mornich."

"Sounds complicated," Samuel said. "Couldn't you just take a written test?"

"Those come much later," Marilla told him.

"You seem pretty out of it yourself," Jorb said to the ambassador's son. "Did you fail a competency test or something?"

"I'm not taking any this semester," Samuel replied. "I signed up for the co-op program and there's been some kind of mistake."

"You too?" Vivian jumped in. "I'm not sure I'm allowed to say anything because, you know, but I didn't get the co-op job I expected."

"Your major is Intelligence and your parents run the Human spy service," Marilla said. "If you wanted to work there for a semester, why didn't you just ask?"

"The Open University gives credit for co-op jobs, plus you get paid. I was sure that they'd assign me to EarthCent Intelligence, especially after I talked my dad into filling out all the forms for them to accept co-op students. My mom warned us that it was too good to be true," she added ruefully.

"But what other intelligence agency would be willing to take on a Human intern?"

"Must be ours," Jorb said, rubbing the side of his nose. "I know someone who knows someone and we work pretty closely with Humans on the station."

"So did you get my slot in EarthCent Intelligence?" Vivian asked her boyfriend.

Samuel held up his index finger while hastily chewing and swallowing a mouthful of pizza. "I wish it made that much sense. I have to report to the Vergallian embassy right after Queen's Day."

"This is starting to sound like that musical chairs game my little sister played when she was on 'Let's Make Friends,'" Marilla said. "If both of you guys ended up sitting in chairs that belong to the other species, who is going to sit in yours?"

"My mom's going to kill me," Samuel groaned. "Our embassy only has three full-time employees and she signed up for the cooperative education program so I could work there. What if the school sends her an alien?"

"Actually, that reminds me of a favor I've been meaning to ask," the Drazen said. "I'm pretty much done taking courses and I've passed all of my competency exams so I'm going to have to get a job. Strangely enough, the main thing I've learned at the Open University is that I like teaching in a dojo. I've been thinking that if there isn't a martial arts studio on EarthCent's circuit ship yet, maybe you could put in a good word for me the next time it stops here?"

"You want to open a dojo on Flower? I'm pretty sure that they'll be happy to have you. You sat on the student committee so you know that the ship took on Open University alumni to start a theatre, a blacksmith shop, an academy—"

"A remedial choral school," Jorb interjected.

"This is about that girl, isn't it," Marilla said. "I should send her a warning."

"Don't do that!" the stricken lover begged. "I figure if I open the dojo on Flower and start getting students, she'll find out there's another Drazen onboard and come to see me. You know that nothing can come of it if I go to see her first."

"I'm aware of your bizarre courting rituals. I suppose I could consider keeping my mouth shut in return for—"

"Just name it," Jorb implored as the Horten girl let the silence stretch.

"Let me have my doily party in the dojo. It's traditional to celebrate and I don't have the money to rent a place."

"I'm not the only instructor there, you know. It's open around the clock. I reserved a four-hour block at the next minor convergence, but there's nothing else available for several cycles."

"Minor convergence?" Marilla asked. "Which species?"

"It's the equivalent of a Friday or Saturday night for Drazens, Hortens, Dollnicks, Vergallians, and Humans," Jorb rattled off. "That's why I snagged it for my competency completion party."

The two aliens glared at each other across the table.

"Why don't you share?" Samuel suggested. "I know you guys like everybody to think that you hate each other, but you share a lot of the same friends, and it's not like either of you are so popular that there won't be enough room for the friends you don't have in common."

"Did you really just say that?" Marilla asked. "I'm beginning to see why the school administration assigned you to the Vergallian embassy. You'll be a quick study at gunboat diplomacy."

"He's right, though," Vivian said, looking down at her student tab. "Even if you found somewhere else to have the party, it's the only calendar convergence for our species in the next two cycles. Either you host the party together or all of your mutual friends will have to run back and forth between two locations."

"What does admin charge for the dojo rental?" Marilla asked.

"With my discount, it's fifty creds an hour," Jorb said.

"Wow, that's still pretty steep," Samuel observed.

"Are you going to have dancing?" Vivian asked.

"I could get Mornich and his band if Jorb pays for the room," the Horten girl offered.

The Drazen grimaced, then shrugged and extended his hand across the table. Marilla looked at it, ostentatiously reached in her purse for a dress glove, pulled it on, and finally shook Jorb's hand.

"What are you scowling about?" Samuel asked Vivian, seeing that the corners of his girlfriend's mouth had turned down. Then he realized that she was glaring over his shoulder and turned to see the Vergallian ambassador's gorgeous daughter approaching.

"Hey, everybody," Aabina said. "No chairs?"

"I was just finished eating," Samuel said, grabbing his plate with the unfinished pizza and dessert and popping up. "Please sit."

20

"Don't be silly," the Vergallian girl said, favoring the ambassador's son with a dazzling smile that set Vivian's teeth on edge. "You should save your manners for work. I just wanted to see if you got the news."

"We heard," Vivian practically growled. "Sam is considering turning it down."

"He can't," Aabina protested. "My mom is counting on him to fill in for me."

"Where are you going to be?" Samuel asked.

"I did the cooperative education option too. I'm starting at the EarthCent embassy the Monday after orientation. The thing is, I asked the station librarian to change my implant to the Human clock so I can get accustomed to your schedule, but it seems like there's something wrong with the way you keep time."

"We're in the process of changing over to Universal Human Time on the tunnel network to match the time at the president's office back on Earth. The station librarian is creeping the clock forward for us so we don't have to jump seven hours all at once."

"Why would you want to be on the same time? I doubt there are two worlds in our entire empire that share the same clock."

"But we're not living on a world," Samuel pointed out. "The change only affects our people living on Stryx stations or space habitats where the time is arbitrary."

Two other students at the table rose from their places and headed off to class, allowing Aabina to take the seat next to Samuel.

"Aren't you eating?" Marilla asked the wasp-waisted Vergallian student.

"I had a piece of fruit for breakfast. I can eat after I'm married."

"When will that be?" Vivian asked eagerly.

"Another twenty or thirty years, I guess. I'm just a girl."

"Hey, everybody," a Dollnick student announced himself, settling his bulk onto the chair next to Vivian. He reached below the seat and hit the height adjustment, bringing it up so his knees weren't higher than his waist. "I was hoping to catch you all in one place. I finally got approved for the visiting alien student slot at the leading Sharf naval architecture firm and I'll be leaving Union Station at the end of the cycle."

"Congratulations," Samuel told Grude. "That's great. It's a fourteen-year commitment?"

"A hundred cycles," the Dollnick confirmed. "I'm hoping that I'll be able to get a job with one of the princely shipyards after I have some experience under my belt, but if not, I can stay with the Sharfs for the full internship of five-hundred cycles. Anyway, I want to invite you all to my going away party. I was thinking of renting a room at a restaurant."

"That's crazy expensive," Jorb told him. "You should split the dojo with me. I've got it reserved for the next minor convergence and a hundred creds will cover your half."

"Or you could pay for the catering," Marilla said. "I'm getting Mornich to play, but his guys are picky eaters."

"I'll split the room rent," Grude said. "Have you decided to start doing advanced work at the Open University, Marilla?"

"I haven't quite worked it out yet," the Horten admitted.

"I thought you took a minor in terraforming along with space engineering so you could go back to that colony ship that your extended family owns shares in and help prepare the new world," Samuel said.

"I guess I still might, but my parents want to stay on Union Station for at least another ten years while my little sister finishes school."

"But you said you need to start earning money and there aren't a lot of entry-level jobs in space engineering on the station," Grude said doubtfully. "I've been working part-time in our repair facility just to get my hands dirty."

"I've pretty much given up on getting technical work here," Marilla admitted. "I don't want to get stuck in a desk job, but my parents would kill me if I started working in retail or food service after passing my competency exams in Space Engineering. If I had any fashion sense, I'd ask Samuel's sister to hire me, but I can't even color-coordinate an outfit."

"That's because you keep changing colors," Aabina observed.

"Do you really want to fool around with repairing old spaceships?" Samuel asked the Horten girl. "I could talk to my dad and my brother. They've got a huge backlog of restoration work from when Gryph auctioned off the abandoned ships in long-term parking around the station."

"Are you serious?" Marilla asked, but then her face fell and her skin flashed bright red. "I can't."

"Why not?" Aabina asked her. "I'm a crown princess and I'm going to work for Humans."

"It's different for me," the Horten girl muttered, and then she blurted out, "What would Mornich's family think?"

"I don't know," Samuel said. "Why don't you ask them?"

"It's not that simple," Marilla insisted. "Mornich's father is our ambassador."

"What if the Open University assigned you there?" Vivian suggested. "It's not too late to sign up for the cooperative education program and Sam can get his dad to file the paperwork."

"But what if instead of sending Marilla the school assigns some alien who looks down on us?" Samuel asked.

"You know that Libby is the one who actually runs the Open University. She's not going to send your dad and Paul a bad match."

"Then why is my co-op job at the Vergallian embassy instead of EarthCent?"

"Let's see," Vivian said, holding up her left hand and starting to tick off fingers. "You speak fluent Vergallian. You started at the Open University with a dual major in Vergallian Studies. You would have won the Junior Vergallian Regional Ballroom Championship if you had a better partner—"

"That's not true," Samuel interrupted her. "You danced better than I did."

"Baloney."

"Vivian has a point," Aabina said. "I was probably assigned to your embassy because I speak fluent English and I got a perfect score on the new tests for EarthCent's diplomatic service."

"You took the EarthCent civil service exam?" Samuel asked. "Why?"

"Curiosity."

"I'm going to miss you guys," Grude said, getting up from the table. "I just wanted to check in before you left, but I'm going to grab lunch now. Good luck with the co-op thing, Marilla."

"I guess it's worth a try," the Horten girl allowed.

Three

Dorothy quietly placed the bassinet with her baby on the counter of her husband's chandlery shop, which was located just a stone's throw from the converted cargo container where they lived. Then she asked in her best piratical accent, "How much will you pay me for the little girl?"

"Already have one at home," Kevin replied, without looking up from his work. "I wish your dad and Paul could find somebody else for these assembly jobs. I'm happy to help when I have the free time, but these tiny screws are driving me nuts."

"You have to remember that they go in at an angle and turn the opposite way."

"It's not righty-tighty, lefty-loosey?"

"Nope. The Verlocks have the contract to manufacture Stryx controller interfaces for tunnel network members and they do everything backward."

"And on an angle." Her husband set aside the alien screwdriver with the L-shaped tip. "It's a good thing that the screws are softer than the parts they hold together or I would have wrecked it already."

"Your days of trying to assemble alien hardware without reading the instructions may be nearing an end," Dorothy informed him. "Dad asked me to fill out the Open University forms to get a co-op student for Mac's Bones."

25

"That would be great. If you're planning on procrastinating, tell me now and I'll do it for you."

"It so happens that I started the process on my tab while I was feeding the baby and I'm going to finish it right now." She fumbled around in the diaper bag hanging from the end of the bassinet and produced the tab that she had never returned to the Open University after her own student days.

"The sooner your dad and Paul hire somebody, the more time I'll have to help you with the SBJ Fashions booth," Kevin encouraged her.

"How are you going to help with that?" his wife asked, activating the tab and paging to the top of the co-op employer's form. "You think that fashion is wearing clean socks."

"It's a trade show, and I'd like to think I know something about trading. Besides, I can carry stuff."

"That is why I married you." Dorothy paused with a finger poised over her tab. "Do you know if my dad is incorporated or any of that?"

"I've never heard him mention it."

"And how many employees does he have?"

"What do you mean? It's just your dad. Paul owns all those ships that Aisha bought, but your father and he aren't even officially partners as far as I know."

"I'm not putting zero, it makes Mac's Bones sound pathetic."

"We're talking about the Open University, right? Run by the Stryx? They'll know if you're lying."

"I'm not going to lie. You're in the middle of putting together a ship's controller for my dad, and I'm filling out business forms for him, so that's two employees already."

"If you're going to count that way, Sam still helps out on weekends."

"So that's three, and Vivian hangs around with him so much that we may as well call it four," the girl continued, pushing the slider higher. "And I'm counting Paul, it would be stupid not to."

"If you're going to count Paul, then you can add his daughter. Fenna may only be ten, but she knows her Sharf socket colors backwards and forwards from assisting him."

"And Beowulf," Dorothy said, raising the total to seven. "He does all of their coolant system troubleshooting with his nose, plus he's in charge of security."

"Does Joe pay him?" Kevin asked.

"Food, lodging, and affection. Cayl hounds don't care about money."

From the other side of the counter, a loud thumping was heard as Beowulf's son, Alexander, began whacking his tail on the deck. Kevin and his wife exchanged a significant look, and then the girl pushed the slider up another notch.

"Who else can we add?" Dorothy asked.

"Who else is left?"

"Well, Aisha prepares food for the employee picnics, and my mom makes the coffee. Dring is away right now, but I've seen him do some fancy welding when my dad needed help. Hey, that's it!"

"What's it?"

"We're up to eleven employees."

"Does it matter?"

"Sure. That's double digits. Now let's see. Type of business?"

"Ship repair and campground rental."

"It's not a choice," Dorothy said, scrolling through the list of options. "I'm going with used spaceship dealership."

"Close enough."

"It popped up a submenu. How many ships do they have?"

"In here for work right now or all together?"

"It doesn't say."

"Well, if you included all of the ships that Aisha bought Paul at the auction, it's in the hundreds, but some of them are just derelicts."

"I'll put nine hundred and two," Dorothy said. "It sounds like we actually counted, and anybody who was going to cheat would have added a little more and put a thousand."

"If you say so."

"What qualifications are we looking for in a co-op student?"

"Manual dexterity and the ability to read alien instructions," Kevin suggested.

"Is there a lifting requirement?"

"You mean weight? I don't think so. Whenever your dad sees me and Paul struggling to pick something up together, he tells us to work smarter, not harder. There's plenty of equipment in Mac's Bones for moving heavy stuff."

"Work hours?"

"I don't know. Negotiable? Your dad starts early, but he takes off afternoons when he's brewing a new batch of beer, and Paul is as likely to be helping Jeeves with the latest Libbyland project as to be working on ships."

Dorothy advanced to the next page, and then moved back one before repeating the sequence to be sure. "I can't believe it," she said. "That was the whole thing."

"So you're done?"

"I just have to certify under the penalties of perjury that I'm Joe McAllister and that all of the information I've entered is accurate," she said, scrawling her father's signature with her forefinger. "All done."

"You signed it for him?"

"Sure. This way, if the co-op student complains that the numbers were exaggerated, my dad can say that he never signed the form."

"But he just did."

"No, I just did. Aren't you paying attention?"

"I'm not sure about your legal grounds here," Kevin said slowly.

"Don't worry about it," Dorothy told him. "I've lived on the station my whole life and ignorance of the law is always the best excuse, especially for humans."

Alexander let out a deep growl. Kevin looked towards the entrance to Mac's Bones and announced, "Baa alert."

"Oh, good. I invited her to consult about the booth."

"You're going to include her enchanted LARPing fashions at the trade show?"

"They're our fastest growing product line and people like the novelty," Dorothy explained. "Can you get Alexander to come around the back? She's allergic to Cayl hounds."

"I thought they were hypoallergenic," her husband said, moving around the front of the counter to corral the dog.

"Don't take him away on my account," Baa called when she saw what Kevin was doing. "The beetle quack was right for a change. My reaction to Cayl hounds was psychosomatic."

"I don't mind bringing him behind the counter. He's gotten a bit nippy with aliens since we had the baby."

"They're possessive about their packs. Do whatever makes you comfortable. I don't nip that easily."

"You don't trust very easily either," Dorothy said, seeing that the Terragram mage's eyes were on the bassinet. "Go ahead and count if it will make you feel better, but I promise you, I would be the first to notice."

Baa folded up the bottom of the blanket to reveal the baby's feet, and working by touch, gently counted Margie's toes. "Ten," she confirmed. "It's still her."

"Were you expecting somebody else?" Kevin inquired.

"She's too cute for her own good," the mage explained. "You really should have her wear the ugly baby mask that Affie gave you at the shower."

"It's what she gives everybody at baby showers," Dorothy said. "The upper caste Vergallians worry that their babies are so beautiful they'll be stolen by the gods or something like that."

"An ignorant superstition," Baa scoffed. "I would never steal a baby. The real threat is one of the fay replacing Margie with a changeling."

"Fairies? Don't you think that you're beginning to take the fantasy role-playing a little too seriously? I mean, I know that it's different for you because you can actually do magic stuff, but still, the fay only exist in LARPs."

"Art imitates life. Of course fairies exist, and while I haven't actually seen one on Union Station, you can never be too careful. They're very good at glamour, you know."

"They're beautiful?" Kevin asked.

"Magical glamour, appearing as something they aren't. I would see right through it, but the two of you would be easily taken in."

30

"Libby would warn me if fairies were coming after my baby," Dorothy said confidently. "She's Margie's godmother, after all."

"That was a clever move on your part," Baa admitted half-grudgingly. She folded the blanket back down over the sleeping baby's feet. "So, Jeeves tells me you're doing a Baa's Bags booth for the CoSHC convention."

"The booth is for the trade show that goes along with the convention, and it's about all of the SBJ Fashions lines, not just your enchanted bags-of-holding for role players. And we're not going there to sell anything."

"Congratulations. Despite my higher intellect, you've managed to confuse me. Why are we participating in a trade show if not to sell merchandise?"

"Human manufacturing reps from all of the open worlds will be there. We're looking for new suppliers."

"I thought Jeeves took care of all of that with his little robot friends."

"The Chintoo orbital is inhabited by artificial people from more than a dozen species—they're artificial intelligences, not dumb robots. And I thought you were the one who wanted to expand into enchanting weapons."

"You've changed your minds about that?" Baa asked, her eyes lighting up from within.

"Jeeves thought that the trade show would be a good opportunity to find a source for noodle weapons. There are human communities living on the open worlds belonging to half of the advanced species now, and many of them manufacture alien technology under licensing agreements."

"Thanks for getting my hopes up and then dashing them," the Terragram grumbled. "I thought you meant real weapons."

"You know the professional LARPing league doesn't allow real weapons." Dorothy gave the mage a narrow look. "You don't bring real weapons into the game, do you?"

"I am a real weapon," Baa said indignantly. "Besides, I'm far too experienced to hurt anybody by mistake."

"So what sorts of enchanted items are you going to display in the booth?" Kevin prompted, hoping to move the discussion back on topic before the Terragram mage felt obligated to give a demonstration.

"That's the thing," Dorothy said. "I never really paid much attention to weapons, but we're going to need some, just to be able to explain to the trade show attendees what we're looking for. And maybe we'll put on some demonstrations to draw attention. It seems like forever since I put together a fashion show."

"You are aware that the enchantments I've been doing for SBJ Fashions only work in the LARPing studios," Baa reminded her. "Even our top of the line five-feather bags-of-holding don't provide weight reduction or more space on the inside than the outside if you aren't in the game space."

"I forgot about that," Dorothy admitted. "Couldn't you enchant a few items so they would work outside of a LARP?"

"Uh, Dorothy?" Kevin cautioned his wife, but it was already too late.

"Done," the Terragram declared. "I'll start with some noodle weapons."

"I'm not sure that—" the ambassador's daughter began, but the feathered mage was already halfway to the exit. "What did I do?" Dorothy asked her husband plaintively.

"One second she was counting baby toes, the next she was pulling that verbal contract trick on me."

"I wouldn't worry about it," Kevin said. "Jeeves has his money on the line here, and even a young Stryx is more than a match for a Terragram mage."

Suddenly Alexander sniffed the air and his ears perked up, but he looked puzzled, as if he recognized a scent but couldn't quite place it. Kevin let the Cayl hound resume his guard position on the other side of the counter below the baby's bassinet, and a half a minute later, an attractive Horten girl approached the chandlery.

"Marilla," Dorothy greeted the girl. "I haven't seen you since our last fashion show. Sam isn't home right now, but I'll tell him you stopped by."

"I'm not here to see Samuel," Marilla said. The yellow shade of her skin betrayed her nervous state.

"Have you decided that you're interested in fashion? We don't have a Horten on the design team yet so I could give you a tryout, but I thought Samuel said you were into space engineering."

"I am. I'm here about the co-op job."

"The one I submitted ten minutes ago?"

"That's when the school admin pinged and instructed me to report immediately for a tryout. The message said something about a Stryx controller interface that requires assembly?"

"Oops, I've got that right here," Kevin said, and moved the box with the partially assembled controller to the counter. "Do you read Verlock?"

"A little," Marilla replied. "I won't need the instructions for this, though." She went to work without another word, setting aside the screws with bunged-up threads, and then dry-fitting all of the parts like a puzzle. Then she found some undamaged screws, took up the Verlock screwdriver, and assembled the controller. Dorothy and Kevin were so intent on the alien's rapid finger-work that they didn't notice the two men arriving at the chandlery.

"I just got a ping from Libby that our new co-op student is here," Joe said. "You must be my son's friend from the Open University."

"Greetings, sir," the Horten girl said, dropping a formal curtsey. "This young one is honored to be under your tutelage."

"Glad to have you. I didn't realize the school would be sending somebody right over so we haven't had the chance to figure out exactly where we'll be using you."

"That's fine, sir," Marilla said. "I didn't expect to be starting so soon myself, but the ping said there was a controller that required assembly."

"You have experience with the Verlock manufactured interfaces for Stryx controllers?" Paul asked. "We just got a kit on evaluation but the screws were too small for my fingers."

"And I could barely see them," Joe added. "We gave it to Kevin here because he has young eyes."

"This controller interface?" Marilla asked, holding up the device she had just finished putting together. "I was about to peel the protective tab off the power pack and run the self-test."

"That's pretty impressive for somebody without any experience," Joe said. "Sam told me that you wanted to get your hands dirty with some repairs before taking a desk job in the design department of a Horten shipyard."

"These controllers are the only bit of space engineering that I do have experience with, and that's limited to putting together the kits. A friend of my father's owns a

34

rental franchise and I used to work there cleaning returns during Open University vacations. When the owner upgraded all of the controllers in the local fleet, he picked me to put together the interface kits because I have small fingers."

"Ship rentals?" Paul asked. "What kind?"

"You know, the regular sort," Marilla replied, sounding slightly confused. "It's a *There Yesterday* franchise, one of the Big Three rental agencies operated by Hortens. *There Yesterday* claims to be the biggest, with over a million ships available for rent around the tunnel network, but that includes all of the leases that businesses take for accounting reasons. There were only a hundred and fifty ships in the Union Station fleet, and there are generally around a dozen available for rental at any given time, though they always run out before the holidays."

"And anybody can go in and rent, what, a small trader?"

"Single cabin excursion craft, strictly for tunnel network use. None of them are jump capable, but that doesn't matter because the franchises only operate on Stryx stations and other places with a tunnel connection. Don't you guys have rental agencies?"

"I've never heard of one," Joe said. "Kevin?"

"There's supposedly a Sharf outfit in Earth orbit leasing two-man traders, but I've heard they demand so much for the down-payment that you're basically buying the ship up-front," the chandler said.

"So what do Humans who don't own their own ships do if they need to go somewhere that doesn't have scheduled space liner service?" Marilla asked.

"They can barter with a trader to take them if there's somebody willing," Kevin explained. "I used to pick up a few loose creds that way, but in the end, it wasn't worth cleaning up after greenhorns who never traveled in zero-G, not to mention having to listen to them. For the main part, people only go places that have regular liner service or employer-provided charters."

"What keeps the renters from stealing the ships?" Paul asked.

"The Stryx controllers," Marilla said. "They're programmed to only accept a tunnel network destination that has a *There Yesterday* franchise."

"What's to prevent me from renting one, bringing it in through our bay doors on the core, and scrapping it for parts?" Joe asked. He correctly interpreted the alien girl's color change and added, "I'm just asking hypothetically because I want to understand the business model."

"Oh. That's a relief. The rental agency tracks the location of the controllers at all times so they would know where the ship was taken. And they wouldn't rent to you to start with since you're not Horten."

"That doesn't sound fair," Dorothy protested. "I thought the Stryx had rules about public resources."

"Rental ships aren't public resources," Marilla explained. "They're more like an extension of the species-specific residential decks. Think about it. What if the agency rented a ship to a Fillinduck trio and one of them was molting? Or to a species who couldn't manage the Zero-G bathroom?"

"Gross," Dorothy said, remembering her own experiences on Kevin's small trade ship.

"Are you thinking what I'm thinking?" Joe asked Paul.

"We do have a hundred smaller ships without jump drives that nobody will ever buy. But we could only rent them for round trips, and we'd have to take a big security deposit like the Sharf for in case we don't get them back."

"You're thinking too small," Dorothy said. "As soon as you launch the business, somebody with deeper pockets will see the potential and out-compete you. Probably Blythe and Chastity with InstaRentals," she added, naming Donna's entrepreneurial daughters.

"I'm not ambitious enough to run a business empire," Paul admitted. "I just want to provide a service and get some use out of the ships that we restore."

"You should talk to Daniel," Joe said. "He's the one who put CoSHC together so he knows everybody who's anybody in the human business community. Maybe we could find partners who are willing to buy or lease ships with controllers restricting them to the open worlds on the tunnel network. Kelly has mentioned that our businessmen complain about having to wait for alien space liners that never seem to be direct flights and charge for using the bathroom."

Four

"Caffeine," Kelly groaned, frantically opening and shutting cabinets in the embassy's kitchen. "Where could Donna have hidden the teabags?"

"Try the wooden box next to the coffee maker," the station librarian suggested over the ambassador's implant.

"Thank you, Libby. And thank *you*, Earl Grey." She ripped the protective foil off of a bag, dropped it in her favorite mug, and hit the red button on the faucet for instant hot water. "I wonder if there really was an Earl Grey or if it's just clever marketing."

"Charles Grey, the second Earl Grey, was a British prime minister and the author of the First Reform Act."

"Oh, that sounds familiar now. Maybe Trollope wrote something about it in the Palliser novels. You wouldn't know if there are any—"

"In the refrigerator," Libby interrupted. "Your steering committee meeting starts in two minutes."

Kelly quickly located the cellophane-wrapped plate of leftover donuts and thanked her lucky star that Daniel hadn't come into the embassy on Friday. She took her spoils back into the conference room where a large hologram of the president's office with the superimposed message 'Be back shortly' was already visible over the jigsaw-puzzle table. The ambassador took a seat in a human-sized chair, and one bite of cold donut and sip of hot tea later, the hologram came to life.

"Welcome one and all," President Beyer greeted the ambassadors who comprised the steering committee for EarthCent Intelligence. "I'm pleased to announce that this is our last scheduled meeting before the change to Universal Human Time, so those of you who woke up early or stayed up late will please keep that in mind and not resort to the usual grumbling. And let's all give a big welcome back to Raj Tamil who has just returned from sabbatical."

"I can't tell you all how disappointed I am to be back," Ambassador Tamil said after their polite round of applause died out. "I loved sabbatical. I wish I could get a job doing it."

"That would be retirement, Raj," the president told him. "You've got another nineteen years in the harness, assuming we don't raise the age again."

"How about you, Stephen?" Belinda asked the president bluntly. "I attended a party at the Frunge embassy this week, and one of their businessmen with interests on Earth approached me and demanded to know if it's true that you're quitting."

"That's the first I'm hearing of it. If I was planning on leaving, I'm sure that Hildy would have informed me by now."

"Spoken like a true man," Ambassador Oshi said. "As long as we're on the subject of retirement, what can you tell us about Stryx Gryph's plans to sell Union Station, Ambassador McAllister?"

"Arurraba," Kelly mumbled with her mouth full of donut. She swallowed quickly and washed it down with a mouthful of too-hot tea. "Sorry. I'm sugar and caffeine loading to wake myself up."

"What time is it there?" Svetlana Zerakova inquired, either forgetting or ignoring the president's plea for the ambassadors not to go off on their usual tangents about the scheduling of meetings. "I'm at eleven in the evening."

"Five twenty-seven in the morning," Kelly replied after checking her implant.

"How can that be?" Raj asked. "It's two past the hour on Echo Station and we're all supposed to be in sync."

"Two past on Middle Station as well," Ambassador Oshi contributed.

"It's exactly noon here, but my grandfather clock runs a bit slow," the president said, getting caught up in the exercise. "Check your implant, Kelly."

"That is my implant time," she said. "Our station librarian agreed to start creeping our clocks forward so we don't have to jump seven hours all in one go."

"So how did you know when to show up for this meeting?" Raj inquired.

"I asked her for a reminder."

"That's brilliant," Ambassador Fu said. "The time difference from Earth to Void Station isn't as large as yours, but I'll ask our station librarian about the feasibility of doing the same thing here."

"I'm more interested in hearing the ambassador's opinion about the pending sale of Union Station," the president interjected.

"Oh, sorry I brought up the whole time issue," Kelly apologized. "I checked with our station librarian and the business about Gryph selling Union Station is just a silly rumor. If anything, he would evict all of the sentients onboard and remain here alone. The Verlock ambassador once explained to me that his people believe the first generation Stryx exist simultaneously in multiple universes and that their stations are the connection points for a multiverse network."

"I can't imagine that the Stryx are slaves to their own stations," Ambassador White said slowly. "If Gryph wanted to leave and transfer his consciousness into a science ship, I'm sure he could manage it."

"The Stryx outgrow science ships after a few million years," Ambassador Fu contributed. "The sheer volume of their knowledge requires ever-increasing infrastructure to contain it."

"Unless they take advantage of the multiverse and spread their minds across more and more dimensions," the Echo Station ambassador chimed in.

"What does that even mean, Raj?" the president asked. "We're all just speculating here. Kelly tells us that Union Station's librarian says it's a rumor and that's good enough for me."

"It's not that simple, Stephen," Ambassador Zerakova objected. "Some of the aliens are taking the rumor seriously, and since we're more dependent on Stryx patronage than any other species, it's affecting our status. I was at an event the other day with the Dollnick ambassador, who's also a member of the Princely Council of Advisers. He asked me whether the council should bother sending an observer to the Conference of Sovereign Human Communities convention, or if it would be cancelled at the last minute."

"Because they're worried that Gryph is selling Union Station," the president surmised. "Alright. I see where that could be a problem, but it's unclear to me what we can do about it."

"I could bring it up at my pre-conference meeting with the alien ambassadors," Kelly offered. "Daniel asked me to invite them all in so we could try to convince them to attend the trade show, and maybe we could prepare a joint statement denouncing the rumor."

"I can see that backfiring in a spectacular manner," Carlos opined.

"Perhaps, but I think it's worth a try," the president said. "I'd like for us to talk a little about the goals of the CoSHC convention, but first, I suspect you'd all like to hear about the results from our recently offered civil service exam."

"That's right," Svetlana said. "My twins both took the test."

"They're interested in joining EarthCent?" Kelly asked.

"Not really. I had to bribe them."

"They did quite well," the president said, looking down at a report on his desk. "Their names showed up in the shortlist for possible cheaters due to the quality and similarity of their answers, but our human resources department concluded that their results were within the statistical range for identical twins."

"How many people took the test?" Raj asked.

"Well, the turnout was a bit disappointing, but Hildy tells me that we made a mistake by not spending anything on promotions. Apparently, our brand value as a potential employer is a bit weak."

"How weak?"

"A little over two thousand individuals sat the exam at all test locations and just over one thousand actually completed it," the president recited, without having to look down again. "The test identified sixty potential candidates for the diplomatic service, of which," a pained look fled across his features, "fifteen were human, including both of Svetlana's daughters."

"You're saying that two-thirds of the candidates who passed the test are aliens?" Belinda demanded.

"Three-quarters," Stephen corrected her. "Fifteen goes into sixty four times, which reminds me that we need to consider deemphasizing math on future exams."

"Why would aliens even take the test? They must all be spies!"

"The last question on the exam asked exactly that. To paraphrase the forty-five aliens who took the test, they were curious."

"Wait, I thought you said that forty-five aliens passed the test," Belinda said. "Oh, you don't mean..."

"I'm afraid so. The pass rate for aliens was one-hundred percent, while the pass rate for humans who completed the exam was less than two percent. And," the president continued, turning to Ambassador McAllister in the hologram, "the only perfect score was achieved by the daughter of the Vergallian ambassador on Union Station. Do you know her, Kelly?"

"Uh, the thing is..." the ambassador fortified herself with another swallow of tea.

"Yes?"

"The thing is, I signed the embassy up for the Open University co-op program."

"To get your son a paying job and some experience in diplomacy at the same time," Svetlana correctly guessed. "I wanted to do that with my girls but they said I've already bossed them around enough for two lifetimes. How does he like working in an embassy?"

"He hasn't started yet," Kelly said. "The Open University has an orientation meeting for co-op students today, and then I think he's going right over."

"Don't be too easy on him because he's your son," Ambassador Fu advised. "Spare the rod, spoil the diplomat."

"He won't be working for me," Kelly confessed. "I was going to bring it up later in the meeting but you caught me off guard. The thing is, the Open University assigned us Aabina, and Samuel is doing his co-op at the Vergallian embassy."

"Could you repeat that?" the president requested.

"There isn't an interview process with the Open University co-op program, they just assign the students to available jobs according to their judgment of the best fit. My husband has a Horten girl starting next week in Mac's Bones, and Clive and Blythe's daughter Vivian is going to be working for Drazen Intelligence."

"Let me make sure I have this straight because I know it's early in the morning for you," the president said, again breaking his own rule about referring to the time. "The daughter of the Vergallian ambassador is going to be working in your embassy—"

"Like you said, she aced our civil service exam," Kelly interrupted.

"—while your son will be working in the Vergallian embassy," the president continued, as if Kelly hadn't spoken. "The daughter of the director and the chief funder of EarthCent Intelligence is going to work for Drazen Intelligence—"

"With whom we have an excellent working relationship," the Union Station ambassador interjected.

"—and a Horten girl is going to be working for your husband in the same hold where he rents space to EarthCent Intelligence for the training camp."

"Marilla is a friend of Samuel's from the Open University," Kelly explained. "Her younger sister was on 'Let's Make Friends' so the family are practically humanphiles. She's very colorful."

"Hortens are all very colorful," Belinda pointed out. "I still get mixed up on the 'philes' suffix. Does that mean they like us or hate us?"

"Marilla definitely likes us. My daughter set her up with her boyfriend, the Horten ambassador's son."

President Beyer groaned and theatrically banged his head on his desk, apparently harder than he intended because he came up rubbing his forehead. "How do you intend to keep track of which side you're on in this soap opera you're living, Ambassador McAllister? You should talk to the Grenouthians about doing a reality program. They could call it 'Let's Make Friends for Adults.'"

"Sounds too much like a hook-up show," Svetlana objected.

"I saw that the Grenouthians are promoting documentary package tours to Earth," Ambassador Oshi said. "Does anybody know if they're for real?"

"That's right," Kelly confirmed, jumping on the opportunity to change the subject. "I saw an advertisement on a corridor display panel. I wonder if they're getting any aliens to sign up."

The president cleared his throat and said, "As it happens, the Grenouthian entertainment group sponsoring the tours sent my office a pair of tickets to the premier as a token of appreciation for my efforts in cutting through the red tape and granting them the required permits."

"What red tape? What permits?"

"The Grenouthians persist in believing that doing business on an alien world requires greasing palms. We've found that it's easier to humor them and accept their little bribes than to explain that no special permits are necessary. Hildy bought me a stack of impressive-looking 'Most Improved Student' certificates that I sign and hand out if they insist on getting something in writing."

"I'm planning on taking the family on a vacation to Earth just to let my kids see the place, and the price I saw advertised for the documentary package tour is cheaper than what I came up with for renting hotel rooms on my own," Ambassador Oshi said. "I was thinking of signing up and just skipping the tour part, but I'd be curious to hear how it went."

"I suppose it was the best vacation I've been on," the president said grudgingly. "We visited a number of locations featured in Grenouthian documentaries about humanity's slow advance towards modernity."

"They took you around to famous universities, and breakthrough infrastructure projects like dams and bridges?"

"The tour started in London on a street where a cholera outbreak was halted by a doctor who convinced authorities to remove the handle from the pump of a contaminated well. We also visited a number of locations where child labor was once endemic, and a museum dedicated to sanitary plumbing. Do I need to continue?"

"So how was it the best vacation you ever took?"

"The food and lodgings were all fantastic, and the young bunny who led the group had the logistics down to a science. We'd no sooner step out of a museum and the bus would be waiting to take us to the next stop, and there were always umbrellas available when it rained. I also got the chance to speak with a number of alien tourists who I suppose were humanphiles of a sort. It seems that we're amassing a cult following among aliens who watch Grenouthian documentaries. The only uncomfortable moment of the whole tour came when I used the bathroom at a restaurant. A Frunge was waiting by the sink when I came out, and he asked if he could capture an image of me washing my hands to prove to his friends back home that we actually understand basic hygiene."

"I hope you gave him a piece of your mind," Kelly said indignantly. "You're the President of EarthCent."

"Actually, I made sure to use the soap dispenser and let him pay for our lunch. Hildy says it was the right move. She's hoping to find time to attend the CoSHC conference, if I hadn't mentioned. She wants to meet face-to-face with the representatives of sovereign human communities to see if they're interested in coordinating their public relations with EarthCent."

"She's welcome to stay with us."

"I'll mention it to her. Will you be participating in the convention, or is Associate Ambassador Cohan carrying the ball for the embassy?"

"A bit of both," Kelly said. "I've been asked to give the keynote address and I'll be sitting on a few panels, but CoSHC is Daniel's baby, and I don't offer my opinions unless he asks first."

"Do you want to try your speech out on us?" Ambassador White asked.

"I haven't exactly written it yet. There's plenty of time."

"Don't leave it too long," the president advised. "I've witnessed some of your extemporaneous efforts from over the years and you have a tendency to go off mission."

"How many sovereign communities are you expecting this year?" Ambassador Fu inquired.

"We're getting official delegates from over three hundred communities plus at least two thousand independent attendees," Kelly said. "The organization has more than doubled in size since Eccentric Enterprises contracted with Flower to serve as a circuit ship. The original members were the large human communities on open worlds, but recently, CoSHC has been adding lots of smaller space-based populations."

"I wasn't aware we had that many people living in space."

"We're talking primarily about groups of human laborers who reach the end of their contract and then lease the facility that employed them. It's very common with mining habitats, ice harvesting operations, really any alien business where the infrastructure is long since paid for and the owners would just as soon receive a regular lease payment. Otherwise, the aliens would have to find new laborers, house and feed them, and provide for childcare and education. Tunnel network members all have to meet Stryx standards to recruit from Earth."

"Except for our own contractors," the president reminded her, "which brings us to the final item on the agenda. Have you all received the latest intelligence assessment about the practices of human contractors recruiting labor for unsafe and often illegal work outside of the tunnel network?"

"It came as a complete surprise to me," Ambassador Zerakova said. "With all of the opportunities available, why are young people from Earth still taking those chances?"

"It comes down to affinity schemes. A young man returns to his old neighborhood, flashes around some money and jewelry, and tells the latest crop of street kids that there's plenty more where that came from. Next thing they know, they're getting off a transport on some world nobody has ever heard of with no way of contacting Earth, not that there's anybody here who could help them."

"I know that Daniel plans to do a panel discussion on the subject, and I think he's just waiting for approval from EarthCent Intelligence in case they want to redact some sections of the report to protect their sources," Kelly said. "I'm planning on attending that session myself."

"Is there any good news from Earth, aside from the Grenouthian tours?" Belinda asked.

"Things have never been better," the president replied. "Our population is showing signs of stabilizing around the four billion mark, and the percentage of communities with public schooling available for at least part of the day is back over fifty percent for the first time in years. Everywhere the aliens build new factories or processing centers, the real estate values go through the roof, and our exports are climbing every year. I'm told that the space elevator is actually turning a profit now."

"How about technology transfer?" the Void Station ambassador asked. "Are the people on Earth learning new skills, or are the alien businessmen just using us as cheap labor?"

"A little bit of both. One of the most successful businesses on Earth is Drazen Foods. They employ over forty thousand people in this state and they're buying the produce from tens of thousands of small farms from across the continent. But bottling hot sauce and poison berries isn't a high-tech business, and the consortium employs dogs to make the decisions in their perfume operation. On the other hand, our scientists continue to work at reverse engineering the original Drazen jump ship, and that wouldn't have been possible without the cooperation of Drazen Foods."

"How about the Verlock magnet academies?" Kelly asked. "I know that their boarding school on Flower has been a great success."

"The Verlocks continue to expand their network of schools as rapidly as they can, which as you might imagine, isn't particularly fast. But the biggest surprise to me has been the success of the Astria's Academy of Dance chain. They have over five thousand locations worldwide, and all of those graceful dance students walking around have had a positive effect on everybody else's posture. They're going to put the remaining orthopedic surgeons out of business."

Five

"Good thing we got here early," Samuel said to his girl-friend as a pair of aliens headed up to the front of the classroom. "It looks like they aren't waiting."

"Early is on time," Vivian replied reflexively.

"Welcome to orientation for first-time cooperative education students," the Verlock presenter droned at a glacial pace. "I am Grynlan, the program coordinator, and—"

"—if you have any problems on your co-op assignment, we're here to help you," the Grenouthian half of the duo interrupted. "In the interest of finishing this session before you're all too old to participate in the program, I'll be doing the talking. Any questions before we begin?" He pointed at a Drazen who raised a hand.

"Do we really have to be here?" the student asked. "I'm going to be working for my family in the same job I had before I started at the Open University. It's just that I'll be getting paid for it now."

"Thank you for making my point. Any of you are welcome to leave at any time, but completion of this orientation session is required for those of you who want to get paid. Any more questions?"

The Drazen made a show of binding his own wrists in front of his body with his tentacle.

"Fantastic," the bunny declared. "I know that none of you want to be here so we'll move as quickly as possible. There are just four topics I need to cover, and the first is—"

"Appearance," Grynlan rumbled.

"Appearance," the Grenouthian repeated. "As participants in the cooperative education program, you will be representing the Open University, so we expect you to dress and groom accordingly. Got that?"

"Was he directing that remark at us?" Vivian whispered to Samuel.

"He's just looking in this general direction," the ambassador's son replied, though it did seem as if the alien was singling them out.

"Then I'll say no more on the subject," the bunny continued. "The next topic is—"

"Allergies," the Verlock boomed.

"Allergies. Some of you will be working for species other than your own, and it's important that you inform us of any known allergies so we can relay the specifics to your employer and make sure that the necessary antidotes are available. Is anybody allergic to Humans? Anybody?"

"I'm sure he's looking at us," Vivian hissed.

"We are sitting in the middle of the room."

"Then let it be on your own heads," the Grenouthian intoned. "Grynlan?"

"Work ethic," the Verlock announced.

"Work ethic. Show up on time, give your employer the same effort you would expect from a family member, and, WAKE UP!" the bunny shouted at the Drazen student, who had dozed off in his seat.

"Whaaa?" the student's response came out in a sleepy yawn. "Have we gotten to the pay part yet?"

"Which reminds me," the presenter continued. "I have a special announcement from the administration of the Open University. If any of you should happen to be working for Humans, make sure to check your starting time with the station librarian every day because their clocks are all defective."

"Beware the Human clock," the Verlock repeated for emphasis.

"Our clocks aren't defective," Samuel spoke up. "We're inching the time forward because—"

"What's all this?" a Dollnick demanded as he strode into the room carrying a large carton. "You two, stop screwing around and sit down. There's always a couple of clowns in every group."

The seated students all groaned when they realized they had been pranked by their fellow co-ops, who exchanged a belly bump before taking their chairs. The real leader of the orientation session continued to the front of the class, and Samuel recognized him as the four-armed clerk he always seemed to get stuck with in the administration office.

"Orientation," the Dollnick declared. "This is Union Station, and the rectangular opening at the back of the room is a door. For those of you who haven't figured it out yet, we live in a centrifuge town. The core is up and the hull is down. The sentients move through tubes in the— never mind." He dumped the contents of the box out on the floor. "These are your co-op student IDs. The station librarian tracks their location and uses the data to compute your pay. No ID, no creds. Got it?"

"Yes," the students replied in a ragged chorus.

"That's it, then," the Dollnick said, scooping up one of the IDs with a lower arm. He flung it at Samuel, who thanks to his fencer's reactions, was able to make the catch. "It's the day after Queen's Day and you're late for work. As for everybody else, these IDs have your pictures on them, so even the dullest among you should be able to figure it out."

"Wait," a Chert student called as the Dollnick started for the exit. "Is that really our whole orientation?"

"You're all old enough to know how to act properly, and if you don't, nothing I can say is going to change that," the Dolly whistled over his shoulder without slowing his pace. "Go forth and make your parents proud."

"You better get going too," Vivian said to Samuel. "I may wait for the process of elimination to whittle down the stack before I look for my ID."

"Stay out of the scrum until the big aliens are gone," he cautioned her as most of the students lurched out of their chairs and mobbed the front of the room. As soon as the aisles were clear, Samuel exited the classroom and headed for the nearest lift tube. He reached the Vergallian embassy before Vivian left her seat, and to his surprise, the main doors slid open at his approach.

"Welcome to the—oh, it's the Human," the liveried doorman cut himself off. "Ambassador Aainda has been expecting you all day."

"I had to attend orientation first," Samuel replied in fluent Vergallian, which drew a raised eyebrow from the doorman. "Is there an event taking place?"

"A reception in the main ballroom. I just pinged the ambassador that you've arrived. She told me to send you through to the office and she'll meet you there. Do you know the way?"

"Yes, thank you. I was here last year."

Samuel made his way through the embassy lobby, which could have easily been mistaken for an art gallery or even a museum exhibition, and took the small corridor that led to the ambassador's office. Somehow Aainda had beaten him there and was waiting by the open door.

"Come in, young McAllister. You've missed the meal but you're in time for the dancing. Are those really your shoes?"

"I didn't know you were having an event. I could run home to change and be back here in less than fifteen minutes."

"That won't be necessary," the ambassador said. She made a subtle hand gesture, and a large panel in the wall of her office slid aside, revealing a closet full of men's formal clothes. "Let's see," Aainda continued, studying Samuel. "I'd say you're a size 11GH Long," She pulled a ballroom dancing suit from the rack and thrust it at him. "Try this on."

"Is there, uh?"

"Don't be shy," the ambassador said. "I'm old enough to be your great-great-grandmother, if not more, and if you had anything I haven't seen before, the co-op office would have mentioned it." She noted the young man's embarrassment and sighed. "Very well, I won't look. Do you know your Vergallian shoe size?"

"It's been too long since I danced competition. I've grown."

"Sit," Aainda ordered, and then to Samuel's shock, she knelt gracefully and pulled an ancient sizing device out from under the couch and quickly removed his shoes. "Always be prepared," she said while positioning the sliders. "The station scouts stole that motto from us."

"I, uh..."

"There," the ambassador declared, pushing the device back under the couch and standing up. "You have a narrow instep and I don't keep your size in the closet so I'll have to go to the storeroom. If you change fast enough, you'll be dressed again by the time I get back."

Samuel practically tore his clothes off as soon as the door closed and made record time getting into the ballroom dancing suit. He was just adjusting the Vergallian version of a bowtie that he'd found in the breast pocket of the shirt when Aainda returned with a pair of dancing shoes.

"I'll have to order more in your size," the ambassador said. "I expect to make good use of your dancing skill at our receptions and the best equipment pays for itself."

"Could I ask who the reception is for?" Samuel asked, sliding his feet into shoes which fit even better than his socks.

"I expect you to ask about anything and everything. It's the only way to learn and not make unnecessary mistakes. The reception is for Ajalah, a senior operator in the Imperial Intelligence Service." Aainda stood back and surveyed Samuel's form. "A little cosmetic surgery and you could almost pass as Vergallian. Have you ever considered removing your back teeth?"

"My molars? Why?"

"It would help accentuate your cheekbones, though you could achieve the same effect with makeup."

"Do I need to pass as Vergallian to do the job?"

"I was just thinking out loud. I hope you don't mind serving as a Gulnick this evening?"

"It's fine," Samuel said, though he winced internally at the Vergallian word, which carried the freighted meaning

56

of a handsome young man who dances with dowagers. "Will they expect me to talk?"

"Some might. Do you have your nose plugs?"

"No," he said, and then the implication struck home. "I'm not sure they'd help anyway. My dad warned me about Vergallian women."

"There are a number of upper caste women present at the reception, and dosing males with pheromones is as natural to them as smiling is to you," the ambassador explained. "Your father is right to be concerned. Do I have your permission to extend my protection?"

"Yes," Samuel said. "I didn't know it was even possible."

The ambassador concentrated for several long seconds, and then she said, "You will ignore instructions from any other women."

"That's it? I don't think it worked."

"You'll be safe until it wears off, though you probably shouldn't mention this to your parents," Aainda said. "Or your girlfriend. Now come and let me introduce you around."

Two hours later, Samuel couldn't believe that his legs were holding up so well. He'd danced with a dozen Vergallian women whose combined ages easily came to three or four thousand years. A number of them had shown clear signs of frustration when he declined their invitations to take a break from the reception to see their lodgings, so he had to believe that whatever Aainda had done to protect him from their pheromones had worked.

"Mind if I cut in?" asked a ravishing Vergallian woman, putting her hand on the shoulder of the matron Samuel was currently waltzing. His partner did a double-take and abandoned him to the newcomer without an argument.

"I'm Samuel McAllister," the EarthCent ambassador's son formally introduced himself in Vergallian.

"I know perfectly well who you are," his new partner purred through an artificial smile as she allowed him to glide her around the dance floor. "I've been watching you. You're quite graceful for a Human."

"Thank you, but I'm nowhere near your level."

"Of course you aren't. I have royal blood on both sides."

"Your Highness," Samuel acknowledged politely, bowing his head. "Is this reception in your honor?"

"It is. Your manners could be worse," Ajalah continued in a speculative tone. "Tell me how you manipulated your way into a job at our embassy."

"The Open University sent me," he replied honestly. "The co-op program seems a bit haphazard."

"I understand that the ambassador's daughter will be working for your mother."

"It seems that way," Samuel answered noncommittally. He was acutely aware that the dance had turned into an interrogation.

"So, how is Ailia doing?"

"The little Vergallian girl who lived with us thirteen years ago?" Samuel replied without missing a beat. "I wonder about that myself."

"That's not what I hear," Ajalah said, tightening her grip on his shoulder. "I know that Ailia's half-sister brought her to Union Station for that ball the Maker arranged for your mother. We have video of you dancing for hours."

"Could I get a copy?" Samuel asked, hoping he wasn't crossing the line into getting his neck broken on the spot.

"Very funny," she said, her thumb digging into his collarbone. "Something tells me that our ambassador foolishly prepped you for this interview, but I waited two hours for the effects to diminish, and now—"

"May I cut in?" the ambassador's daughter requested, putting her hand on Ajalah's shoulder. The girl and the woman stared at each other for several long seconds, and then Aabina tilted her head slightly towards the back of the ballroom. The Imperial Intelligence officer glanced in the direction indicated and took note of the handsome man dressed in black who was cleaning his fingernails with an ornamental dagger. She released Samuel.

"I look forward to meeting you again," Ajalah said with an icy smile. "Both of you."

"Ta," Aabina said sweetly, but she kept her eyes on the older woman until another couple waltzed between them. "Scary, isn't she?"

"Terrifying," Samuel agreed. "You know her?"

"I sat next to Ajalah at dinner and spent the whole meal watching her hands out of the corner of my eye to see if she would try to poison me."

"Why would your mother invite a woman like that to the embassy, much less throw her a party?"

"Imperial Intelligence is one of the balancing forces in the empire," Aabina explained. "It's better to welcome their operatives as guests than to have them skulking around undercover. I even have some relatives in the service."

The song came to a close and the orchestra segued into a slower and more subdued piece, indicating that the evening was drawing to an end.

"When are you starting at my mom's embassy?" Samuel asked.

"Tomorrow, I hope. It's the strangest thing, but I don't think that your girlfriend likes me."

"Why do you say that?"

"After the Dollnick dumped all of the IDs on the floor, Marilla and I got into a conversation about the problems we could expect working for Humans. We went up to find our badges at the same time as Vivian, but mine was missing."

"Did you ping Libby?"

"The station librarian? No, I just waited and chatted with your girlfriend until she had to leave for her job, and you know what? It turned out she was standing on my ID the whole time, as if she didn't want me to work in the EarthCent embassy. Isn't that funny?"

"I'm sorry," Samuel said. "She has this idea in her head that I'm attracted to Vergallian girls."

"Isn't everybody?" Aabina replied without the slightest hint of self-consciousness.

"I'm hoping she'll stop worrying when we're officially engaged. Vivian originally wanted to get married on the Sunday after her eighteenth birthday, but for some reason she changed her mind. Now I'm supposed to make a formal proposal instead."

"Are you waiting for something?"

"She wants me to do it on the last day that she's seventeen. I don't argue with her about stuff like that. The truth is, it doesn't matter to me. I'd just as soon take her down to the Elvis chapel and get married right now."

"You sure know how to put a damper on a romantic dance," Aabina said, causing the young man to blush.

"I just hope that Drazen Intelligence doesn't teach her to kill because I'd be a dead man if she could see me right now."

"From what I know of Drazens, they're probably fitting her with a prosthetic tentacle so she doesn't feel left out."

60

Three decks above the Vergallian embassy, in a theatrical shop on the Drazen deck, Vivian scrunched up her nose and repressed a shudder.

"It feels weird," she complained to her newly assigned handler, "like I'm going to fall over backward."

"That's because you have it extended directly behind you. Try curling it up on your shoulders, like this." The Drazen woman demonstrated by extending her own tentacle above her head, and then bringing it down so that a thick loop fell over each of her shoulders. "Just be careful not to get your neck in the middle or you could strangle yourself."

Vivian concentrated on the control panel for the prosthetic tentacle which had been linked with her implant to appear on a heads-up display. There were over a hundred individual joints to manipulate and she ended up tugging on her own ponytail.

"Ouch!"

"Maybe the tentacle isn't absolutely necessary," her handler said. "Korg?"

The Drazen proprietor, who had been pretending to straighten a nearby display of back braces, dropped what he was doing and returned to his customers. "At your service, ladies."

"The tentacle seems to be a bit much for her right now. Is there anything you can do for her hands?"

"I have just the thing," Korg declared, leading the women over to a rack of odd-looking gloves with the fingers cut off. "A salesman convinced me to give these a try, even though they're manufactured by Humans, and they've been selling like hot peppers to the five-fingered species who want to play our musical instruments."

"We make these?" Vivian asked, accepting a pair of the gloves and slipping them on.

"On an open world owned by the Two Mountains consortium," the shop owner confirmed. "Personally, I can't imagine what it would feel like going through life with only one thumb on each hand, but it will probably take you a while to get used to them."

"Hey," Vivian said, her eyes lighting up as she gripped her left forearm with her right hand. "It actually works!"

"There's a sensor that picks up the nerve impulse to the little finger next to the prosthetic thumb," Korg explained. "I've been told that most humans lack the discipline to move their pinkies independently, but the musicians who come in seem to have no problem with it. Mind you that the prosthetic isn't as strong as your natural thumb, and leverage is dependent on the tightness of the glove, but they're very useful for operating Drazen equipment that requires six fingers."

"We'll take them," the handler said. While the proprietor cashed them out, Vivian's companion helped her remove the prosthetic tentacle rig and told her, "You can roll up a towel and stuff it in the back of your blouse or dress where it will look like a tentacle hump for the time being. We'll come back and try again after you get used to having the right number of thumbs."

Six

Marilla spent almost an hour sticking her head into various parked spaceships and calling "Hello?" before she concluded that there must have been some mistake about the starting time for her first official day of work at Mac's Bones. Her shoulders sagged in disappointment and her skin began showing some dull blotches as she gave up and headed for the exit. At the last minute, she decided to risk being rude and ascended the shallow ramp of the converted ice harvester, where she knew that Samuel lived with his family.

"Come in," Kelly welcomed the Horten girl. "Joe told me you were starting today and asked me to get you settled in, but I have to leave for work in a few minutes."

"I'm so sorry," Marilla said. "I got here early but I didn't want to disturb anybody in your house. I've been looking for Mr. McAllister out in the parking area."

"Joe, Paul, and Kevin all went out in the tug before I woke up. They must have taken the dogs with them or I would have gotten a report from Beowulf as soon as you entered the hold. Do you drink tea or coffee?"

"I couldn't let you serve me," the Horten girl said in horror. "I'm your husband's employee!"

"We don't have that rule," Kelly said. "Libby? Can you estimate when Joe and the boys will be returning?"

"The Nova is in the core and making its final approach," the station librarian replied. "The bay doors have already started opening."

63

"Oh, I can't get enough of watching this," Kelly said, grabbing the surprised alien's arm and pulling her towards the door. "You'll want to see it too."

Marilla followed the ambassador back down the ramp of the ice harvester, and both of them craned their necks to watch as the bay doors opened to their fullest extent. The shimmering atmosphere retention field gave the approaching ship the appearance of a desert mirage. A jury-rigged tow rack holding six small ships in a grid was suspended below the tug as it settled into the hold, but the only sound was a warbling 'Beep, beep, beep," vaguely reminiscent of the back-up warning Joe had added to all of the heavy equipment in Mac's Bones.

"Where's that noise coming from?" Kelly asked, looking around. "Oh. There you are."

Dorothy made one final 'Beep' sound to the delight of her baby before greeting the co-op student. "Hey, Marilla. Do any of those wrecks look familiar? Kevin said he was going out with my dad and Paul this morning to find some Horten ships to get you started."

"They're bringing in those six ships for me to work on?"

"Well, mom and I certainly aren't going to fix them. We already have jobs."

"That's right," Kelly said. "I have to get going. Our Vergallian co-op student is starting at the embassy today." She turned to her daughter. "Give me some sugar."

Dorothy dutifully held out the baby for her mother to kiss, and then the ambassador walked quickly to the exit, leaving the hold just as the tow-rack touched the deck. The rigid coupling holding the rack to the tug opened, and then the Nova lifted a little higher and maneuvered to its usual parking spot.

"Let's go see what they brought," Dorothy said. "Are those Horten numbers on the two pink ones?"

"Yes," Marilla replied nervously. "Do you really think your father is going to expect me to restore those ships by myself? All I have experience with is cleaning up after customers and assembling Stryx controller interfaces."

"Then you can learn on the job. You really put a bee in their bonnets with that rental talk. Paul has been trying to figure out what to do with all of the little ships for years. It wasn't worth fixing them up, because traders only want ships with cargo capacity. He didn't want to sell anything for scrap," Dorothy continued in a lowered voice, "because they were all a gift from his wife. Your timing is great too, with the CoSHC conference coming up."

"I think the pink ships with the numbers once were rentals or leases," Marilla said. "I don't recognize the models so they must be pretty obsolete."

"What's obsolete for Hortens is advanced technology for us. Watch out for the dogs. They look excited."

Alexander skidded through a wide turn as he changed course towards the girls, and then, claws scratching at the deck, built up speed again as he bounded right at them. Beowulf lagged behind the younger dog but didn't over-shoot the turn as badly. Neither of the Cayl hounds showed any sign of slowing as they approached, and Marilla was sure she was about to be knocked on her back when Alexander leapt clear over her.

"Is he going to do that every time I—" the Horten girl began, but she was cut off by shrill whistling.

"Alexander! Come here!" Dorothy yelled, but the Cayl hound ignored her and instead began barking and snapping at a newly arrived Dollnick who was backed up against the chandlery counter.

The four-armed alien fended the hound off with a piece of equipment mounted on a tripod and remained surprisingly calm in the face of his attacker. Then Beowulf arrived, clamped his jaws around the loose skin on the back of Alexander's neck, and began to slowly drag his son away.

"Sorry, sorry," Kevin panted, sprinting into the scene thirty seconds behind Beowulf. "Alexander! Down!"

The younger Cayl hound finally stopped trying to claw his way forward, but he continued to snarl and bare his teeth at the Dollnick, who was whistling what sounded like a lullaby in an attempt to calm the situation.

"Sorry," Kevin repeated once again when he was sure that Alexander wasn't going to lunge at the stranger. "We have a new baby in the family and these Cayl hounds can be overly protective of their packs."

"Perfectly understandable," the Dollnick said. "He caught me by surprise, is all. Normally, I carry treats on this job, but I had nothing to offer as a bribe."

"What job is that?"

"Property assessor," the Dollnick said, producing a holographic cube that served as his business card and offering it to Kevin. "I'm Blure. I didn't really expect to encounter any Cayl hounds on Union Station."

"Could I ask what you're doing here?"

"Surveying," Blure replied, giving the tripod he still gripped in his lower set of arms a shake. "The public spaces on the station are fully documented, but my employer wanted to get some measurements of the privately leased spaces with access to the core. Are you the owner?"

"No, but he'll be here in a minute," Kevin said, placing a calming hand on Alexander's head. "My father-in-law has leased this hold for over thirty years, but the owner is Gryph, of course."

"And that's why I'm here. I work for Prince Drume, who is currently the president of the Princely Council. They're planning to bid on Union Station at the auction."

"What auction?" Dorothy demanded, coming up behind the dogs with the baby. "Don't tell me that the Dollnick princes believe the crazy rumor about Gryph selling Union Station."

"I assure you that we are expecting an announcement of the auction date any day now. I've been working overtime to get my report in."

"Well, you can ask a Stryx yourself," Kevin said. "Jeeves is the one who warned me that our hound had you cornered, and here he comes now with my father-in-law and Paul."

"Jeeves went out with you guys this morning?" Dorothy asked.

"Paul invited him to come along and identify the Horten ships. They look the same as the Drazen family craft from the outside, and both species copied the design from the Frunge."

"Did not," Marilla muttered under her breath.

"Any harm done?" Joe asked, coming up and offering the Dollnick his hand. "No pieces missing?"

"All part of the job," the alien reassured him, producing another holographic cube to give to Joe. "Blure. I'd like permission to survey your hold."

"Didn't you check with Dollnick Intelligence? I'm sure they have more detailed plans than I do."

"Oh, I got a floor plan from them that shows the layout of your training camp, but those espionage types couldn't tell you the three most important factors in valuing real estate if their nests depended on it."

"And what are those?" Joe asked.

"Location, location, location. See those bay doors?"

"Just came in through them."

"Exactly. Most of the hold space on the core is reserved for the large shippers and passenger lines. There are only six-hundred and thirteen private leaseholds with exterior access on all of Union Station, and your facility is one of the nicer ones I've seen so far. Do you mind if I ask what you pay for rent?"

"I won't take offense, if that's what you mean."

"And you won't reply. I understand. It was just a shot in the dark."

"Jeeves," Dorothy addressed the young Stryx who floated up alongside Paul. "Tell this Dollnick that Gryph isn't selling Union Station."

"Gryph isn't selling Union Station," Jeeves repeated dutifully. "And if he does, I've been wasting a lot of time and creds working up the new Libbyland attraction."

"Is that your home?" Blure asked the ambassador's husband, pointing at the converted ice harvester with his tripod.

"Now that I look at it from here, it could use a little dressing up," Joe admitted. "We just redid the shipping container that my daughter lives in so our place is looking a little scruffy by comparison."

"You insist that Gryph isn't selling the station, but I can't help but notice that you're moving out."

"You mean the furniture and things? It's not even all ours. We're planning a multi-family tag sale and some of our friends have been dropping off their things. The more stuff you list in the ad, the more people will show up."

"If you say so," the Dollnick whistled skeptically. "Do you mind if I confirm the interior dimensions and take a few notes about the lighting and such?"

"Knock yourself out," Joe said. "Beowulf, you stick with Blure and make sure that Alexander doesn't jump him from behind."

The older Cayl hound, who had been planning on a snack and a nap, let out a long-suffering sigh as he fell in behind the Dollnick.

"Good morning, Marilla," Jeeves greeted the girl. "I picked out the six ships from Paul's collection that are the closest to what you've worked on at the Horten rental agency."

"I really only cleaned them and plugged in new ship controllers," Marilla protested.

"That's more than most people ever do," Paul said. "The two of you know each other?"

"Stryx Jeeves taught the educational LARP course at the Open University," the Horten replied. "I took it with Samuel, Vivian, and—some Drazen."

"And you passed with flying colors," Jeeves said.

Marilla groaned at the terrible pun, which recalled her experience growing wings and suppressing her skin's coloring response to emotional states.

"I'm helping Jeeves in Libbyland today but you can ping me if you need anything," Paul said. "See everybody later."

The little crowd broke up, with Kevin keeping a grip on Alexander's ruff, and half leading, half dragging the hound into the chandlery. Dorothy went back to their container to feed the baby, and Marilla was left with Joe, who tried to hide his awkwardness at having an employee who wasn't a family member.

"We're really enthusiastic about your rental agency idea and we hope you can tell us more about it as we get these ships into shape," he said to the Horten girl. "But the first thing is to get you introduced to everybody."

"Was Paul serious about helping Jeeves?" Marilla asked. "What can a Human, I mean, anybody, do to help a Stryx?"

"Libbyland is adding a game for young sentients to develop their career goals, though to tell you the truth, it sounds too educational to be fun," Joe explained. "Paul and Jeeves have worked together on several Libbyland attractions, but you'd have to ask them yourself if you want to know who comes up with what. Even the Stryx can't think of everything."

"Do you really mean that or is it just a Human saying?"

"The Stryx don't have a reason to think of everything," Joe told her. "When you know the best way to get to the best answer, there's not a lot of point in exploring alternative paths to reach solutions that can't work as well."

"I've never heard it put that way before," the Horten girl said slowly. "I'll have to think about it."

"I see Thomas, Chance, and Judith have arrived, and we should tell them about the Dollnick so they don't mistake him for a spy."

"Maybe he is a spy."

"You see? I didn't even think of that, and I've been in the business."

"Do they all work in Mac's Bones? The information sheet from the co-op office showed that you have eleven employees."

"Eleven?" Joe asked in astonishment. "There's just me and Paul. Samuel and Kevin help out when they can, but for Dorothy to get to eleven she must have counted everybody who lives here, including Dring. She's the one who filled out the forms."

"Fewer is better," Marilla said. "I'm actually kind of shy around aliens because of the whole color thing. If Thomas, Chance, and Judith don't work here…"

"They do work here, but not on ship repair," Joe told her. "Thomas and Chance, she's the taller woman, run the EarthCent Intelligence training camp. Judith is on maternity leave, but she took over unarmed combat training from me when I retired. I'm not sure what she's doing here today."

"I remember all three of them from Dorothy's fashion show. Thomas and Chance move very gracefully for Humans," the Horten said, and then turned a molted yellow when she realized the implication of her words. "I mean—"

"Don't worry about it, we have thick skins. And you should know that Thomas and Chance are artificial people."

"They're artificial intelligence? And they work for EarthCent?"

"Human-derived artificial intelligence. It's not like EarthCent Intelligence would hire outside our species, unless they passed the civil service exam, I guess," Joe corrected himself. "I'm not a big fan of politics so I don't worry about it."

"Morning, Joe, Marilla," Thomas greeted them.

"Nice coveralls," Chance said to the Horten girl. "Do they come in black?"

"Just the safety colors," Marilla replied. "Green and violet."

"That's a nice picture of you on the badge," Judith said.

71

"It's kind of embarrassing, but we have to carry them with us to get paid."

"There's a Dollnick wandering around the hold taking measurements for in case Gryph sells Union Station," Joe told the training staff. "Beowulf is keeping an eye on him. What's scheduled for the camp?"

"We're setting up this morning for a kidnap avoidance course," Chance replied. "The Galactic Free Press has been saving up new employees for a while so it's going to be a big class."

"Thomas offered to teach me holographic programming," Judith said.

"Where's your baby?"

"Bob is watching him this morning. The paper put him on half-days after I gave birth. It's a pretty sweet benefits package."

"Hi, Grandpa Joe," Fenna announced her presence. "Mikey and I are going to water Dring's garden."

"Do you want to bring Marilla along and show her?" Joe asked. He turned to the Horten girl and added, "The Maker is away, but you're going to be working here so you should be familiar with his area."

"Come on," Mike said, grabbing Marilla's hand and pulling her along. "You can attach the hose. Fenna is afraid of it and I always get wet."

The Horten girl allowed herself to be led through the short tunnel in the barrier mound of old metal scrap that isolated Dring's corner of the hold from the rest of Mac's Bones. The area inside was a veritable sculpture garden, filled with the fruits of the Maker's artistic labors from the past two decades. A large bare spot on the deck bore witness to the absence of the gravity surfer, a metamorphic vessel filled with living matter that was all more or less associated with Dring.

"Why do you remove the hose after watering?" Marilla asked, looking down at the coiled rubber tubing right below the faucet. "The valve stops the water from coming out."

"Does it?" Mike asked. "I always thought you have to unscrew the hose first or it will explode."

"Mikey's imagination has gotten too good since he was on my Mom's show," Fenna explained to the Horten girl.

"My little sister Orsilla was in the same cast," Marilla reminded her. "She misses telling stories about witches."

Mike got the hose screwed on and found the other end, but Fenna stopped him from turning on the water.

"My mom wants us to harvest some of the carrots and celery first," she told him, and then explained to Marilla, "The vegetables just go bad if you let them grow too long. We keep planting new seeds so Dring will have fresh food when he gets back."

"Won't the soil be tired?" the Horten girl asked.

"We have the compost from three houses to mix in," Fenna explained. "And Grandpa Joe adds the leftover stuff from brewing beer. I can show you how to pick carrots if you want," she added shyly.

Mike remained behind to guard the hose, just in case, and a minute later, the ten-year-old girl and the Horten co-op student heard the water start spraying, followed by loud whistling.

"Turn it off, Mikey," Fenna shouted. "You're getting the Dollnick all wet."

"He's sneaking around," the boy objected.

"Mr. McAllister gave him permission," Marilla told the boy. "Look, Beowulf is with him."

73

Mike turned off the water, but he continued scowling at the towering Dollnick, who seemed to be quite amused by the whole situation. The Cayl hound had a different point of view. Stalking over to stand next to the boy, he shook himself vigorously, showering Daniel and Shaina's son with water.

Seven

"Who's that?" Kelly asked the Drazen ambassador, inclining her head towards a tall figure wearing an environmental suit.

"The Fillinduck ambassador," Bork replied, as he edged around his host towards the buffet. "Just let me grab something to eat and I'll fill you in."

The Grenouthian ambassador darted forward to block the Drazen's access to the fruit salad, but both of them were beaten to the punch by the Chert, who had snuck up to the buffet before turning off his invisibility projector.

"Animals," the Frunge ambassador remarked, shaking his finger at Crute, who used his upper set of arms to clear a space while loading a plate with the lower set.

"Not hungry today, Czeros?" Kelly inquired.

"I just came from a wedding and it would have been rude not to eat anything." He popped the cork from the bottle of wine that Donna had thoughtfully set out at his place and poured himself a glass. "Will you be joining me, Ambassador?"

"Never before lunch," she replied, though given her expectations for the first part of the meeting, Kelly felt tempted. It was clear from the deep green shade of the Frunge ambassador's hair vines that he'd gotten an early start on drinking at the wedding. "I hope Srythlan gets here on time. I'm counting on him to keep the others on an even keel."

"I passed him right after I came out of the lift tube so he should be arriving in a few minutes," Czeros said. "If the Verlocks walked any slower they'd need bots to carry them around."

The Horten ambassador, who had been first to reach the buffet, deposited two loaded plates at his place. Then he surprised Kelly by catching her eye and indicating the embassy's reception area with his chin. The EarthCent ambassador discretely pointed a finger at her own chest to make sure that Ortha was signaling to her, and when he nodded in the affirmative, she made her excuses to Czeros and worked her way around the table to follow the Horten.

"Can you spare a moment?" Ortha asked, surprising Kelly again with his polite manner.

"Certainly, Ambassador. What is it?"

"This is a bit awkward for me, but I presume you know that my son has permission to begin courting the young woman who is now employed by your husband."

"Marilla. Yes, Dorothy told me all about it."

"Please give this to Joe," Ortha said, thrusting something in Kelly's hand.

"A programmable cred?"

"To reimburse him for whatever the Open University charges for co-op students these days. Some of the elders in my family may be uncomfortable with the idea of accepting a girl who works for aliens, but this way I can show that her position was officially funded by my embassy."

"And that would make it kosher?"

Ortha gave Kelly a funny look. "What do the dietary restrictions of a Human religious sect have to do with anything?"

"It's another way of saying 'legitimate' or 'admissible.'"

"Strange language," the Horten ambassador remarked. "Don't tell Marilla, but I've signed her up for the Peace Force. If my elders make problems, I'll use the Stryx statements for my embassy's programmable cred to prove that she was doing outreach work to a primitive species."

"I'm sure Joe will be thrilled to—" the EarthCent ambassador began before she realized that Ortha had already started back for his seat. Kelly grimaced, but the Horten ambassador had calculated correctly on her unwillingness to stand in the way of romance, and she resisted the urge to return the coin.

"Ambassador," a familiar voice called, and she turned to see Aainda coming out of Daniel's office. "I haven't had a chance to thank you for hiring my daughter. She and your Associate Ambassador are working up quite the presentation."

"Daniel has been monopolizing Aabina's time so I've hardly had a chance to say two words to her," Kelly said. "I hope it won't be awkward for you when they join our meeting."

"Not at all. I would have brought your son along but the other ambassadors might have taken it the wrong way."

"I still haven't gotten over how the Open University swapped children on us. I assume it's one of Libby's schemes."

"I think their co-op assignments fit them perfectly. Aabina has been studying up on Humans since we arrived on Union Station, and I'm pleased she's getting a chance to practice her new language skills."

"Do you mean she speaks English? I assumed I was hearing her through my translation implant."

"English and Chinese. She's fluent in both."

"Ambassadors," a low voice grated out behind the two women. The Verlock didn't pause as he passed, making his way directly to the ravaged buffet. Kelly noticed Srythlan's head slowly turning back and forth as if he was searching for something, and she went to investigate.

"Is something wrong, Ambassador?" she asked the leathery alien.

"It seems that somebody got to the salt cod before me," Srythlan replied sadly, gazing at the empty wooden box. "Did you expand the guest list for this meeting?"

"No, but the Fillinduck came for the first time. I have no idea what he eats."

"Salt cod, apparently."

"I'm sure there's another box in the kitchen," Kelly said. "You go and sit and I'll bring it to you." She waved off Srythlan's objection that he was fine and slipped into the attached kitchen where she quickly located a new box of the dried and salted fish. The EarthCent ambassador reached the Verlock's place at the conference table before he did.

"Sit," Bork called to her, gesturing to the open chair between the Frunge ambassador and himself. "I know you've already had breakfast but I made you a plate of crackers and cheese. If you don't want it, I'll eat the crackers and Czeros can eat the cheese.

"I think I'll just get started because we have a lot to discuss," Kelly said and re-pitched her voice for public speaking. "I want to thank you all for—"

"Get to the point," an unfamiliar voice cut her off. She looked over and saw the Fillinduck ambassador resealing his face mask. From the action of his jaws, it was apparent that he'd taken advantage of the opening to stick another piece of hard salt cod in his mouth.

"And I especially want to thank our Fillinduck colleague for gracing my embassy with his presence," Kelly continued pointedly. "In just a few minutes, my associate ambassador will be giving a presentation on the upcoming CoSHC convention and trade show. But first, as I promised in the update to your invitations, I want to address the rumor about Gryph selling Union Station."

"Next Tuesday," the Dollnick ambassador spoke up.

"What?"

"That's what I'm hearing for the auction date."

"My information put the auction on the last day of the current cycle," the Grenouthian ambassador contributed.

"Ditto," Ortha added.

"Why would Gryph sell his station?" Srythlan asked, tapping the table with a piece of salt cod to increase the cadence of his speech. "Our intelligence offers no independent confirmation."

"Timing is everything in business," Crute said. "Maybe Gryph has identified the top of the Stryx-built station market and knows he'll never get a better offer. Prince Drume is on his way here to bid on behalf of the Princely Council."

"My own people are on the fence about this," Czeros said. "The report from our rumor analysts suggests that for so many species to be talking about this at the same time, there must be something to it. On the other hand, our economists can't figure out what Gryph would possibly want in return for the station."

"Capital for investment," Crute suggested. "Maybe he wants to pull out the equity so he can build more stations elsewhere."

"He's a Stryx, not a real estate magnate," the Vergallian ambassador objected.

"What do your intelligence people say?" Bork asked her.

"Nothing that merits repeating," Aainda replied. "I hate to agree with practitioners of the dismal science, but my instincts tell me that the Frunge economists have it right. Unless somebody can explain what Gryph could possibly want in exchange for Union Station, I have to believe that it is simply a rumor after all."

"As do I," Kelly said. "I know that all of you are reticent to speak directly with the Stryx so I've taken it upon myself to do it for you. Libby?"

"Yes, Ambassador," the station librarian responded.

"Is Gryph available to make a statement?"

"I'll tell him you're ready."

"Now you've done it," Czeros muttered to Kelly. "Snatched defeat from the jaws of victory."

"This is an all-decks, all-species public announcement," Gryph's synthesized voice thundered. "I've been requested to address the rumor that I intend to sell Union Station. The probability of that event occurring is zero. Any tenants who fail to pay their rent in the theory that I won't be around to collect will find their possessions in the corridor. And the recycling bins are here for a reason. Use them."

"I think I just heard the price drop," Crute said, rubbing all four of his hands together.

"What?" Kelly practically shouted.

"Stryx Gryph has never made a public announcement about a rumor before," the Dollnick pointed out. "Why start now, unless it's true and he's covering up?"

"I'm sticking with the first of the new cycle, but I'll keep next Tuesday open," the Grenouthian ambassador said.

"Gryph denied the rumor at Ambassador McAllister's request," Srythlan pronounced laboriously.

"Exactly," the Chert said. "It doesn't even count as lying if somebody asks for it."

"Not what I meant," the Verlock protested, but the conversation had already left him behind.

"Stop!" Kelly begged. "This is silly. The Stryx don't do things because I ask them to."

"Right," the Grenouthian said. "They're using you as a tool."

"So you're all going to insist on believing that Union Station is on the market?"

"My information is that you're running a tag sale so you'll have less to pack when the time comes to move," Crute said. "It's in your best interest for everybody else to believe that Gryph isn't selling the station because they'd never buy your junk otherwise."

"I have a report that you're even selling your plumbing fixtures," the Chert chipped in.

"Joe redid the master bathroom for our anniversary and the old sink is in great shape," Kelly protested. She resisted the urge to slam her fist into the table for emphasis since she knew just how thick the onyx puzzle pieces were. "What can I say to prove to you that we're just trying to reduce the clutter and we took a few things from friends to make the tag sale more attractive?"

"I'm sure I have some items lying around the embassy that I won't be taking with me if we lose the bidding war," the Grenouthian ambassador insinuated. "If you'll accept them on consignment, that would go a long way to convincing me that you're telling the truth."

"Fine, whatever," Kelly snapped. "Bring all of your junk. But if something doesn't sell and you don't pick it up, I'm going to charge you to get rid of it."

"Does that apply to all of us?" the Chert ambassador inquired. "A whole corner of my living room is off limits with furniture my wife got tired of looking at."

"And now she never turns her head in that direction?"

"We set up an invisibility projector so nobody can see it, but the space is lost."

"I can visualize the advertisement in the Galactic Free Press," Bork said, gesturing with his hands as if he were smoothing out a poster. "Giant eight-species tag sale at Mac's Bones."

"If you put it that way, I feel obligated to bring something," the Dollnick ambassador chimed in.

Kelly glimpsed Daniel and Aabina coming out of the associate ambassador's office and decided it was time to get back on topic. "We can talk about the tag sale later. The primary purpose of this meeting is to give you all a heads-up about what will be happening at the upcoming CoSHC convention and to invite you to participate in the trade show."

The Fillinduck noisily pushed back his chair, rose, and left the conference room by way of the corridor exit without another word.

"Who ate the food and didn't stay for our presentation?" Daniel inquired.

"The Fillinduck ambassador," Kelly replied. "Apparently he was just here for the Gryph rumor."

"You wouldn't believe this, but I just got a ping from the Dollnick who manages the Empire Convention Center. He offered me a gift certificate good for one free event in the Meteor Room at a future date in return for confirming our convention reservation."

"Did you try for cash back instead?" Crute inquired.

"I passed it on to our embassy manager. We sponsor a mixer every month and it's usually in the Meteor Room, so a gift certificate is as good as cash to us."

"Why is your daughter here?" the Chert ambassador asked Aainda. "If I knew it was 'Bring your offspring to work day' I could have saved what I'm paying the InstaSitter."

"The EarthCent ambassador and the Vergallian ambassador have exchanged children," the Dollnick said. "Your intelligence people must be slipping."

"Aabina is working here and my son is working at the Vergallian embassy because that's where the cooperative education program sent them," Kelly explained, and then she attempted a smooth segue into the CoSHC presentation. "It's a good example of how we can work together rather than against each other. Daniel?"

"Thank you, Ambassador. Let me begin with a brief overview. The Conference of Sovereign Human Communities is an umbrella organization that was set up to facilitate trade among our people living in independent communities all around the tunnel network. Some of the most successful communities are found on open worlds administrated by the species represented here today, especially the Drazens, Frunge, and Dollnicks."

"Fyndal hosts a fine community," the Verlock ambassador interjected.

"Yes, Srythlan, and the human population there has joined CoSHC and will be presenting about their academy at our convention. Unfortunately, the temperature extremes and volcanic activity common to worlds favored by your species discourage many of our people from experiencing the famous Verlock hospitality. I believe Aabina has the numbers."

"CoSHC has three member communities on Verlock open worlds," the Vergallian ambassador's daughter said, without referring to her tab.

"Thank you. Every year Union Station hosts a convention for CoSHC representatives to get together and discuss the challenges they face, in addition to signing trade agreements and coordinating activities. This year we're opening the trade show to other species who wish to promote their goods and services to our growing market, and we're willing to provide free booth space for any of you who wish to advertise your open worlds to humans."

"We've experimented with allowing your people who complete labor contracts to remain on some of our worlds," the Horten ambassador commented. "I'm told that one of those communities took out a large loan from a local benevolence society and later defaulted."

"You're talking about the agricultural settlement on Gump Four," Aabina said. "According to a report we received from the CoSHC representative, the mayor ran up a large personal debt gambling on sports, and her Horten bookies arranged that loan from the benevolence society and then intercepted the money. Our legal aid people are pursuing the matter with the local authorities."

"Vergallian legal aid?" Ortha asked in disbelief.

"CoSHC legal aid," the Vergallian girl replied. "I've adjusted my pronoun usage in accordance with my employment."

"What benefit would we derive from opening worlds to Human settlements that we don't already get through hiring contract workers?" the Grenouthian ambassador demanded. "Are you seeking a quid pro quo for our business activities on Earth? I've seen that contract and it makes no stipulations about equal access."

"Every CoSHC community represents economic activity that wouldn't be there otherwise. On Drazen and Frunge open worlds, our people have rehabilitated housing stock and brought back to life abandoned mines and foundries that weren't sufficiently profitable to continue operation with native employees. We also have numerous communities on Dollnick open worlds manufacturing custom goods under license for export to human markets."

"If the Dollnicks want to cut their own throats, that's their business. I don't see the Vergallians rushing to open their worlds to Humans, and you're practically the same species. Why would we want to share our monopolies?"

"First of all, I'll remind you that the most popular show produced by Grenouthians on Union Station is 'Let's Make Friends,' which is hosted by Aisha McAllister," Aabina replied. "Second, Vergallians employ more of our mercenaries than all of the other species combined. Third —"

"By 'our' mercenaries, does she mean Humans?" the Grenouthian interrupted. "I'm getting confused."

"Aabina got the top score on the EarthCent civil service exam," the Vergallian ambassador announced proudly.

"It all comes down to different standards of living," Bork informed the giant bunny. "Our consortiums have found that it's actually less expensive to let Humans set up their own communities and operate facilities under lease than to hire them as contract workers with all of the protections and benefits the Stryx impose."

"That's right," Czeros said. "A colleague of mine has an ownership interest in the Break Rock asteroid belt. The find was considered to be played out thousands of years ago, and there wasn't enough demand for a beat-up old mining habitat to move it elsewhere. When Human contract labor became available, they reopened the mine, and since leasing the facility to the workers after the contract expiration, the shareholders have seen a jump in dividends."

"You're saying that the Humans are better at managing themselves than we are?" the Grenouthian ambassador asked skeptically. "I find that difficult to believe."

"No, I'm saying that Humans are willing to work longer hours under worse conditions than we would ask of them."

"We're planning to introduce labor and safety regulations for our communities, but the standards are less stringent than those of the advanced species," Aabina volunteered.

"Just think about it," Daniel said to the ambassadors. "I have free passes to the convention and the trade show for all of you. We don't require a commitment up front."

The Grenouthian ambassador asked for more examples, and Daniel allowed his Vergallian co-op student to carry the ball. By the end of the meeting, Kelly could barely remember which species was which, much less who lived where. As usual, the Verlock ambassador remained in his seat when the others rose, giving them time to get away before blocking the exit with his slow-moving bulk.

"What did you think, Srythlan?" the EarthCent ambassador asked.

"Aabina is an excellent addition to your embassy," the Verlock pronounced slowly. "It proves the value of your civil service test."

"We had a, uh, little problem with the pass rate for humans," Kelly confessed. "Between you and me, it was less than two percent."

"Closer to one and a half percent, and it would be less than one percent if you include the test takers who gave up early."

"You spied on our civil service exams?"

"Not personally," Srythlan said, his heavy features splitting into a wide smile. "I have a fourth cousin who is planning to open a chain of cram academies for Humans who want to take the EarthCent civil service exam and he showed me a prospectus. Perhaps you can mention something to your president?"

"Give me your cousin's contact information," Kelly said resignedly. "Somebody suggested grading on a curve, but that's not going to work if aliens keep taking the test for the entertainment value."

Eight

The large banner over the dojo was hand-printed in three languages, and it translated to, "Farewell, Grude. Congratulations, Marilla. Good luck, Jorb."

"Is that Yvandi in the corner?" Samuel asked Vivian. "I can't tell Sharf girls apart."

"That's because you're always too busy ogling the Vergallians," his girlfriend replied, glancing across the room. "Yes, that's her. She finished her competency tests a while ago but she stayed around the Open University to teach a lab and do research. When she heard that Grude got the visiting alien position at that Sharf naval architecture firm, she decided to go back with him."

"That's very nice of her."

"They're splitting a yacht delivery rather than taking a space liner and they'll be doing a little exploring along the way. Maybe they'll strike it rich."

"Why would somebody in Sharf space be taking delivery on a yacht from Union Station?"

"Don't tell anybody where you heard this, but Drazen Intelligence has identified a huge market opportunity for personal ship delivery and furniture-moving businesses due to the Gryph rumors. The yacht belongs to some rich Sharf who had it parked here, and he figures he better get it home before Union Station changes hands."

"Crazy," Samuel said, shaking his head. Then he pointed down at the mats covering the floor. "I wonder if there will be a martial arts demonstration for entertainment."

"I heard that Jorb threatened to toss that rude Dollnick princeling out on his butt if he shows up at the party to give Grude a hard time," Vivian said. "Besides, leaving the mats down should help prevent drinking injuries."

"I never understood why anybody would get inebriated to the point of falling down or throwing up."

"That's because you aren't any fun," Aabina said, putting a hand on Samuel's shoulder and drawing a reflexive scowl from his girlfriend. "Hi, Vivian. Don't worry. Sam and I are practically foster siblings now."

"Sounds like the band is getting ready to start," Samuel announced in an obvious attempt to change the subject. "I see Mornich, but where's Marilla?"

"She, Jorb, and Grude are going to make a grand entrance," the Vergallian girl told them. "They even hired that pair of jokers from the co-op orientation to do an introduction."

"I'm going to get a glass of wine before it's gone," Vivian said. "When I put the bottle I brought down on the table, it was the only thing I saw there that we can drink."

"I'll get it," Samuel volunteered immediately. "Can I bring you anything, Aabina?"

"I have to be at work in three hours."

"But it's a convergence weekend and our embassy is closed."

"I promised your associate ambassador I'd go in and moderate a conference call for his CoSHC members."

"You have access to the EarthCent embassy when nobody else is there?" Vivian asked in astonishment.

"I'm an employee," Aabina replied simply.

"And I suppose that Sam can just wander into the Vergallian embassy any time of day or night…"

"Of course, though keep in mind that my mother and I live there."

"You never mentioned that," Vivian growled, rounding on her boyfriend.

"I'll just get that drink," Samuel said and fled into the crowd. He didn't look back until he reached the table set up as a bar, and was shocked to see his girlfriend and Aabina laughing so hard that they were holding each other up. He ducked out of sight behind a Dollnick and waited for the music to start before returning. Vivian was standing in the same spot he'd left her, but the Vergallian ambassador's daughter was nowhere to be seen.

"What was that all about?" he shouted over the music, handing Vivian her glass of wine.

"I don't know what you're talking about," she replied, and without even tasting the wine, put the glass on the floor against the wall where it would no doubt get knocked over. "Let's take off our shoes and dance."

After a few songs with a steadily increasing tempo that the Horten musicians employed to kick the party into high gear, the music came to a sudden halt. The odd couple of a Grenouthian and a Verlock in formal dress climbed onto the improvised bandstand.

"Attention," the Verlock bellowed, and the crowd fell silent.

"Welcome one and all to a celebration in honor of our dear friends," the bunny announced, and then made a show of squinting up at the banner, "Grude, Marilla and Jurb."

"Jorb," his partner interrupted.

"Right. Grynlan and I have known Jurb—"

"Jorb," the Verlock boomed.

"—ever since we began training at the dojo, and I want to say that he's the finest Frunge—"

"Drazen!" Grynlan thundered.

"—that I've ever had the joy to meet in martial combat." The Grenouthian paused and threw a few ineffectual jabs at the Verlock, which bounced right off the leathery alien's hide. "We both wish Jurb and Marilla well in their marriage—"

"He's not marrying Marilla, you idiot," Mornich shouted, his skin turning purple.

"My mistake," the bunny apologized. "We wish Grude and Jurb a fruitful union—"

"Jorb," the Verlock howled.

"And may their children be a blessing on us all. Without further ado, let's get them out here."

The students formed a double line extending to the dojo's office where the three honorees were waiting. The Grenouthian started a drum roll on his belly, and the students set up a rhythmic clapping and stomping, though the mats rendered the latter ineffective. Grude came out first, clasping both pairs of his hands together, and giving the victory shake of a successful martial artist to the left and the right at the same time.

"I give you Marilla," the Grenouthian announced.

"Jorb," the Verlock roared.

"Grude!" the students shouted in unison.

"He's got a fifty-fifty chance of getting the next one right," Vivian remarked to Samuel.

"I saw a bunny doing stand-up once," the ambassador's son replied. "Their usual jokes are way too complicated, so this guy may be a comic genius."

Marilla came out next to the continuing applause, dropping Horten-style curtseys in all directions.

"I give you Jorb!" the Grenouthian shouted, looking pleased with himself for pronouncing the name correctly. Mornich jumped on the bunny's back and wrestled him off the stage, where the mats proved their value. The Verlock member of the comedy duo attempted to take bets while the skinny Horten and the giant bunny flopped around on the floor, and then Jorb rushed out to break up the fight.

"That was unexpected," Vivian commented. "I hope Mornich isn't too mad to keep singing."

"Marilla is laughing," Samuel pointed out. "Look how brown she is. All of the Hortens got a big kick out of the act."

"When we finish at the Open University, let's not throw a party." She pointed at the wall below a poster showing a two-dimensional frame grab of an immersive featuring the leading Drazen martial arts actor. "Didn't I leave my wine right next to our shoes?"

"I'll get you another one," Samuel offered, but a minute later he was back with the bad news. "Empty."

"That's alright," Vivian said as the music started up again. "Let's dance."

Mornich and the band must have been putting in a special effort for Marilla because they never stopped for a break until the lights in the Dojo began to flicker on and off. Exhausted dancers collapsed on the mats as the musicians rushed to pack their equipment. The three honorees took the stage.

"Thank you all for coming, but our reservation is almost up," Jorb announced. "Please make sure to take your personal belongings and your trash with you. We don't have much time to clean and I don't want to lose the deposit."

"If anybody finds themselves in Sharf space, give me a shout," Grude added.

The dojo emptied out rapidly, but Samuel and Vivian stayed behind to help with the final clean-up. As soon as the musicians moved their equipment out to the corridor, Jorb gathered his friends in the office. The Drazen used his tentacle to pull a ceiling-mounted controller into reach and said, "Watch this."

For a moment nothing happened, and then a long metal pipe, just shorter than the width of the large room where the party had taken place, emerged from a slot at the top of the wall. Jorb jabbed at the controller, and hundreds of nozzles began blasting steam at the floor. The apparatus moved rapidly across the whole room, and to the students in the office, it looked like the dojo had filled with clouds.

"Now a little ventilation," Jorb announced, hitting a different button. The clouds of steam formed into vortexes as they were sucked up through ceiling vents, and in less than a minute, the only sign that the room had been cleaned was the glistening mats.

"How long will it take the mats to dry?" Grude asked.

"Just getting to it," the Drazen said, and after thumbing a different button, he pushed the controller back up to its parking position at the ceiling. The metal pipe began its return trip, and the nozzles that had previously spewed steam now blasted hot air at the mats, causing dimples as they passed over.

"I wish I had one of those at home," Samuel exclaimed. "What a way to clean a room!"

"But you have to take everything out first," Vivian said. "What are those mats made of, Jorb?"

93

"It's the same stuff the Verlocks use for flexible armor. It would take a railgun pellet to cause any damage. I've seen guys hacking at it with axes and all they do is put a little crease in the cover that goes away as soon as somebody walks over it."

"Hey, we can't just go home," Grude said. "What time is it for you guys?"

"Time to eat," Jorb replied. "I'm starving."

"Works for us," Vivian said. "We skipped supper because of the timing."

"I could do with a snack after all that dancing," Marilla admitted, and then pointed at her ear. "Mornich just asked me if I want to go and grab something in the Little Apple. He's been teasing me about going Human since I started working for Samuel's dad."

"Have you guys ever been to Pub Haggis?" Samuel asked. "It's my treat."

A group of tough-looking bunnies wearing silk belts rather than banners entered the dojo and immediately started throwing each other around.

"Let's go," Jorb said. "We overstayed our time. Stick near the walls and they should leave us alone."

The students cautiously made their way to the exit and found Mornich waiting for them in the corridor.

"The guys let me off roadie duty, so I owe them at the next gig," the Horten singer said. "But, listen. I looked up haggis while I was waiting and I don't think I want to eat any."

"Don't worry," Vivian assured him, "it's just the name of the place. They don't even serve haggis unless somebody orders it ahead of time."

"Last one in the capsule has to carry me home," Jorb declared, and raced for the nearest lift tube. His friends

94

jogged after him, and Grude made a point of letting the Hortens and the Humans enter the capsule before him.

"Won't be the first time I've carried him home," the Dollnick said. "I've gotten used to you guys."

"You'll have fun in Sharf space," Samuel told him. "It's only a hundred cycles, and that's not long with your lifespan."

"I imagine the two of you will be married with a kid in the Open University by the time I finish my internship. How old were you when you started here, Vivian?"

"Fourteen, but I'm going to make our children stay in the station librarian's experimental school until they figure out what they want to do. I wasted my first three years at university."

"Alright, so you'll be married and living in a fancy apartment by the time I get back."

"Shipping container," Marilla corrected the Dollnick. "Young married Humans live in shipping containers."

"That's just Dorothy and her husband," Vivian told the Horten. "Samuel's family isn't typical."

"But when you get married you'll belong to them so you'll have to follow their traditions," Grude said.

"We're not Dollnicks," Samuel rushed to tell their four-armed friend before Vivian could get worked up. "Humans who get married belong to each other."

"Sounds complicated from a legal perspective," Jorb said as the lift tube doors slid open. "We settled everything long ago by having singing competitions."

"But most Drazen males can't even read musical notation."

"That's what I'm saying. Which way is the stuffed intestine place?"

"Pub Haggis. Just go straight."

"I never thought I'd say anything positive about Drazens, but I think that establishing who's in charge with singing competitions makes perfect sense," Mornich said.

"Dream on," Marilla retorted. "Are you sure they'll have something we can eat, Samuel?"

"Before we expanded the embassy my mom used to host meetings with the other ambassadors here. Ian knows what all of the oxygen-breathing species on the station eat."

"As long as he knows what we drink," Jorb said. "Do you think he can make a Divverflip?"

"No, but he buys the beer that my dad brews and you like that."

"It's tasty, but it's impossible to drink enough to numb your tentacle, if you know what I mean."

"Not really." Samuel led the others to a table with six seats, making sure that the furniture was carbon fiber to bear Grude's weight. Then he went up to the counter and caught Ian's eye.

"Hello, Samuel. Celebrating something with your friends?"

"They've passed their competency tests, and our Dollnick friend is leaving the station. Can you send out something that everybody can eat?"

"Not a problem. Is the Drazen going to want something strong to drink? We can order in."

"I'll take two pitchers of my dad's ale. How's it been selling lately?"

"The last few barrels were on the fruity side but it's been going fast," Ian said. He held a pitcher under the tap with one hand and began arranging beer mugs on a tray with the other hand. "Any idea what he put in there?"

"Cherries, I think. At least I remember there being cherries with breakfast, lunch, and dinner a while back. Donna gave mom this chocolate fountain thing for her birthday and they had a cherry-dipping party." Samuel lowered his voice. "My dad had to hide it. He said she can use it on holidays or when we have special guests."

"Here, take these." Ian placed the full pitcher on the tray with the glasses. "I'll send the waitress out with a refill as soon as she finishes with that other table."

Samuel returned to his friends with the beer, and the pitcher was emptied into six mugs.

"A toast," the Drazen announced, raising his glass. "To beer."

"Beer," the other students echoed dutifully. Jorb and Grude drained their mugs in one go and looked around for the next pitcher. Samuel sighed and returned to the bar for a refill.

"Faster than I thought," Ian said. "Food is going to take a little while. Do you want some snacks?"

"Maybe something salty?"

"Nuts should do the trick. You can't get the Frunge to eat them, but all of the other species seem to like cashews and pistachios." He reached under the bar and came up with an unopened can, studied the label, then broke the seal and poured them out in a wooden bowl. "Got to be careful with the Hortens and peanuts. They're allergic."

Samuel returned to his friends with the new pitcher and the large bowl of nuts. He filled the empty mugs before returning to his seat, where Vivian promptly informed him, "It's your turn."

"What's my turn?"

"To tell a co-op experience story."

"What about you and Marilla? I missed yours?"

"You missed the discussion of who goes first."

"I've only been working one week."

"You must have done something by now other than dancing with old ladies."

"The ambassador mainly has me studying for the CoSHC trade show."

"But isn't that a Human thing?" Grude asked.

"Yeah, but they're accepting booths from the other species this year, and I'm going to be representing the Vergallians."

"That doesn't make any sense," Marilla said. "You have a conflict of interests."

"That's what I told them but they wouldn't accept it," Samuel said. "The ambassador said that she's confident in my—she used a Vergallian word that translates to something like a code of ethics and loyalty to the queen—and that I have as much right to represent them at the convention as her daughter has to represent us, I mean, Humans."

"Did you just say 'Humans' with a capital 'H', Sam?" Vivian demanded.

"I know, it's confusing. I can't imagine what Libby was thinking by sending me there and Aabina to mom."

"That wasn't much of a story," Marilla said. "You guys are never going to believe mine. On my second day at work, Mr. McAllister asked me to help him change out the blue box in one of the Horten ships they're trying to convert into a rental."

"What's a blue box?" Grude asked.

"It's a heat exchanger that we use in small craft for cooling ion drivers. I've seen them before when cleaning rental returns, but I never cracked one open and I was worried that the fluid might be toxic. Mr. McAllister called Beowulf in, he's a giant Cayl hound, and cracked the seal just enough to let Wolfie get a sniff."

"Wolfie?" Vivian asked.

"He's kind of adorable, don't you think? Anyway, Beowulf gave Mr. McAllister the nod, and we took off the cover, drained the old fluid, and scraped off the crud. Then we put it in a Verlock hot tank, took a lunch break, and by the time we came back, the coils looked like new. By the end of the day, we had it reinstalled and tested. I never did anything like that before."

"How did you choose a replacement for the thermal fluid?" Grude asked. "Those systems are sensitive."

"Oh, Wolfie picked it out for us. Mr. McAllister stocks all of the common lubricants and thermal fluids behind their ice harvester and he says the dog knows them all by smell."

"Your turn, Vivian," Jorb said, pouring himself a third beer. "Anybody else? Grude?"

The Dollnick, who was juggling nuts in an intricate pattern using all four hands, made a slight adjustment so the nuts all ended up in his mouth, then chased them down with his beer and gave the Drazen the empty mug.

"Well, I'm not supposed to talk about what I'm doing on my co-op job, but I guess I can tell you about my first test," Vivian said.

"Did they put you in spy school?" Marilla asked.

"It's not like that, exactly. I have a sort of a trainer, and she has me carrying out assignments that they evaluate to see what kind of work I have an aptitude for. But there's one test they make everybody take, which is talking your way into a stranger's apartment."

"What do you mean?" Mornich asked. "That could be dangerous."

"On Union Station? In any case, the only rule is that I couldn't tell anybody that I was taking a test, and if they guessed, it didn't count."

"Who would guess?" Samuel asked.

"Every Drazen with an apartment near the Intelligence headquarters," Jorb told them.

"That's pretty much what I found out," Vivian said. "And they gave me some suggested scripts, like, to pretend I was doing a safety inspection for station maintenance or that I needed to use the bathroom, but nothing seemed to work. A couple of aliens let me in because they thought I was the InstaSitter they ordered, but that didn't count."

"So you failed?" Samuel asked.

"Until I tried the Dollnick deck. Then it was so easy that I got into four apartments in a row and my trainer gave me extra credit."

"How'd you do that?" Grude asked. "Most of my people are very private and protective of their nests."

"I told them I was there to count rooms," Vivian said and grinned at the blank faces of her friends. "You know, to put a value on the residential deck for Gryph's auction."

Nine

"Where's our baby?" Flazint asked Dorothy.

"Margie? Kevin is babysitting. When I brought her to the office last week to get acclimated, she never settled down because you and Affie spent the whole time playing peek-a-boo."

"I wouldn't hold out on you if I had a baby."

"I don't know where you're going to get one as long as you and Tzachan are afraid to be alone in a room together."

"We're not frightened of each other you know," the Frunge girl protested indignantly. "It's just our culture. Tzachan is worried about my reputation."

"That and a half a cred will buy you a cup of coffee," Dorothy retorted. "Do we have any?"

"Coffee? Aren't you nursing?"

"Skip the lecture, I'll have fruit juice."

A gorgeous young Vergallian woman entered the conference room and demanded, "Where's our baby?"

"At home," Flazint told her. "Dorothy thinks we can't control ourselves."

"I'll have you both know that my royal training included building up a resistance to cute babies," Affie said. She stared into space for a moment as if trying to remember something, and then added, "I might have failed that part."

Brinda arrived with her older sister Shaina, and after a brief scan of the room, asked, "Where's Margie?"

"Kevin wouldn't let me bring her," Dorothy lied.

"I don't blame him," Shaina said. "They grow up so fast. My Grace is starting on 'Let's Make Friends' this afternoon and she's so excited that I could barely get her to go to school. And the little Stryx friend Libby assigned to Grace is even more nervous than she is, if that's possible."

"Aisha mentioned that this is the first time a younger sibling of a former cast member is joining the show," Dorothy said. "I'll be watching from home."

"Is Jeeves here yet?" Brinda asked.

"He's probably hiding out in the corridor waiting for Baa to come in first," Affie said. "You know how those two are always playing power games."

"We aren't playing," the Terragram mage announced as she joined the meeting. "We're positioning. There's a difference."

"Ladies," Jeeves said, floating in right behind Baa and assuming his accustomed place at the head of the table. "The reason I asked you all here today is to discuss our strategy for the CoSHC trade show. I also want to take this opportunity to welcome Dorothy back from maternity leave. SBJ Fashions is a baby-friendly business, and in that spirit, I've added a changing station to the all-species restroom. Please return the fold-down table to the upright position against the wall after use."

"Does that mean you're going to approve my new line of infant clothes?" the new mother asked hopefully.

"No. We've been through this before, and while I'm willing to help you start a new business if you're passion-ate about the idea, baby apparel does not fit with the SBJ Fashions brand image."

"He's right, Dorothy. If you want to try licensing your designs to another manufacturer, Tzachan can help with the legal stuff," Flazint said.

"On his own time," Jeeves cautioned them. "While we're on the subject of manufacturing, I've heard back from Chintoo and it's too expensive for our supplier there to gear up for noodle weapon production on a small scale. In addition, the technology originated with the Grenouthians, and they have a contract with the professional LARPing league that imposes limitations on the promotion of generic noodle weapons."

"Those bunnies are getting too big for their sashes," Baa muttered.

"Be that as it may, I've contacted several Grenouthian manufacturers, and after I made it clear to them that I was shopping in my capacity as the buyer for SBJ Fashions and not as a Stryx, they fobbed me off on their authorized distributors. I've discussed the necessary price points with Shaina and Brinda, and we aren't going to get there if we have to pay the same price as retailers for the raw stock."

"Let me negotiate with the manufacturers," the Terragram mage begged.

"Don't forget the deal under which Gryph allowed you to remain on the station," Jeeves cautioned her. "In some ways, your restrictions are even tougher than mine."

"Shaina and I have been looking into this, and since noodle weapons aren't forged or hand-finished, they're basically sold by weight," Brinda said. "The Grenouthians are charging an outrageous amount for the material, but the weapons themselves are produced by 3-D printers."

"Can we find some humans on a Grenouthian open world who manufacture noodle weapons under license?" Dorothy asked.

"The bunnies don't allow us on their open worlds," Shaina told her.

"Well, they should. My mom said something about Grenouthians making a fortune on a new business taking aliens to Earth on documentary tours. Maybe that will give us leverage."

"Ai-hem-sha," Jeeves said as if he was clearing his non-existent throat. "I seem to have picked up a bug somewhere. Ai-hem-sha."

"Do you mean, Aisha?" Flazint asked.

"I couldn't venture to say because my parent is threatening to send me to my room for interfering in the competitive balance between tunnel network members."

"Aisha does host the Grenouthian network's most profitable non-news show, and the local ambassador has a point in the production, so maybe he'll listen to her," Shaina mused. "I'll ask when I see her this afternoon and maybe she can get the producer on our side. We could offer them exclusivity on shooting our commercials."

"But we've always hired Grenouthian production crews for our ads," Dorothy said.

"Offering something they already have is a veiled threat, the bunny will understand. In the meantime, Baa could get started with enchanting some noodle weapons that don't weigh much, like daggers. Maybe that would help persuade the bunnies that it's worth getting their paws wet."

"Baa already has my honor dagger," Flazint said.

"And my rapier," Affie added. "Have you done anything to them yet, Baa?"

"Enchanting weapons, even noodle weapons, takes a lot more energy than creating bags of holding or adding magical protection to a cape," the feathered mage replied.

"I try to keep the draw on the station infrastructure below the point where Gryph starts adding surcharges."

"It shouldn't take that much power to get the effects you want in a LARP studio," Jeeves said. "Are you up to something I should know about?"

"It was Dorothy's idea."

"What was my idea?" the ambassador's daughter asked.

"Enchanting some of our products for use outside the LARP environment," Baa replied. "I know, I know. I promised Gryph that I wouldn't employ my abilities on the station in a way that the other species could interpret as hostile or intimidating, but giving some stat boosts to toy weapons that I'm not personally wielding can hardly be considered a violation."

"What kind of stat boosts?"

"You know, the usual," Baa said evasively. "I'm working on Samuel and Vivian's swords as well, since they're our best bet for putting on a demonstration duel in the booth."

"Is there anything else you want to share with us?" Jeeves asked in an icy tone.

"I borrowed a noodle axe from Samuel's Drazen friend because I wanted to practice on something with a little mass. And the Horten girl working in Mac's Bones let me have her sword as well."

"Are there any former participants from our LARP fashion shows whose weapons you aren't enchanting for real-world use?"

"Judith wasn't at Mac's Bones when I stopped by to pick up Thomas and Chance's swords, and Tzachan wanted me to sign something, so I told him to forget it. I'm thinking of loaning him a staff if he'll agree to appear at Dorothy's booth."

"What's done is done, but I don't want you putting on any demonstrations without my knowledge in case something goes wrong," Jeeves said. "In fact, I want to be there when you return the weapons to their owners to make sure they can wield them safely."

"I've got good news about the trade show," Shaina announced. "My husband wanted to stick us in the back corner, but the embassy's Vergallian co-op student is taking over booth assignments for CoSHC. I talked her into giving us space on the main aisle, not far from the entrance."

"How many folds?" Dorothy asked.

"And what's a fold?" Affie added.

"A folding table," Dorothy explained. "It's the universal standard for trade shows. I'm surprised it never came up in your royal education."

"I asked her for two folds," Shaina said. "Aabina suggested eight set up in a square, so our booth will have access on two aisles rather than being backed up against somebody else who only took two tables. It means that if we keep the center area clear, there will be just enough space for a duel."

"So eight folds only cost twice as much as two because the interior tables don't have aisle access?" Jeeves asked.

"Well, it wasn't cheap, but it's in the budget, particularly now that we don't have to buy Baa any noodle weapons to enchant."

"Plus, there will be plenty of room for my boothmates," Dorothy said. "Marilla and Kevin can take one side to drum up interest in the ship rental business, and Thomas and Chance can take the other side to recruit for EarthCent Intelligence."

"Which side does that leave us with?" Brinda asked.

"Oh, that's a good point. Do you think we can get the square at the beginning of the aisle so we have access on three sides?"

"I'll check with Aabina," Shaina said.

"How much are we charging EarthCent Intelligence?" Jeeves inquired. "Paul asked me about sharing the booth to explore the spaceship rental market, but I haven't heard an offer from Blythe."

"Thomas and Chance can work it off by putting on demonstrations with the enchanted noodle weapons," Dorothy said. "Don't you love it when everything just sort of fits together?"

"I love it when I actually get a return on my investment," Jeeves grumbled. "Do you have a program in mind for the demonstration?"

"Since it looks like we have to please the Grenouthians, musical accompaniment won't do. I'm not going to play one of their twangy ballads, and they hate our music. I guess I'll have to write a script and find an announcer."

"We better get back to work then," Flazint said, standing up and pulling Dorothy along with her. "Come on, Affie. Baa. Our employers probably have important financial matters to discuss."

As soon as the door of the design room slid closed behind them, the Terragram threw a ball of fire at the wall above the bench where she did most of her enchantments. It dissipated harmlessly, though the metal surface glowed briefly.

"That young Stryx gets me so frustrated!" Baa declared. "I wouldn't mind as much if he was a few hundred thousand years older, but having a child for a minder makes me crazy. Does he really think I'm stupid enough to put dangerous enchantments on weapons that could get me kicked off the station?"

"I think he's just trying to be helpful," Affie said. "Besides, he's the one that Gryph would hold responsible in the end."

"So now I'm a charity case."

"None of us would ever think that," Dorothy told the irate mage. "You know that without your enchantments our sales wouldn't even be growing at this point. The only reason we're even taking a booth at the trade show is to expand your part of the business."

"That was interesting what you said about tapping into the station's power grid," Flazint said. "Does that mean if you arranged with Gryph ahead of time you could enchant items faster?"

"Depends," Baa replied. "If you're talking about a simple enchantment, like increasing the available space inside of a purse for LARPs, I could handle a hundred at a time if I wasn't worried about power consumption. But the bonuses that I'm adding to the noodle weapons are specific to each, so I can only do one at a time."

"That's the oldest question in fashion," Dorothy said. "Is it better to be exclusive and sell at high prices, or to mass produce and capture market share?"

"Unless another fashion house can get a Terragram mage to come work for them, we're probably safe on being exclusive," Affie pointed out.

"I watched too many Vergallian dramas while I was home with the baby and there are tons of commercials for cross-over fashions now. You see plenty of kids wandering around the station in costumes these days. Just a year ago, they would have changed into their regular clothes after the LARP before going out in the corridors, but now, I swear people who aren't even role players are wandering around dressed as elves and barbarians."

"I've noticed that on the Frunge deck as well," Flazint said. "It's like every day is Sun Day."

"That reminds me," Affie said. "There's a festival on the Vergallian deck this weekend and you guys should really come and hang out. Everybody will be wearing the latest fashions from the empire and it's always fun to see drama fans acting out their favorite scenes. Let's pick a time that works for all of us."

"When is your weekend?" Dorothy asked.

"Starts in a couple of hours, but the real fun isn't until tomorrow. Say, nine in the evening on your clock?"

"I can go, but it's morning for me so I won't drink," Flazint said.

"Baa?" Affie asked.

"You're inviting me?" The Terragram mage placed the purse she was about to enchant on her workbench and turned back to the girls. "You want me to come with you?"

"Sure. Does the time work for you?"

"Anytime works for me, I don't sleep." Baa hesitated for a moment, and then asked, "Does this mean you think of me as a friend?"

"I do," Dorothy replied without hesitation. "What's the big deal? You must have had friends before."

"Not since my heart was stolen," Baa replied. "There were a few girls I used to hang out with in a pantheon back on—it's not important. It didn't end well."

"What did you do for fun?"

"Fight, mainly. You know, thunderbolts and proxy armies of worshippers. When I look back at it now, I have to wonder if I was sane."

"You spend too much time working," Affie said. "It will help with your creativity to get out and have some fun. Just don't, uh—"

"I won't," the Terragram mage promised. "If I wear one of my LARPing outfits with a veil, nobody will even know that it's me."

"I'll see you all tomorrow, then," Dorothy said. "I told Kevin I'd come home and watch his chandler's shop and the baby so he can help with the rentals they're trying to get ready before the conference."

Flazint followed the ambassador's daughter out into the corridor before asking, "Can I talk to you for a minute before you go, Dorothy?"

"Sure. Why so serious?"

"It's about Tzachan."

"You're having problems? You want me to straighten him out?"

"What are you—no, just listen. I've been hinting to my ancestors for cycles that I want them to get a move on and start some preliminary negotiations with Tzachan's family tree, but you know what old Frunge are like."

"Creaky," Dorothy acknowledged.

"So Tzachan and I have talked about trying to speed things up by getting a matchmaker involved."

"What's the point of hiring a matchmaker when the match is already made? You'll just be throwing your money away."

"We don't get married without a matchmaker's help, it's just a question of when you bring one in. Most Frunge attorneys won't even talk to you about a marriage contract unless you have a draft prepared by a matchmaker first. And the matchmakers are the ones who administer all the tests."

"Why does love have to be so complicated?"

"Love isn't complicated," Flazint said. "Family is complicated. I hate bringing up how much longer than you we live, but we have to deal with the consequences of our choices for hundreds of years. It's worth taking the time to get it right."

"So when are you going to the matchmaker?"

"I can't go!" Flazint exclaimed, her hair vines turning dark green. "It isn't done that way."

"So when is Tzachan going?"

"He can't go either. You're going to make me come right out and say it, aren't you?"

"I guess so, since I don't really know what you're talking about."

"If I wanted the matchmaker to find me somebody it would be different. But when there's already a potential suitor, a responsible matron who knows both parties has to vouch for the match."

"Isn't that like a woman who runs an orphanage? I think I remember some matrons in my mom's old books."

"Is there something wrong with your implant?" Flazint asked in frustration, stamping her foot for emphasis. "A matron is a respectable married woman with a child."

"I think this is one of those cases where we don't have exactly equivalent words," Dorothy mused.

"Are you being purposely obtuse? I want you to go to the matchmaker for us."

"Me? Would a Frunge matchmaker even talk to an alien? I thought they were super traditional."

"They are, but you aren't just any alien. You work with me, your mother is an ambassador, and most important-ly—" Flazint hesitated for a moment, "—you got married under Frunge law."

111

"I thought we agreed never to bring that up again," Dorothy hissed.

"It didn't make any difference in the end. You still had your big wedding, and you have a beautiful baby to prove it."

"Do you really think this will work?"

"It has to work. If it doesn't, I'll be lucky if Tzachan and I get married before Margie does."

"Ouch, that is a long time to wait. Well, I don't suppose the matchmaker will eat me. Ping me with her contact information."

"Thank you, Dorothy. I'll owe you forever. Oh, and don't forget to bring the baby with you, I'm counting on her to close the deal."

"Bring Margie to Frunge matchmaker. Got it."

"And your companionship contract, with the scroll from Ailia witnessing that the conditions were met. Better bring the dog too, just to be safe."

"How about Kevin?"

"Of course you have to bring your husband. What would the matchmaker think if you showed up without him?"

"I don't know, Flazint. I'm not a Frunge matchmaker. You better have Tzachan brief us on what to expect before we go in or we could end up making matters worse."

Ten

Shaina found her husband's hand on the armrest and twined her fingers through his. "I haven't been this nervous since we got married."

"How about Mike's first day on the show?" Daniel asked.

"That was different. Your son is an extrovert."

"My son? What did he do now?"

"He and Fenna went backstage with Grace to keep her company, but I just know that he's giving her bad advice."

A large Dollnick lifted up the armrest between two seats to Shaina's left and dropped his bulk down with a groan. "Why are we so close to the stage?" he complained. "I'm going to get dizzy turning my head back and forth to take it all in."

"Actually, you're in the wrong seat," Shaina told him. "I know because they're reserved for my son and Aisha's daughter."

"Aisha's daughter sits here?" The Dolly sprang up, but then he looked at the tag on the edge of the seat and thrust a plastic chit at Daniel with one of his lower arms. "The numbers match up."

"Eighteen and nineteen," the associate ambassador agreed. "The Grenouthians must have made a mistake."

"Let me see," Shaina said, pulling her husband's whole arm over rather than taking the tickets from him. "Upper level. You're in the first row on the balcony."

"Balcony?" The Dollnick scanned the back of the studio and clapped both sets of hands in relief. "Excellent. I'll have a much better view from there."

"Why would he complain about sitting in front?" Shaina asked her husband as the towering alien moved away.

"Field of view, I guess. I've heard that some of the Dollys from the old engineering families develop a sort of tunnel vision from staring at the details on large structures all of the time."

"That doesn't sound like much of a survival skill."

"I think their peripheral vision is fine, better than ours, but when they concentrate on a particular object, their field of view narrows and the magnification increases."

"I'll stick with squinting."

"Aisha's almost ready to start," Mike reported excitedly as he took the seat next to his mother. "I thought that Grace was going to cry, but she's too busy keeping Twitchy from panicking to remember to be scared herself."

"If you keep calling your sister's Stryx friend by that name the poor thing will end up with a complex," Shaina said.

"She *is* twitchy," Mike reiterated stubbornly. "Just like Spinner always spun around when he got nervous or excited."

"I miss Spinner," Fenna said. "Why'd he have to go away?"

"All of the young Stryx go off to explore the multi-verse," Daniel said, speaking across Shaina and Mike. "Jeeves is the exception."

The lights in the giant studio blinked three times, and a harried-looking bunny hopped up on the stage.

"All right, calm down," he shouted at the audience, all of whom were already settled in their seats and waiting quietly. "Some of you have been here before, but I'm going to run through the rules for the newcomers. That—" he pointed dramatically at a blank display above the stage, "—is an applause sign. When it comes on, you applaud. Shall we do a test?" The display lit up with 'Applause' in a dozen languages, but nobody responded. "Very funny," the bunny growled. "So funny that I might have to cancel the traditional free catering after our new cast debut. Shall we try again?"

This time, the applause sign was met with storms of clapping, whistling, foot stomping, and belly drumming. It took the Grenouthian almost a minute of patting down the air with his outstretched arms to get the audience to stop.

"That's better. The name of the show is 'Let's Make Friends,' so if you're here for the news, you're in the wrong studio." A smattering of polite laughter met this poor attempt at a joke. "Right. Anybody who disrupts the show will be removed, and don't get any smart ideas about becoming famous across the galaxy by running onto the stage because security *will* stop you with extreme prejudice."

"Is he new?" Daniel whispered to his wife.

"He looks familiar. Maybe he was the assistant to the assistant when Mike was on the show."

"I'm the assistant director, which means I'm in charge here," the bunny continued. "If you have any questions or emergencies, remember that our feed is going out live on the Stryxnet, so save them for after the show."

A loud chime was heard, and the Grenouthian turned away from the audience and hurried over to the stage entrance. A moment later, Aisha came out in her favorite show sari, and the audience exploded with genuine applause. She gave everybody a smile and a wave, exchanged a few words with the assistant director, and ducked backstage again. Another chime sounded, and the status lights on immersive cameras positioned around the stage lit up. A few seconds later, the theme music started to play, and the bunny dove off the stage just as Aisha made her entrance.

"Welcome to Let's Make Friends," the host began to speak as the music faded. "Tonight we have a new cast rotation, plus special surprise guests, one of whom has never been on the show before. Also for the first time, the younger sibling of a former cast member will be joining our new rotation, so why don't we all give her a big round of applause."

Shaina's grip on her husband's hand tightened to the point that he was certain that the bones were grinding together. Their six-year-old daughter peeked around the curtain at the audience and then ran out to where Aisha was standing. It appeared that the little girl wanted to get the introduction over with as quickly as possible.

"Do you want to tell us your name?" Aisha asked, putting a comforting hand on the girl's shoulder.

"Princess," she said in a loud whisper.

The audience gave her a friendly round of applause, though there was also a certain amount of whispering among the Dollnicks and Vergallians, for whom royal titles carried significant meaning.

"This is your fault," Shaina hissed at her husband. "How many times have I told you that if you always call her 'Princess' she'll think it's her real name."

Aisha waited for the applause to die down before asking, "Do you have another name?"

The girl scrunched up her eyes and tried to guess what the host was fishing for. "Cohan?"

Offstage, the assistant director tapped his furry foot impatiently, and Aisha decided it wasn't fair to make the other children wait.

"Do you have a special friend of your own who you'd like to introduce?" she prompted Grace.

"Twitchy," the little girl said, looking hopefully at the curtains. For a moment nothing happened, and then a little Stryx floated out on an odd angle, as if her robotic body had been knocked off kilter by a shove. "Over here," Grace called, waving excitedly.

Twitchy's pincer was snapping open and closed so rapidly that it sounded like an old-fashioned door buzzer, and after floating unsteadily to the center of the stage, the little Stryx settled to the floor with a clunk.

"Are you okay?" Aisha asked.

"Nervous. So many sentients watching."

"My brother said to imagine them counting on their fingers," Grace suggested.

"They all look silly now!"

The loud buzz from the chattering pincer came to an end and Aisha breathed a sigh of relief. The next cast member to be introduced was a confident Dollnick boy, who immediately dropped to the floor and did a set of four-armed pushups.

"Do you want to tell the audience your name?" Aisha asked.

"Brule, and I'm a gymnast."

"Are not!" a voice cried from backstage, and a Drazen girl rushed out. "I told him that's what I was going to say. He stole my line!"

"What's your name?" Aisha asked her.

The little Drazen girl sang a few clear notes that didn't translate to anything, but Grace seemed to get something out of it, because she ventured, "Binka?"

"Close enough," the alien said.

A Vergallian boy came out next, his poise and finely chiseled features giving away his ruling class status. "I'm Pietro," he introduced himself with a bow.

"And our first Vergallian cast member in a long time," Aisha said. "Can you tell us why you wanted to be on the show?"

"Just following orders," the little boy replied with a shrug.

The final two cast members came out together, a squat Verlock boy with a Frunge balanced on his shoulders.

"Careful!" Aisha warned. "You could fall and hurt yourself."

"I'm very steady," the Verlock boy said, shuffling slowly towards the center of the stage.

"We're gymnasts too," the young Frunge added.

"And what are your names?" Aisha asked.

"Plynyth," the Verlock grunted.

"Gzera," the Frunge shouted, then promptly lost his balance and did a belly flop on the stage. "I'm okay. I'm okay," he said, scrambling to his feet.

"I'm the gymnast!" Binka reiterated.

The status light on the front immersive camera began to flash. Brule pointed and asked, "Is that broken?"

"That's our cue for a commercial," Aisha told them, and then spoke to the audience. "We'll be right back after these brief messages."

The assistant director hopped up on the stage and crouched low on his haunches. "Does anybody have to use the bathroom?" he asked. The little Frunge hesitated and then raised his hand. "It's always the shrubs," the bunny muttered under his breath. "Go quickly," he said, waving for a furry stagehand to accompany the boy. "The stage manager will send you back out when you return."

"Is 'Princess' your real name?" Pietro asked Grace.

"It's one of my names," the girl replied.

"That's what her father calls her," Twitchy informed the Vergallian.

"Where are the actors doing the commercials?" Binka asked, looking around in confusion.

"The commercials for the different species are all prerecorded and the Grenouthians show them according to who is watching," Aisha explained.

"Doesn't everybody like hot peppers in their breakfast porridge?"

"Yuck," several of the other cast members chorused in reply.

The new assistant director placed the children where he wanted them for the opening shot, quietly threatening to glue their feet to the floor if they moved. Then he hopped down off the stage and began the countdown. Aisha waited to speak until the status lights on the immersive cameras went from blinking to solid.

"Welcome back to Let's Make Friends. It's fun to start a new rotation by asking our cast members what they want to do when they grow up, and today, we have some special guests who want our help with a new attraction they're building for Libbyland. First allow me to introduce my husband, Paul McAllister."

The audience applauded loudly as Paul came out on stage, pushing a cart with high canvas sides before him. He left the cart behind the children and went to stand next to his wife, trying not to show how nervous he felt.

"Working with Paul is somebody you all know from his time filling in as one of the hosts when I was on maternity leave," Aisha continued. "Stryx Jeeves."

The studio audience made even more noise than they had when the bunny insisted on testing the applause sign, and large sections began chanting, "Spiral Slide of Death," the name of a physics-defying playground apparatus that Jeeves had introduced on the show during his tenure. The stage manager took advantage of the chaos to send the young Frunge back out without anybody noticing.

"Thank you. Thank you," Jeeves acknowledged his fans. "As Aisha told you, Paul and I are working on a new game for Libbyland which we hope will help young sentients learn about career options. It's never too early to get started."

"But there's also no rush," Aisha felt obligated to tell her audience.

"Right," Jeeves unexpectedly concurred. "So who wants to start us off?"

"Me," Brule declared, raising all four of his hands. "I want to be a construction engineer."

"Excellent. Can you tell us why?"

"Because my whole family are construction engineers going back forever. Well, I have one uncle who is a musician, but we don't talk about him."

"Would you like to play an engineering game?" Paul asked the young Dollnick.

"Sure."

Aisha's husband pulled a case labeled "Engineering" from the box and opened it up to display a colorful construction kit.

"Who would like to go next?" the host prompted.

"Me," the Drazen girl said. "I want to be a composer."

"Could you tell us why you want to be a composer?" Jeeves asked her.

"All girls want to be composers," Binka replied matter-of-factly. "Don't you?" she asked Grace.

"I don't know. I'm only six."

"How about you?" the Drazen boldly asked Twitchy.

"I don't know either," the little Stryx admitted. "What do composers have to do?"

"Write music, I think."

"Would you like to play a composition game?" Jeeves asked.

"Yes," Binka replied. "You guys can play too if you want."

Paul retrieved another case from the cart, this one labeled "Music." He removed an instrument that resembled a xylophone from the padded case and plugged in a two-sided display panel that would show the musical notes being played.

"Do you want to explain the games that my husband is setting up for the children, Jeeves?" Aisha asked.

"We tried to come up with fun ways that children can find out what it's like to work in the careers they think are interesting. Paul and I did a lot of homework ourselves to generate ideas, so I'll give you an example. Every species on the tunnel network has toys like building blocks. Sometimes it's fun to just pile the blocks as high as you can and knock them down, but we can also ask children to

121

build something they think would be useful, like a house to live in."

"That does sound like work," the hostess said cautiously. "Do you really want to put limits on their imaginations like that?"

"Our staff will watch how the children play their games and tell them about the related careers," Jeeves continued, choosing to ignore Aisha's question. "When they return to Libbyland the next time, we'll give them new games to help them explore the areas they like, always taking into account what was learned on the previous visit."

"We want to play too," Gzera said.

"And what do you want to be when you grow up?" Aisha asked.

"A metallurgist," the Frunge replied immediately.

"A scientist," his Verlock companion said.

"I've got a kit you can work on together," Paul told them, hauling out another case. "It's important in science and technology to learn how to work as part of a team."

"How about you?" Aisha asked the young Vergallian boy. "What do you want to do when you grow up?"

"Serve my queen with honor."

"I'm not sure they'll have a game for that."

"Of course we do," Jeeves said, and pulled a case out of the cart, keeping the label side turned away from Aisha.

"What is it?" she asked.

"Let Pietro play and see if you can guess."

The assistant director gestured frantically at the production crew, and it was a miracle that none of the cameras crashed into each other as their controllers maneuvered them about trying to capture the action as the children played with the kits. The studio audience began growing restless after a few minutes without any of the cast saying anything, and only a few random notes played on the xylophone to break the silence. Finally, the assistant director called an emergency commercial break, barely giving Aisha enough time to say, "And we'll be right back."

"What is this?" the bunny wailed. "It's so quiet on set that I can almost hear our ratings falling. Is there some law nobody told me about where finding careers for the children means you have to sacrifice mine?"

"It's actually going very well," Jeeves said. "In a few hours—"

"We don't have a few hours! Aisha, go to 'Storytellers' after the break."

"Jeeves is just teasing you," Paul said. "The children have already done enough to start asking questions. That's where the learning happens."

"I never knew you agreed with me," Aisha whispered to her husband as the furious bunny began counting them back in. "Children do learn best when they're encouraged to ask questions."

"Actually, Jeeves is going to do the asking," Paul replied just before the immersive cameras lit up.

"And welcome back again," the hostess said in a bright voice. "The children played right through the commercial break so you know they must be having fun. It looks like Brule is building quite the tower."

The young Dollnick barely looked up as Aisha examined his construction, but Jeeves got Brule's attention by pulling out a column from the twisting triangular tower and tossing it back in the case.

"What are you doing?" Brule demanded, followed immediately by, "Why didn't it fall down?"

"That column wasn't supporting any weight," Jeeves explained. "Do you remember why you put it there?"

123

"I thought I needed it."

"Why is that?"

The young Dollnick shrugged. "I remember seeing something built this way, and it had extra columns, maybe on the top."

"Like this?" Jeeves asked, and moving at blinding speed, he rearranged most of the components of the construction. The resulting building consisted of twelve stacked triangular floors, where each story was offset by a five-degree angle from the slightly larger floor below.

"That's it," Brule said excitedly, as the Dollnicks in the audience broke out in loud whistles of admiration. "I see it when I'm sleeping sometimes but I can't remember where it's from. What is it?"

"That's the traditional cake served at the wedding of a prince."

"I remember now," Brule cried. "I got a piece and it was soooo tasty. I wish I could make cakes like that."

"You could, if you became a baker."

"That's what I want to be when I grow up. A baker."

"You don't have to decide right now," Aisha reminded him, but the young Dollnick was already deconstructing the tower and returning the pieces to the case. Jeeves floated over to where Binka was hesitantly striking notes on the xylophone, aided by Grace and Twitchy.

"Composing music is hard," the Drazen girl piped up. "The notes don't want to go together."

"That's good," Jeeves told her. "A feel for which notes don't fit with each other is just as important as understanding which ones do. How do you like being a composer, Princess?"

"I just wanted to help," Grace said. "It doesn't sound like the music mommy plays."

"I like the harmonics, the counting, and the scales," Twitchy contributed nervously. "They remind me of math. I like math."

"You're all set then because you're going to get plenty of it," Jeeves told the little Stryx.

"How are you two progressing?" Aisha asked the young scientists.

"He's so slow," Gzera complained, and to illustrate his point, made a series of moves in the string game related to cat's cradle they were playing. The Verlock was unable to keep up. "It keeps getting tangled."

"You skipped the fourth sequence," Plynyth replied slowly. "I don't think you read the instructions."

"Did you read the instructions?" Jeeves asked the young Frunge.

"Maybe not all of them," Gzera admitted. "They were so long, and there weren't enough pictures."

"Do you think that metallurgists have to follow lots of instructions?"

"I never thought about it. Do they?"

"I'm afraid they do," Jeeves said. "But you can work with metal without becoming a metallurgist. There are blacksmiths, and welders, and sculptors—"

"I want to be all of those," Gzera interrupted.

"What are you working on?" Aisha asked the Vergallian boy. She crouched down to look at the small figurines Pietro was arranging on the deck. "Are those soldiers?"

"They're alien mercenaries. I'm setting up a defensive perimeter," he added, stumbling over the last two words.

"What are the mercenaries going to eat?" Jeeves asked.

"Food?"

"But where is it? All I see are soldiers and weapons."

"Do you mean the supply train? I didn't take any of those pieces out because they're boring."

"And so they are, but your soldiers still have to eat," Jeeves said.

Pietro chewed on his lower lip and nodded. "I'll do better next time."

The assistant director started counting them to another commercial break, and Jeeves rushed to say, "Free entry to the Career Game at Libbyland this cycle for anybody who mentions my name."

Aisha helped her husband and Jeeves repack the toys during the long commercial break, and when the cameras went live again, she led the children through a successful round of Storytellers, one of the show's most popular features. Then it came time for the closing segment, and Jeeves reappeared with the xylophone from the career kit and began playing the theme music. The cast members, all of whom had watched the show countless times, launched into their song:

Don't be a stranger because I look funny,
You look weird to me, but let's make friends.
I'll give you a tissue if your nose is runny,
I'm as scared as you, so let's make friends.

"That's a wrap," the assistant director concluded when the camera lights blinked off. "New rule, and this is from the booth. No more career planning on the show—we're already getting complaints from the parents."

Eleven

Joe finished stacking the used breakfast dishes on a tray and asked his wife, "What are your plans for today, Kel?"

"I have to write my keynote speech," she replied grumpily.

"You don't have anything you can recycle?"

"I wish. The last time I reused a speech at a conference the Galactic Free Press reporter left out all of the parts the paper had already reported."

"Bob did that to you?"

"Judith's husband takes being a correspondent a little too seriously sometimes."

"When's the last time you wrote a speech from scratch?"

"Ugh," Kelly groaned. "Decades? I don't want to think about it."

"Take your tea out to the patio and I'll finish cleaning up," Joe offered. "And it's the weekend, so don't work too hard."

"I really should start putting prices on our things for the tag sale. Donna found me a huge roll of sticky labels."

"There's no hurry. It's not like we have to worry about rain, and you haven't even submitted the ad yet. Prices can wait until the kids are available to help."

Kelly rummaged around the living room until she found a pad of paper and a couple of EarthCent Intelligence branded pencils that somebody had liberated from the training camp. Joe's stepping in to clean up after breakfast had blown her procrastination plans out of the water so there was nothing left for her to do now other than to get down to business. The lawn furniture in the patio area in front of the ice harvester proved to be more comfortable than she remembered, and a few minutes later, she dozed off with a pencil in her hand.

Her dream of finding a lucky rabbit's foot that magically wrote speeches was interrupted by a voice insistently repeating, "Ambassador. Wake up."

"I'm just resting my eyes," Kelly lied reflexively as she jerked awake.

"Are you going to stab me with that little spear?" the Grenouthian ambassador inquired.

"It's a pencil. I was just working on my keynote speech for the CoSHC convention."

The large bunny picked up the blank notepad and flipped a few pages to make sure he wasn't missing something. "So you're going the minimalist route."

"I compose everything in my head before writing it down," Kelly lied again. "It saves a lot of editing."

"Whatever you say. Where should I put my things?"

"What things?"

"A few items from the embassy I brought for your tag sale. My cultural attaché suggested this morning for the drop-off. Did he get it right?"

"I guess so," Kelly replied, looking around to see if the Grenouthian ambassador had set a box somewhere before waking her. "Do you have the things with you now?"

"My secretary is waiting in the corridor. I wanted to make sure you hadn't changed your mind."

"No, of course you're welcome. Just put it all over there on one of the folding tables next to the sink and the old games."

"Good morning, Ambassador," Joe called from the top of the ramp. "Can I get you anything? A drink?"

"Some of that bubbly stuff you make would be acceptable," the Grenouthian replied, choosing a lawn chair that was constructed from carbon fiber tubing that could support his bulk.

"I should go see if my daughter is around to help set up your things," Kelly said, sensing an escape from speech writing. "She has a flair for marketing."

"No need, no need. My staff will handle it."

"You only mentioned your secretary."

"She's supervising the staff, of course. I've just pinged her with the go-ahead." The bunny leaned forward to pull another chair close and put up his feet. "Why don't you tell me your opening joke?"

"I'm sorry?"

"For your speech. You must have an opening joke."

"I, uh, I save that part for last."

"You end with a joke?" The Grenouthian ambassador turned his large black eyes on her and his furry features formed into a frown. "You should always end a speech with a call to action."

"I meant, I write the speech first, and then I come up with the opening joke," Kelly fibbed. "You know, to fit it with what comes after."

"I've never seen it done like that before." Shifting slightly in the chair, the Grenouthian accepted his drink from Joe. "Thank you, kind Human."

"You're welcome, Ambassador," Joe replied. "Are you helping my wife with her speech?"

"Just a few pointers," the bunny said. He took a long pull from the pilsner glass and let out a satisfied belch. "You should consider selling this beverage."

"I do, but only in small batches. I'm getting too old to shift the kegs around and none of the kids are that interested in brewing."

A group of burly bunnies pushing floating pallets led by a petite Grenouthian wearing a pink sash padded their way up to the patio.

"Put those things on the tables near the sink and hurry back for the second load," the Grenouthian ambassador instructed his subordinates. "We don't want to intrude here all day."

"Yes, Ambassador," the staff chorused, and set to work unloading the pallets.

"Interesting collection," Joe commented as he watched the bunnies work. "Looks like you brought some of everything."

"When opportunity knocks," the Grenouthian ambassador said, and rapped his knuckles on the table. "A large number are decorative pieces, as you can see, though I'm told that the trash of one species can be the treasure of another."

"Is it really all from your embassy?" Kelly asked, recovering from her initial shock at the quantity of merchandise the ambassador was dumping on her.

"And from my tenure. Gifts have a way of piling up, you know. Whenever we have a meeting at your embassy, I'm amazed at how clean you've kept the place."

"It's my policy not to accept—Good morning, Bork."

"Evening for me," the Drazen ambassador said, setting down a heavy sack. "I was weeding out some of my old reenactment costumes and I thought they might give a little color to your tag sale."

"I don't know if they'll sell, but you're welcome to display them."

"Excellent. I'll just leave these here for a minute and be back with the rack."

"Rack?"

"No help required. It's on wheels."

"Some aliens," the Grenouthian ambassador commented as Bork hurried off. "Give them room to breathe and they'll suck all of the air out of the room."

"Can I refill that for you?" Joe offered, pointing at the bunny's empty glass.

"Yes, that would be very nice. You wouldn't have any of those green and orange sticks that the Gem caterers put out at our meetings, would you?"

"Celery and carrots," Kelly said, rising to her feet. "I'll get them."

By the time the EarthCent ambassador and her husband had returned with the vegetable platter and a pitcher of fresh beer, Czeros had arrived pulling what looked like a child's wagon. Unfortunately, twenty more wagons trailed behind the first like a train.

"Good morning," he greeted everybody cheerfully. "I knew I would find you at home today so I thought I'd bring a few things for your tag sale. I see that our colleagues have beat me to the punch."

"I'm helping the ambassador with her speech," the Grenouthian said. "She was going to end with a joke."

"That won't do," Czeros told Kelly, his voice taking on a serious timbre. "Let me just park these wagons by those tables and I'll be happy to offer my expertise. And if somebody wants to buy the wagons, it will save me a trip back to pick them up."

"I'll get you a glass," Joe said, to which the Frunge ambassador replied with a thumbs-up.

"So what's the major thrust of your speech?" the Grenouthian ambassador inquired. "What's the value proposition?"

"Value proposition?" Kelly repeated.

"What are you trying to sell them?"

"The attendees will be leaders and businessmen from our sovereign human communities, plus a sprinkling of news correspondents. I'm not trying to sell them anything."

The Grenouthian ambassador choked on the celery stalk he was inhaling and thumped himself on the chest ineffectually. Kelly was about to yell for Libby to send help when Crute arrived and began drumming on the bunny's back with all four fists. A stringy length of masticated vegetable shot out of the choking ambassador's mouth and hit Srythlan, who was shuffling slowly towards the table, a large box in his arms.

"Are you trying to kill me?" the Grenouthian ambassador demanded. "Who ever heard of giving a speech without a sales pitch? It's like a drama without a plot."

"Sorry," Kelly said. "It's just the keynote to open the convention."

"That's the most important speech of all." The bunny glowered at the EarthCent ambassador, and then consoled himself by downing his refilled glass. "Somebody else explain it to her."

"I see I arrived just in time," the Dollnick ambassador said.

"Thank you for saving him," Kelly acknowledged.

"I meant in time to save your keynote address." Crute took the chair on Kelly's other side and yelled to his embassy staffers, "Just pile the stuff over there next to the Grenouthian junk. If you run out of space, they keep more folding tables out back."

"You gentlemen do remember what I told you about items that don't sell," Kelly said.

"Sure, sure. You'll charge us for disposal. How much of the speech have you written so far?"

"Zilch. Nothing. Nada," the Grenouthian answered for Kelly. "She doesn't even know why she's giving the speech."

"I remember now," the EarthCent ambassador snapped. "I need to convince a certain furry species with big floppy ears to open some worlds for CoSHC and to license the manufacture of droopy swords."

"Noodle weapons," Crute corrected her.

"SBJ Fashions has invited me to a demonstration on the final day of the CoSHC trade show and I'll be putting together a delegation of our businessmen to attend," the Grenouthian ambassador said. "I wish I had recorded their presentation for you, it was given by the two sisters who ran the Kasilian auction. They opened with a joke, proceeded to their value proposition, and closed with a call to action."

"Statistics," Srythlan suggested, setting his heavy box filled with commemorative plates on the table next to Kelly's notepad. "Provide a hand-out with a mathematical proof of what you're saying."

"I was just going to welcome everybody to the convention and tell them about all the great sessions," Kelly said. "Maybe I'll offer a few pointers about things to see on Union Station."

"Before Gryph sells it," the Grenouthian ambassador grunted.

"I'll just leave the rack right here," the Drazen ambassador called from the edge of the rapidly expanding tag sale area. "Is this axe for sale?"

"Axe?"

"A hundred creds," the Grenouthian ambassador shouted back. "It's a steal."

"Done," Bork replied. He slung the battle axe over his shoulder and joined the other ambassadors. "Here you go, Kelly," he said, handing over a one-hundred-cred coin. "Do I get a beer with my purchase?"

"Coming right up," Joe told him, and returned to the ice harvester for another pitcher and more glasses.

"Aren't you forgetting something?" the bunny asked Kelly.

"You'll get your money after the tag sale," the ambassador replied, holding onto the coin. "I don't want to have to chase after anybody for disposal fees."

"Where did you get this axe?" Bork asked the Grenouthian. "It's one of the nicest replicas I've seen in ages."

"Probably a gift from your predecessor or the Drazen ambassador before him. I also brought a collection of swords and some very old bottles of liquor that I believe were bribes from the Frunge and the Hortens."

"Be right back," Czeros said, spinning around and heading for where the Grenouthian embassy staff had just finished dumping off their second load.

"Did you ever visit a doctor on Earth?" the Dollnick ambassador asked Kelly out of the blue.

"Sure, when I was a girl. I grew up there."

"Start your speech with one of those stories about being bled for your health. Human medical practices are always good for a laugh."

"You've been watching too many Grenouthian documentaries, Crute. Bleeding went out of fashion almost two hundred years ago. That's ancient history."

"Srythlan and I have been ambassadors on Union Station longer than that," the Grenouthian ambassador pointed out. "It doesn't feel like ancient history to us."

"Alright, I've got one for you," Bork said. "A drunk Horten walks into a bar and—"

"I hope you're ready to use that axe," Ortha interrupted the Drazen.

"Ambassador Ortha. Welcome," Kelly said. "These gentlemen were just trying to help me write a keynote speech and we've been trying to come up with a joke."

"A Drazen with a sword," the Horten ambassador shot back. "That's the funniest joke I know."

"Easy, easy," Joe said, slipping between the two diplomats and handing Bork a beer. "Is that a self-propelled dumpster trailing behind you, Ambassador? I'm surprised it fit in the lift tube capsule."

"I took the service tube. It's just a few things for your tag sale," Ortha said, realizing he'd better play nice if he wanted to get rid of his junk. "Sorry if I lost my temper there for a minute."

"Is that the lava sculpture I gave you?" Srythlan asked slowly, pointing to a glassy oblong rock sitting on top of the jumble in the low-walled dumpster.

"How did that get in there?" Ortha asked, his skin turning yellow. "I specifically told the staff I wanted to keep it."

"That totem looks very familiar," the Grenouthian ambassador added.

"I swear you didn't give it to me," the Horten said. "I got it from Srythlan with the rock."

"Guilty," the Verlock ambassador said. "If not for re-gifting, I'd have brought a lot more than this one box of commemorative plates."

"Where do they come from?" Kelly asked.

"Us," Aainda announced her presence. "Our diplomatic service discontinued the practice of supplying plates to ambassadors for use as gifts when the imperial council found out how much they cost. There was a stretch of a few hundred years when embassies received a regular supply of plates to commemorate the coronation of every new queen around the empire. A complete set is quite valuable these days."

"I just brought these to show Ambassador McAllister," Srythlan said slowly. He followed up by moving the box to the floor and guarding it with his legs.

"How does it happen that all of you are showing up at the same time?" Kelly asked. "Did you coordinate?"

"A note from our intelligence people suggested it was a good time," Bork said. "I can check the exact wording." He stared off into space for a moment, reading something on his heads-up display. "Something's not right here. Let me confirm."

The alien ambassadors all fell silent for a moment as they either pinged their own embassies or rechecked messages on their implants, and the Grenouthian actually slammed his paw down on the table.

"Spoofed," he exclaimed. "The message wasn't from my cultural attaché after all. But why would anybody—"

"Is that who I think it is?" Kelly interrupted, pointing at the backs of several figures wearing environmental suits fleeing rapidly towards the exit. "Hey!"

"Our intelligence confirms that the message originated at the Fillinduck embassy," Bork said. "Their ambassador must have wanted to gather a crowd here so they could slip in and drop off their unwanted items without being noticed."

"He could have just asked," Kelly said as the Fillinduck ambassador and his cohorts disappeared. "There's no need to sneak around."

"Really?" a disembodied voice asked, and the Chert ambassador materialized, along with a floating sled loaded with an assortment of knickknacks. "I'll just put these things out and be with you in a minute."

"I don't get what the big deal is," the EarthCent ambassador complained. "Is it that hard to get rid of each other's gifts?"

"None of the merchants on Union Station would take them," Crute admitted. "They're afraid to offend the diplomatic service of another species."

"If you don't want the stuff you give each other, why not re-gift, like Srythlan?"

"We didn't know that's what he was doing until just now," the Grenouthian ambassador replied.

"All lava over the dam," the Verlock ambassador said. "What's important now is Kelly's speech."

"Start with a joke," the Chert ambassador called over his shoulder.

"Doesn't EarthCent have speechwriters on staff?" Crute inquired.

"I never knew there were such people," Kelly replied. "I can hire somebody?"

"A good one is invaluable," Czeros said, returning to the table with several dusty old liquor bottles, the seals still intact. "They can help you establish a coherent theme for your presentation and make sure that the message comes across clearly. There's nothing worse than a speech that draws applause for every sentence and is forgotten before the audience leaves the room. Not that I've ever needed to employ a ghostwriter myself," he concluded as the other ambassadors peered at him suspiciously.

"Good speechwriters pay for themselves in the invitations you'll get to host business gatherings once you build a reputation," Bork added. "Not that I use one either."

"Of course not," the other ambassadors muttered.

"Our Guild of Speechwriters guarantees anonymity and is bonded by the Tharks," the Grenouthian ambassador contributed.

"Speechwriting is part of Vergallian royal training, but most queens still keep one or two ghostwriters on staff," Aainda said. "After all, giving speeches is a huge part of what we all do."

"Does that mean Aabina is trained in speech writing?" Kelly asked eagerly.

"Of course. I'm sure she'd be happy to help you."

"When are you planning on holding the sale?" Czeros asked, examining the labels on the dusty bottles of liquor he'd found. "Can I take these with me today or do I have to come back and bid on them?"

"It's a tag sale, not an auction," Kelly explained. "We'll put prices on some of the bigger items if we can figure out what they are, but with all of the new inventory that showed up this morning, I think we'll just have to sort it into price ranges."

"You mean, like the one-cred store on the market deck?" Bork asked.

"Except almost everything they sell costs more than a cred. I used to take the children there but it was always a disappointment."

"Maybe you could have an exclusive viewing before the tag sale to get the best prices for some of the more expensive items," Czeros suggested. "I'd go two hundred creds for this lot."

"That's because it's worth at least five hundred," the bunny grunted. "I'll have my staff come back and mark prices on the bottoms of our items. I don't want any of it back because it will just cost a fortune to move when Gryph sells the station, but there's no reason to give it away. I suggest the rest of you do the same."

Twelve

"You must have started practicing again," Ailia complimented Samuel after their first dance. "The last time we visited together I thought your hologram was going to step on my toes."

"It's my co-op job. The ambassador makes me dance with all of the unescorted Vergallian women who come to embassy dinners. My starting times for work are all over the place since our clocks don't match, but she usually doesn't even want me coming in until mid-afternoon on their time."

"Most formal balls in the Empire don't begin until long after the farmers are in bed. Vergallian royalty are expected to keep late hours. Shall we try a new ballroom piece?"

Samuel nodded in the direction of the supposed robot toy supplied by Jeeves which made their cross-galactic visits possible. He stepped towards her hologram and assumed the classic starting position. The modified magnetic flight suits from the Physics Ride they both wore provided tactile feedback that made the holograms feel real.

"Yellow Star Memories," the princess announced. Music swelled from their quantum-coupled bots, and for the next eight minutes, the pair traced the complicated figures of the dance, Samuel in his bedroom, and Ailia hundreds of light years away in her study.

"How did I do?"

"You really have returned to form. I can't say I blame Vivian for losing interest in Vergallian dancing after the way you were treated at the competitions, but it would be a shame to give it up altogether after you're married."

"We went to a party last cycle and I caught her doing the steps a few times," Samuel said. "I think when she's a bit older she'll miss it enough to start again."

"In the meantime, we can thank my father's cousin for paying you to practice," Ailia teased him.

"Ambassador Aainda treats me really well and my mom says she's been helping EarthCent on the sly. It's too bad they can't visit you without risking political consequences. I thought I understood how complicated your situation was, but you've been holding back on me," Samuel added in an accusatory tone.

"I didn't want you to worry for no reason. Baylit has proved more than equal to foiling the plots contrived by the Imperial faction." Ailia gave a wry smile and let out a sigh. "I just wish I could see my cousins. My half-sister is the only member of the family I've ever met."

"Do you want me to introduce you to Aabina?"

"It's too risky. Somebody might see her going into your house."

"But she's already here," Samuel said. "My mom found out that speech writing is part of Vergallian royal training and she didn't want Aabina helping her at the embassy because she's afraid it's bugged."

"Your old ice harvester is more secure than the embassy?"

"I think Jeeves cheats and takes care of it for us. He's over here all the time, and the dogs have a nose for surveillance technology as well."

From his guard position sprawled in the doorway, Beowulf nodded his agreement.

"If your mother won't mind your stealing her ghostwriter for a few minutes, I'd love to meet Aabina. What will you say to them?"

"I'll come up with something. Be right back."

Samuel stripped off the Physics Ride flight suit which he wore over his clothes, squeezed past the Cayl hound, and found his mother and Aabina at the dining room table.

"How's the speech going, Mom?"

"Aabina is a genius. I'm just going through and checking some of the numbers she included. I think she already knows more CoSHC statistics than I do."

"I read my Mom's intelligence reports," the Vergallian ambassador's daughter admitted. "She likes me to keep up on everything so I can act as her sounding board."

"That's just what I need—a sounding board," Samuel said. "Can I borrow her for a few minutes, Mom?"

"You can't talk here?"

"Vergallian embassy business. It wouldn't be right to discuss it in front of you."

"Oh, go ahead. As long as you don't let her sneak out the back way."

Aabina gave the ambassador's son a strange look, but she followed him to his bedroom, where the dog stood up and blocked the door.

"It's okay, Beowulf," Samuel said and lowered his voice. "She's Ailia's family."

The Cayl hound sniffed Aabina carefully, tilted his head as if to slide an old odor profile into place, and then broke into a tongue-lolling grin.

"Thank you," Aabina said, slipping by Beowulf into the room. "What did you—Ailia?"

"Aabina!"

"How is this possible?"

Samuel pointed to the little robot toy with the glowing green eyes. The Vergallian ambassador's daughter nodded. "Stryx technology. I might have guessed."

"There are so many things I want to ask you," Ailia said, her voice choked up with emotion.

"I should give you two some privacy," Samuel mumbled, backing in the direction of the door. "Just call me if you need anything."

"Wait! Let me see the two of you dance first. Something short would be fine. There's no faster way to get to know somebody than watching them dance."

"Don't be shy, Sam," Aabina said. "We've danced before. How about Orion's Waltz? That's fast."

The two took the starting position, and Samuel requested Orion's Waltz, which immediately began to play. The Vergallian ambassador's daughter wasn't used to dancing in such a confined space, but Samuel was an expert lead and would have completed the waltz without a single false step if not for Vivian entering the bedroom.

"Okay, let's hear it," Blythe's daughter growled, folding her arms across her chest.

"It's not what you think," Samuel said reflexively. "I can explain everything."

"It's better that you don't try," Ailia spoke up, her voice coming from the little robot even though her hologram was on the other side of the room. "I've been hoping for an

143

opportunity to speak with Vivian for years. Could you give us a little privacy, Samuel?"

"That's a good idea," Vivian said coldly. "Could you take your arm off of Aabina's waist and give us a little privacy? Your dad was looking for you when I came in."

Samuel slumped out of his bedroom, giving Beowulf a hard stare for not sounding the alert when Vivian arrived. The Cayl hound winked in return.

"Where's my co-op student?" Kelly asked, without looking up as her son passed the table.

"She and Vivian are talking, I guess. They kicked me out."

"My little boy is all grown up. Ask your father if he knows any good jokes. That's the only part I'm missing."

Samuel saw welding flashes coming from the area where Paul and his father were working on the nascent rental fleet and headed in that direction. Before he got there, he spied the two men helping Kevin replace the main thruster in the next ship over and realized that the person welding must be Marilla. A moment later the Horten girl completed the bead and flipped up her visor.

"Are you coming to help me, Samuel? I need somebody to hold the hatch in place so I can scribe the upper hinge leaf."

"Sure, I can do that. Since when do you know how to weld?"

"Since last week. Your dad taught me, but you can see I'm still using the Dolly student rig so it's almost impossible to do a bad job."

"I don't remember it being that easy."

"I can't tell you how much I'm loving this. If I ever do start working at a design firm, I'm going to know more

144

about how ships actually stay together than any of the other newbies."

Samuel held the escape hatch in position while Marilla inserted the bottom pin and then scribed the location of the upper hinge leaf with a fine marker. Then she pulled out the lower hinge pin again and motioned for him to set the hatch back down on the deck. Finally, she pulled the upper pin and held the newly liberated hinge leaf up against her scribed outline to double check the alignment with the opening.

"Do you need me to hold that in place while you weld? I can grab the channel-locks."

"I've got a magnetic clamp," she said, fitting it into position over the hinge leaf and activating the electromagnet.

"Okay. I heard my dad was looking for me so I better check what he wants."

Marilla flipped her face shield back down, waited until Samuel turned away, and then started welding the hinge leaf into place. Joe looked up at the initial flash, and seeing his son approaching, said a word to the other two men and left them to finish bolting the thruster down.

"You were looking for me, Dad?"

"I was hoping to get Beowulf back and I knew he was with you, but Alexander jumped right in and did the sniff test on the coolant system. I'll have Beowulf double-check later, just to be sure."

"He's standing guard on my bedroom," Samuel said. "I think I'm in trouble."

"Oh?"

"Vivian came in when I was dancing with Aabina because Ailia wanted to watch us."

"Stop right there," Joe said, holding up his palm. "You know I'm always happy to give you advice, but when I was twenty years old, I wasn't juggling two Vergallian royals and one of the heirs to InstaSitter. I'm not in your class, son."

"You know it's not that," Samuel protested before he realized that his father was teasing him. "Anyway, they let me know that I wasn't wanted."

"When do you have to be in work? We could use some help with cleaning up the old starter shells."

"From that Raider/Trader game that was popular before I was born? Is it making a comeback?"

"We're going to bring them to the CoSHC trade show. Your mom's Vergallian co-op student sweet-talked the Dollnick who runs the Empire Convention Center into letting us put them in the lobby, near the entrance to the Nebulae Room."

"Why?"

"We can't bring real examples of rental ships to the show. There's enough clearance in the lobby, but they wouldn't fit in the freight lift tube unless we cut them in half. It's just not worth the effort."

"So you want to set up game simulators to let people see what it would be like flying a rental ship?"

"Yup. Jeeves is coming by later to help reprogram the controllers with the same parameters we'll use for rental ships. They won't get the effect of being weightless or pulling G's on acceleration, but that's just as well since a lot of the conference attendees will hit the trade show right after breakfast or lunch."

"Sure, I can help with that. I'll go get the cleaning stuff."

"It's already over by the shells. I started earlier but my knees gave out. We only need to bring four, and there are seventeen to choose from, so pick out the nicest ones."

Samuel spent the next hour vacuuming out flight simulator shells, some of which plainly hadn't been entered since he had played in them as a small boy. After cleaning the deck and wiping down the interior surfaces of the last of the four he'd picked out, he noticed that the upholstery of the command chair was cracked.

"Can I help?" Marilla asked, sticking her head in the hatch. "You know that I'm an expert at cleaning rentals. Isn't it ironic that your dad has me welding and you vacuuming?"

"I thought I was just finishing up but the fake leather on this chair is cracked. I guess we'll have to pick another shell, though these four have the best exteriors."

"Are the chairs standard? We could swap it out for one from another simulator."

"Why didn't I think of that?" Samuel said. "Sure. If I remember correctly they're held in by four bolts."

The Horten girl got down on her hands and knees, and producing a small flashlight, looked under the seat. "Sharf sizes. I'll grab some tools and find a good chair while you take out this one."

"Deal." The ambassador's son waited for Marilla to climb back out of the shell before following, and then the two of them broke into a sprint for the closest tool chest. Samuel got there first, but then he realized he hadn't sized the bolt heads. He pretended to busy himself selecting a ratchet while watching the Horten girl make her choice out of the corner of his eye.

"Blue pent head," she told him. "The light blue, not the dark blue."

"Thanks," he said, embarrassed at having been caught peeking. He waited for her to choose a ratchet and start back towards the shells before digging into the collection himself. "Hey, there should have been two light blues here! Did you take both?"

"Finders keepers," she called back, and then broke into a jog. "Besides, I have to pick out a good chair."

Samuel raced to the back of the ice harvester where his father kept a large collection of tool chests. He quickly found a light blue pent-head socket and grabbed a ratchet wrench. On his return, he saw Marilla come out of one shell and disappear into another, so he knew she hadn't located a replacement chair yet. After he climbed through the hatch and started feeling for the bolt heads under the chair, it occurred to him that the Horten girl might have lied about the socket size, but the blue pent head fit perfectly. Ten minutes later, after some tricky maneuvering, he succeeded in getting the chair out the hatch. Then he went to check on the last ship he'd seen Marilla enter.

"What took you so long?" she asked.

"You've been waiting?"

"I had the bolts out ages ago but I can't lift the chair myself."

"Sorry, I didn't think of that." Samuel helped the slender Horten remove the command chair from its mounts and the pair carried it to the other shell. Each of them put in two of the bolts, but when Marilla started to get up, she lost her balance and flopped on her stomach.

"Are you alright?" Samuel asked.

"Something pulled me down. Oh, I can't believe this. I got the sleeve of my coverall pinched under the chair rail."

"I'll get a knife."

"Are you crazy? All I have to do is loosen the bolts on this side and it will come right out."

"You do the front one, I'll do the back one," Samuel offered. He lay down beside her, felt for the bolt head, and seated the socket. "Wow. You really torqued this down."

"I used the quick-drying thread glue. Didn't you?"

"It's just a simulator," he said, reaching over her to brace his other hand on the front of the chair so his body wouldn't slide forward as he applied force to the ratchet wrench. "Got it. Let me pull your sleeve out."

Some instinct made Samuel glance towards the hatch and he saw Vivian glaring daggers at him.

"I suppose you can explain this too?" she asked sarcastically.

"What did I do now?"

"We have a saying in Drazen Intelligence that if it looks like a Brulock and chirps like a Brulock—Oh no," she interrupted herself, clapping a hand to her forehead. "I'm late for my debriefing."

"What's wrong with Vivian?" Marilla asked after Samuel's girlfriend disappeared.

"I don't know. Maybe the Drazens are working her too hard. I've got a couple more hours before I have to be at the Vergallian embassy, so let's get the hulls of these shells shined up and it will all be done except for the programming."

Samuel and Marilla worked together, applying Dollnick polish to the exterior of the metal shells, and then buffing it out with a long cloth that they pulled back and forth over the surface as if they were working a two-man saw. They were just finishing the fourth shell when Paul and Jeeves arrived.

"The controllers are all identical," Samuel informed them. "I turned them on an hour ago so they could sync up and download updates from the Stryxnet. Who knows the last time they were actually used."

"I do," Jeeves said. "The usage parameters are permanently stored, which turns out to be a handy feature in the rental business."

"Permanently?" Paul asked. "But I thought that Stryx controllers lasted more-or-less forever. I've certainly seen some old ones."

"They can't function without Stryxnet access so storage isn't an issue," Jeeves explained. "It wouldn't be fair to the other species if I reprogrammed the controllers using best practices for rentals, so you tell me what changes you want and I'll make them."

"What does he mean?" Marilla whispered to Samuel, as Paul climbed into the shell to switch the controller mode to 'Maintenance,' which would unlock the program memory.

"You know that the Stryx don't help us with technology when it could impact the business operations of other species. It's part of the whole tunnel network deal," Samuel replied.

"You don't have to whisper, Marilla," Jeeves said. "It doesn't work in any case because I have superior hearing."

"It's just that I thought the Stryx only held back sharing the advanced technology, like faster-than-light travel and nanobots. Who cares about excursion craft rental software?"

"The competing species that invested the time and money into developing successful business models. I can get away with reprogramming the controllers for Paul because he's my friend and it's just saving him a few days of tedious coding, but I won't step in and do the product development as well."

"All set," Paul said, emerging from the shell. "We want to limit the simulation to navigation in systems connected to the tunnel network. Did I already send you the thrust profile for the drive units we're installing in the actual rentals?"

"Yes," Jeeves replied. "Did you decide on whether you want a charge meter to show on the main display at all times?"

"I don't think that would be a good idea. How did the Hortens do it, Marilla?"

"You could ask for a verbal price check at any time, but the amount was never displayed. I've heard that the Verlocks are the only species who show a running total on their rentals, but they're just weird."

"I don't think I could fly a ship that was telling me how much it cost every second," Samuel added. "Are you going to charge strictly by time, or does distance come into it as well?"

"Time and reaction mass," Paul said. "It's not like the customers can refuel the thrusters themselves, and we wouldn't want to encourage it if they could."

"We always took a cleaning deposit," Marilla said. "It's hard to collect after they leave with their programmable cred."

"How about insurance?"

"For what?"

"If they get into an accident."

"With a Stryx controller? Not unless you allow them to turn off the automatic docking function."

"Time and reaction mass, cleaning deposit, disable manual docking mode," Jeeves recited. "Have you figured out the rates yet?"

"We don't really have a clue," Paul admitted. "Could you just stick in some dummy figures for now? They don't have to make sense, but keep them low so we don't scare off potential partners."

"Why is it so hard to come up with a rental rate?" Marilla asked. "All of the Horten agencies charged pretty much the same, though they used loyalty rewards to keep their customers."

"We don't know what the costs will be on the other end or what kind of profit margins our partners will need. It's easy for us to make money because we already own the ships and we got them for a song, but we don't have enough for a rental fleet, which means somebody will have to buy new ships."

"Or old ships," Joe pointed out, taking a seat in the ripped command chair his son had removed from the shell. "We weren't in any hurry to fix ours up until Marilla gave us the rental idea, so maybe there's an endless supply of used excursion ships up for auction somewhere."

"You should check with EarthCent Intelligence," Samuel said. "Vivian told me they keep track of that kind of information for their business subscribers, and they might be interested in the idea as a way to gather more information."

"What sort of loyalty rewards did the Horten agencies give customers?" Paul asked Marilla. "Do you mean discounts for more rentals or hotel stays?"

"They said I was too young to work the counter so I don't really know much about that end of the business. I remember somebody telling me that the salesmen always went for the cash because their employers were paying for the rental so it was like getting something for nothing.

Besides, why would anybody who travels for a living want a free trip?"

"How about the customers who weren't traveling for business?"

"I don't think most of them rented enough times to earn rewards. Keep in mind that even though we're far more populous than Humans, most of our communities have been in the same place for tens of thousands of years, so they have good passenger liner service."

Thirteen

Flazint and Tzachan were waiting for Dorothy and Kevin in front of the entrance to the honor court on the Frunge deck. "Thank you so much for doing this," the Frunge girl said. "I feel awful about making you drag the baby out at this time of night on your clock, but it was the only slot the matchmaker had available. She's very popular."

"Margie sleeps everywhere, providing that she wants to sleep," Kevin said, adjusting the baby carrier strapped across his chest. "Alexander is the one who's making a fuss."

As if to confirm Kevin's point, the Cayl hound yawned like a hippopotamus, then collapsed to the deck and pretended to fall asleep.

"You brought all of your legal documentation?" Tzachan asked.

"Got the companionship contract and Ailia's affidavit right here," Dorothy replied, patting her shoulder bag. "Why are we going to Hazint's legal shop? Are you and Flazint ready to get your own contract?"

The Frunge girl made a choking noise and turned away to hide her embarrassment, but Tzachan's training as an attorney helped him maintain his poise.

"Mizpah rents an office in Hazint's and they share administrative staff," he explained. "We're still a good ten years or so away from a contract, providing everything goes well."

"Are you coming in with us?" Kevin asked.

"Technically, we're not even supposed to be here, but there's a bit of wiggle room when an alien species is involved. I'll bring you in and make the introductions, but Flazint and I can't be seen entering the office together at this stage in our relationship. And take this," he said, offering a change purse. "I collected the fee in high denomination coins because a programmable cred would have been traceable."

"How much is in here?" Dorothy asked, accepting the purse. "No, don't tell me. It's better that I don't know."

"This sum is just the down payment," Tzachan said. "When Mizpah asks you for a sign that you're serious about arranging a match, hand her the change purse, and say, 'That's not the end of the story.'"

"What story?"

"It's a legal expression," the alien attorney explained patiently. "Frunge aren't supposed to charge each other interest, but when we pay for something in installments, it's acceptable for the payments to add up to more than the whole, which implies an internal rate of return."

"What?"

"It's not important. Just remember to say, 'That's not the end of the story.'"

"Got it," Kevin answered for Dorothy. A loud snore coming from below their knees testified to the fact that Alexander really had fallen asleep. "Anything else we need to know?"

"I'm pushing the envelope by telling you as much as I already have. Just answer her questions honestly and remember that you're our only hope."

"No pressure there," Dorothy muttered. "We may as well get this over with before carrying our companionship contract around gives me a compressed disc. It's twice as heavy as Margie and not half as sweet."

Tzachan took a deep breath and then led the way next door and through the massive set of gates into Hazint's legal shop. Kevin had to nudge Alexander with his foot several times to get the Cayl hound up and moving, so they trailed behind Dorothy. The group minus Flazint, who waited in front of the honor court, met up again at the lengthy reception counter. Behind the row of clerks, dozens of craftsmen were working with high-tech equipment to churn out contracts engraved in stone tablets.

"Are you hiring the Humans?" the receptionist asked Tzachan. "The infant looks too young to sign a contract, and you must know that we don't recognize alien power-of-attorney agreements."

"We're here to see the matchmaker," Dorothy told her.

The receptionist's hair vines turned pale, and she reached for the security button on her desk.

"Not for she and I," Tzachan reassured the horrified Frunge woman. "These two are already married and they're here to see Mizpah about arranging a match for me. They have an appointment."

The receptionist let out her breath and moved her hand away from the alarm button. "That's better," she said. "I'll tell Mizpah you've arrived. Please take them to privacy booth—" she glanced down at a screen on her desk "—seven and I'll bring the matchmaker out."

Tzachan led the group to the privacy booth and then he waited by the door until the matchmaker arrived. Mizpah allowed him to make the introductions and then shooed him towards the exit before activating a privacy field.

The elderly Frunge woman was tiny, but she had an air of authority about her that led the humans to undergo her scrutiny in silence. When she finally spoke, it was to request that Kevin place the baby on the table.

"What are you going to do to her?" Dorothy asked.

"If it hasn't been explained to you, the child is your primary qualification to act as a matron for this match. I have to check that she's not a changeling."

"Oh, that's okay, she's used to that. Here, I'll pull off her socks for you."

"That won't be necessary," Mizpah said, counting Margie's toes through the cloth. "You can't be too careful in this business. I have to make sure you're serious about the match after all."

"Of course," Dorothy said, and then frowned when Kevin nudged her. "What?"

"Money," he hissed out of the side of his mouth.

"Sorry, right." The ambassador's daughter handed over the heavy change purse and added, "That's not the end of the story."

"It better not be," the matchmaker said, weighing the purse in her hand. "Why don't I start with the Cayl hound so he can leave and we'll have some more room in here. I assume he's your pack leader?"

"In his mind he is," Kevin replied.

Alexander thumped his tail on the floor and sat up straighter, as if he were on the parade grounds for a military review.

Mizpah pulled out a small tab, activated the screen, and scrolled down to the information she was looking for. Then she held both hands up in front of the dog and began flashing signs by folding down a number of fingers on each hand simultaneously. She held each signal in place for a few seconds, and then produced a different combination. Alexander watched the show intently, and after several minutes of this, he nodded and presented a massive paw. The matchmaker solemnly shook it, and then opened the door for the dog to leave.

"What was that all about?" Dorothy couldn't help asking.

"He agreed to extend his protection to the young Frunge couple if I place them in your care. You can ask him to explain the contract terms when you get home."

"But I don't know Cayl finger speech."

The matchmaker shrugged. "So don't ask him. Do either of you have anything you want to tell me before we begin?"

"I don't think so," Kevin said. "Is there a specific answer you're looking for?"

"Very good. Very clever. Let's start with your proof of marriage."

Dorothy pulled the companionship contract out of the custom shoulder bag that Flazint's cousin Barzee had given her when they visited the Frunge world where the latter lived. She placed the heavy stone slab on the table, and then fished out a document which read, "I, Ailia, heir to the throne of Avidiya, daughter of Atuba, granddaughter of Avilia, great-granddaughter of Aagra, do solemnly witness the fulfillment of a Frunge companionship contract engraved in the names of Kevin Crick and Dorothy McAllister of Union Station. They exchanged their vows in the presence of myself and the Cayl hound Alexander in the private dining room of the Mercenary Tavern in the ninth year of the reign of Royal Protector Baylit, my half-sister."

"Very good," Mizpah said. "A Vergallian princess and a Cayl hound as witnesses. I have no further questions about the validity of your marriage."

Dorothy replaced the stone contract in its carrier and rose to her feet. "So that's it? We can go? This wasn't half as bad as—"

"Sit down," the matchmaker interrupted. "Establishing your eligibility to act as chaperones is only the first part of the process. Now tell me. How do you know the intended?"

"I met Flazint on the job at the station's lost-and-found and we've been friends ever since. We work together in SBJ Fashions now, and Tzachan is our outside legal counsel for intellectual property."

"Have you ever seen them alone together?"

"No, of course not," Dorothy fibbed. "What kind of Frunge do you take them for?"

"I have to ask," Mizpah said, fixing the ambassador's daughter with a hard stare. "I've received a report that the subjects were seen together Live Action Role Playing. That sounds awfully close to unauthorized dating to me."

"It's part of our business," Dorothy said. "We sell enchanted bags-of-holding. Flazint participates in LARPs to get design ideas and assess our product performance, while Tzachan is on the lookout for trademark and patent infringements."

"Your fashion business holds trademarks and patents? Remember," the matchmaker cautioned before Dorothy could answer, "I can have your story checked."

"Cross my heart and hope to die," Dorothy said.

"That's acceptable," Mizpah concluded, and turned to Kevin. "How do you know the subjects?"

"I know Flazint because she's been my wife's friend since before we were married, and I've met Tzachan a few times at Dorothy's work-related events."

"I see. Very good." The matchmaker drummed her fingers on the table for a moment, coming to a decision. "Alright. The baby and the dog were impressive, and your contract is in order, so we can proceed to the initial round of testing."

"That's great," Dorothy said, rising from her chair again. "I can ping them if—"

"Sit down. The testing is for you. Don't you know anything about Frunge matchmaking?"

"Not really."

"I can do this verbally or let you take a multiple choice test on a tab. What's your preference?"

"Verbally," Kevin said, at the same time that Dorothy answered, "Multiple choice."

Mizpah frowned and made a note on her tab.

"Multiple choice," Kevin tried again, while Dorothy changed her answer to "Verbal test, please."

The matchmaker made another note on her tab. "Both it is," she said. "I'll give you the preliminary verbal test now and the multiple choice test at our next meeting, unless you prefer to take it at a proctored exam center."

"Would we have to schedule that?" Kevin asked.

"No. Once I put in the order you can show up at any time. Do you read Frunge?"

"I'm afraid not."

"Then expect the exam center to charge a translation fee. Now, which one of you wants to go first?"

"I will," Dorothy volunteered.

A few seconds later, the matchmaker said, "Well?"

"Well, what?"

"Are you going or not?"

"Do you mean you want me to leave?"

Mizpah sighed in frustration, then rose and opened the door. "There's a waiting area in front of the reception desk. Your husband will come out and get you when it's your turn. And take the baby with you, she's too young to hear this."

Dorothy left the contract carrier, took Margie, and headed out to the reception area. Alexander had waited rather than heading home by himself, and he was enjoying the attention of two Frunge children, who were climbing all over the Cayl hound like he was a statue at a park.

"Are you waiting for your husband to finish a test too?" Dorothy asked the mother of the children, who was intent on the door of a privacy booth.

"A test?" the Frunge woman replied. "No. My husband is just having the terms of our lease checked so we'll know where we stand when Stryx Gryph sells the station. What is a Human doing here, if you don't mind my asking?"

"We're trying to sponsor a match for our Frunge friends. So far the matchmaker tested my baby and our dog, and then she sent me out so she can ask my husband some questions."

"Did you practice?"

"Answering questions? We're just going to be honest."

"Oh, there's my husband." A Frunge man emerged from a privacy booth and lifted the smaller of the two children off of Alexander, who looked liable to fall asleep again without the distraction. The woman who Dorothy had been chatting with grabbed the hand of the larger child and gave the ambassador's daughter an apologetic smile. "I have to run. Good luck with your test."

As the couple with their children left the law office, Dorothy overheard the woman telling her husband, "They're taking the verbal test for sponsoring a match and they didn't practice."

Kevin emerged from the privacy booth and came over to the waiting area. "That was easy," he said. "She just asked me a few questions about—"

"No kibitzing," Mizpah called from where she stood in the doorway. "I'm on the clock, you know."

Dorothy passed the baby to her husband and hurried back to the privacy booth where she shut the door behind her and resumed her seat.

"What's your husband's favorite food?" Mizpah asked without any preamble.

"Hamburgers?"

"Which side does he sleep on?"

"His back, but I'm trying to get him to stop because he snores," Dorothy answered confidently.

"Does your husband like your hair vines long or short?"

"Short. And it's just hair, not vines."

"What was your husband's last dream?"

"He doesn't tell me his dreams."

"Really?" Mizpah looked up sharply. "How do you know what he's thinking?"

"I suppose I could ask him if it was important. I think I have a pretty good idea what he's thinking most of the time."

"Are you a mind reader?"

"No, not like you mean."

"Tell your husband to come back in with the baby and the dog."

"Did I pass?"

The matchmaker ignored Dorothy and busied herself making notes on her tab until the whole family was back in the privacy booth. Then she announced, "We have a problem."

"What's wrong?" Kevin asked.

"Your wife thinks that your favorite food is hamburgers, that you like her hair short, and that you're the one snoring."

"At least you know we didn't cheat," Dorothy said.

"Obviously. The problem isn't that you guessed the wrong answers, it's that neither of you were offended that I would ask such intimate questions. How can you supervise the behavior of a young couple when our value systems don't align? I've never worked with Humans before and I can see that our usual tests won't apply."

"So can we just skip them?" Dorothy asked hopefully.

"It isn't done that way. You need to find a Human matchmaker to vouch for your basic suitability before I can proceed."

"But we don't know any matchmakers," Dorothy said. Then a thought occurred to her, and she asked, "Would Eemas count?"

"The all-species matchmaking service run by the station librarian?" Mizpah asked in disbelief. "Was your match made by the Stryx?"

"No," Dorothy said, beating Kevin's "Yes" by a microsecond.

"You two really are bad at this. If the Stryx are willing to guarantee your suitability, I can accept that."

"Libby?" Dorothy asked out loud. "Can you tell Mizpah that Kevin and I are fit sponsors for Flazint and Tzachan?"

"I have to turn off the privacy field first," the match-maker told her. "Some people would use their implants to cheat on the verbal tests otherwise. Try it now."

The station librarian replied to Dorothy's second attempt in the affirmative, and Mizpah put aside her tab.

"That's it, then," she said. "The artisans will have your contract prepared in a few minutes. Carry it with you whenever you are chaperoning your charges."

"Is it going to weigh as much as our companionship contract?"

"Yes, but you don't need to carry both at the same time as long as you're on the station. If you want to chaperone your charges in Frunge space, it would be best to bring your proof of marriage, along with your baby and the dog."

Kevin and Dorothy thanked the matchmaker and were on their way to pick up the new contract when Mizpah called after them, "And read *Frunge for Humans*. I'll be testing you on acceptable dating behavior at our next meeting."

Five minutes later, after a short argument over who would carry what, they left Hazint's law office with Dorothy holding the baby and Kevin and Alexander each burdened with a stone contract.

"You got it!" Flazint squealed when they emerged. "Let me see the calendar."

"What calendar?" Dorothy responded.

"You didn't ask for a calendar? Mizpah will want to see a record of our dates, and you'll need it to make sure we aren't going out too often. The calendar handles all of the calculations."

"Calculations?"

"You don't have to repeat everything I say. Anyway, it's better this way because the calendars the matchmakers sell in their offices are the same as the ones in the shops, but the matchmaker charges a markup."

"As long as I don't need to do math," Dorothy replied philosophically. "Are we going to have to bring it on dates with us?"

"Of course, and as the chaperones, you start and stop the built-in timer."

"So it's not made of stone," Kevin concluded. "That's a relief."

"I don't want to sound pushy, but when can we see each other?"

"We're seeing each other right now," Dorothy said.

"Not us," Flazint said in frustration, pointing back and forth between herself and the ambassador's daughter. "Me and Tzachan."

"Oh. Well, you just saw each other now."

"That didn't count. I mean a date!"

"I was kidding. We need to buy a calendar first, right?"

"You need to have the calendar in time to bring it along, but we can arrange the date now. I'm free whenever."

"How about Tzachan?"

"He's free whenever too."

"Where do you want to go?"

"We don't care. Pick something you and Kevin will like."

"How about a restaurant?"

"Except a restaurant. No eating on first dates."

"We could go to an immersive," Kevin suggested.

"No sitting in the dark," Flazint told them.

"I guess we could do a LARP," Dorothy ventured.

"No holograms."

"How about you choose the place and we'll choose the time?"

"Bowling?" the Frunge girl asked hopefully.

"Bowling it is," Dorothy agreed. "I know my mom will be home to babysit Friday night, so you can take me shopping for the calendar before then, and it's a double date."

Fourteen

"—and if you sign up today to participate on one of the new planning committees, you'll receive a complimentary year of the ad-free version of the Galactic Free Press. Thank you."

Thunderous applause followed the EarthCent ambassador as she stepped away from the rostrum and returned to her seat on the stage. Kelly could no longer remember which parts of the speech were ghostwritten by her talented Vergallian co-op student and which were her own, but she made a mental note to have Donna contact the Open University to check if they could give Aabina a raise.

Daniel let the applause run a few more seconds before motioning for the audience in the half amphitheatre to let him speak. "For those of you who have never attended a conference at the Empire Convention center, most of the session rooms are located below the stadium seating in this half of the Galaxy Room. The trade show is taking place in the Nebulae Room, which can only be reached through the upper exits from the amphitheatre, as the lower exits come out on the deck below."

Aabina hurried up to Daniel, showed him something on a tab, and then retreated back into the wings.

"I want to take a moment to thank the *For Humans* publishing arm of the Galactic Free Press for providing these printed versions of the convention program," the associate ambassador continued, waving a glossy booklet above his head. "Please note the single sheet addendum tucked inside the back cover which lists changes in room assignments and schedules since the program was printed. I also want to inform you that due to unexpectedly high demand, the session titled, 'Alien Import Duties – Is Bribery A Better Option?' will be held right here in the Galaxy Room rather than its assigned location. The first session begins in ten minutes, so let's carry Ambassador McAllister's inspirational message into our day, and don't forget the free cocktail hour sponsored by EarthCent Intelligence in the lobby area after the last session."

Approximately half of the audience remained in their seats and began talking with each other, while the other half headed for the lower exits that led to the smaller conference rooms. Kelly accepted the effusive praise of the senior CoSHC representatives who had also been seated on the stage and then studied her dog-eared program booklet to refresh her memory as to her own schedule. Before she knew it, she found herself standing in the rapidly emptying corridor below the stadium seating, trying to decipher the signage.

A Grenouthian correspondent accompanied by a cameraman approached and addressed her. "An impressive speech, Ambassador. My producer has already informed me that they'll be rerunning part of it on our main update loop throughout the day."

"Uh, thank you?" Kelly said, temporarily flustered over receiving a compliment from one of the furry aliens. "Could I ask which part of the speech worked for you?"

"The whole thing. I ran it against our SpeechCheck application, just as a precaution, you understand, and the only part that was listed as possible plagiary was your opening joke."

"I got that from my husband, actually. He said it was old."

"All basic types of jokes are old, or perhaps it would be more accurate to say that new types are never funny. Do you have time for a quick interview?"

"I was planning to attend a session," Kelly replied, brandishing the program guide as evidence. "Could we do it during the lunch break?"

"Which session are you attending? I've been assigned here for the convention and they're still setting up the trade show so the sessions are the only action."

"The Grenouthian news is covering the entire convention? I thought you normally rewrote a few stories from the Galactic Free Press for your text feed and maybe bought video from the station librarian if there was an accident."

"If I had to guess, my producer must have a stake in some potential new business venture that involves CoSHC. I just go where they send me." The Grenouthian's cameraman whispered something in the reporter's ear. "We need more video of your associate ambassador. Is he participating in any of the sessions?"

"Thank you, I knew I was forgetting something," Kelly said. She paged quickly through her booklet, paying attention to the presenter names rather than the session descriptions. "He's on a panel about abusive labor contracts in the first session and I told him I'd attend. It's room B12, this way."

The EarthCent ambassador set off down the corridor, but within two steps she realized that the bunnies weren't following her, so she turned and looked back over her

169

shoulder. The Grenouthian correspondent took the opportunity to point at the sign over the door they had been standing in front of, which read, "B12."

A chime sounded telling attendees they had thirty seconds before the doors would be closed, so Kelly hurried back and entered the room on the heels of the reporters. Daniel was seated at the panel table, along with Shaina's husband Walter, Donna's daughter Blythe, and Aabina. A volunteer wearing a CoSHC T-shirt closed the doors, and Kelly slipped into one of the few untaken folding chairs. The burly bunnies remained standing at the back, along with a Verlock who apparently didn't trust the human-sized chairs with his weight.

"Welcome to our panel discussion titled, 'Affinity Schemes in Contract Labor.' Our panel this morning consists of Walter Dunkirk, the managing editor of the Galactic Free Press, Blythe Oxford, the co-founder of InstaSitter and co-director of EarthCent Intelligence, and Associate Ambassador Daniel Cohan, who you all know. My name is Aabina and I'll be moderating the discussion. Yes?" the co-op student said, pointing towards a person with a raised hand.

"Aren't you Vergallian?"

"I am, but I work for the EarthCent embassy. Yes?" she pointed at another hand.

"I heard that some of the peripheral star systems of the Vergallian Empire were considering opening their planets to sovereign human communities. Is that true?"

"The Vergallian embassy is sponsoring a booth at the trade show and I'm sure they'll be happy to answer your questions," Aabina replied primly. "I'm here representing EarthCent."

170

"Can you comment on the news that Ambassador McAllister is replacing President Beyer?"

"I was with Ambassador McAllister all week and I can assure you that she has no intention of leaving Union Station."

"Even when the Cayl take over? I just heard that Gryph cancelled the auction and is swapping the station for—"

"I think you may have misread your conference program," Aabina interrupted. "The session on rumors is scheduled for the Galaxy Room this afternoon."

"Well done," Kelly muttered to herself under her breath.

"After our panelists each give a brief summary of grey-area contracting from their professional perspectives, we'll open the session up to questions from the floor. Could you start us off, Mrs. Oxford?"

"Thank you, Aabina," Blythe said. "If anybody here plans to establish a field office on Union Station and is looking for high-quality temporary help, I can't say enough good things about the Open University cooperative education program. They sent us a Verlock student two weeks ago who has already reorganized our filing system, in addition to helping pull together the data for this presentation."

Kelly turned again to look at the Verlock standing against the back wall and noted that he was wearing a co-op badge identifying him as Wrylenth.

"Why do I recognize the name of Blythe's co-op student?" she subvoced to the station librarian.

"Wrylenth was on Samuel's student committee for Flower," Libby replied over the ambassador's implant. "The experience made him an excellent candidate for the co-op job at EarthCent Intelligence, plus he was only one correct answer away from a perfect score on the civil service exam. He ran out of time."

"I understand you placing Vivian with Drazen Intelligence since we work together," Kelly continued to subvoc as Blythe started talking about the categories of affinity schemes, "but as much as I like Srythlan, I'm not sure that I'd want a young Verlock running around—alright, shuffling around—with our secrets."

"As opposed to a Vergallian?"

"Aabina is different. Her mother is on the other side of the schism in their Empire, and the enemy of my enemy is my friend."

"Wrylenth won't be sharing EarthCent Intelligence secrets with anyone because it would be a violation of the Verlock code of honor," Libby explained. "In addition, all co-op students sign a contract agreeing to put their employer's interests above their own."

"Samuel didn't mention that."

"It was in the small print. Aren't you going to pay attention to Blythe's presentation at all?"

"I'll ask Aabina to summarize it for me later," Kelly said, but she broke off her conversation with the station librarian.

"...so while we're hopeful that the trend is moving in the right direction, we don't intend to let down our guard until unethical labor contractors become a footnote in a future Grenouthian documentary," Blythe concluded.

As soon as the polite applause for the co-director of EarthCent Intelligence died down, Aabina announced, "Next we have Mr. Dunkirk to tell us about how the Galactic Free Press has been covering this issue."

"Thank you, Aabina. And if you decide that the embassy isn't for you, just tell the Open University and we'd be happy to have you on the paper."

"He can't do that!" Kelly subvoced the station librarian again. "We have a contract."

"Did you read it?" Libby asked in reply.

"You know perfectly well that I don't read contracts when you're involved. Is there really a chance that I'm going to lose her?"

"Cooperative education assignments aren't a new form of slavery, whatever some students may think. She can quit at any time, though it's unlikely that the co-op office would agree to send her on a new assignment."

"But the Galactic Free Press is a business. They could just pay her more than we do. I was going to ask Donna to check with the Open University about giving Aabina a raise, but as long as I'm talking to you…"

"The program compensates all first-time co-op students on a scale that reflects their financial need and the general expectations of their species. Aabina is still an adolescent by Vergallian standards, which is why you're able to afford her."

"Joe said that his Horten co-op student is a bargain at any price. She really enjoys the work, but he worries he might be teaching her the wrong way to do things since he never had any formal training himself."

"…and we will continue our investigative journalism of shady labor practices until the problem is stamped out," Walter concluded to a polite round of applause.

"Our final panelist is Daniel Cohan, the associate ambassador here on Union Station, and the driving force behind the creation of the Conference of Sovereign Human Communities," Aabina announced.

"Have you been watching little Grace on Aisha's show?" Kelly subvoced as Daniel began his presentation. "I always thought that Dorothy and Samuel were as different as two siblings could be, but you would never guess that Grace and Mike are from the same family."

"I was a bit concerned about Twitchy, but she's settled in nicely," Libby replied. "Her parent is the Echo Station librarian and we go back hundreds of thousands of years together, so I feel personally responsible."

"Do you think the show is making a difference?"

"It's certainly done wonders for the Grenouthian ambassador's financial situation."

"I meant in terms of helping the species get along together."

"The demand for Let's Make Friends related merchandise has opened up some new trade relationships with civilizations who aren't even members of the tunnel network."

"That's not what I meant either, but how do they even watch the show if they aren't on the Stryxnet?"

"Piracy. I know what you're asking, Ambassador, but the answer isn't that simple. It certainly doesn't hurt for children around the galaxy to be able to put a name with an alien face and to watch the cast interacting with one another. But if you're asking me to quantify the effect of watching a children's show for a few years as opposed to the influence of family and society, it will take a few generations before I have a definitive answer."

"You can't make a prediction?"

"I expect there will be a positive effect, but it's small enough to fall within the margin of error based on the limited data set. Keep in mind that Samuel was in the original cast rotation and he's still in school himself. The children from the other species who were at the same stage of emotional development when they appeared on the show with your son won't reach adulthood for several more decades."

"...but thanks in large part to cooperation with ISPOA, the Inter-Species Police Operations Agency, we now see the light at the end of the tunnel," Daniel concluded his prepared remarks.

"Before we open the floor to questions, I see my boss in the back of the room and I should ask if she has anything to add," Aabina said. "Ambassador McAllister?"

"I'm just here to listen and learn," Kelly responded, straightening up in her chair as the other attendees turned in her direction. "Please carry on as if I wasn't present."

"Very well," the Vergallian girl said, and a number of hands shot up. "Yes, in the front row?"

"Janet, I'm on the delegation from Dolag Twelve, where a group of us coming off a thirty-year contract was recently given permission to set up our own community. Many of us are nearing retirement age ourselves and we've been looking into bringing in picking crews for the harvest, but we don't want to end up with a contractor who's exploiting the labor. Is there such a thing as a list of good human contractors?"

Aabina nodded and turned to Blythe. "Mrs. Oxford?"

"EarthCent Intelligence does offer our subscribers ratings for a variety of human-run businesses but I have to admit this is the first time I'm hearing your question. Our focus to this point has been on chasing down the bad actors in labor contracting, but I'm sure we must have the data to be doing the opposite. Wrylenth?"

"I created a list of ethical contractors while organizing the data for your presentation," the Verlock co-op student said, though the sentence took him almost a half a minute to get out.

"I think we can provide that information outside of our subscription model," Blythe said. "Would the Galactic Free Press be willing to run it in a supplement, Walter?"

"Glad to be of service," the managing editor responded.

"All set?" Aabina followed up with the woman who had asked the original question. "Great. The man in the back wearing the glove with the prosthetic thumb?"

"Horm. I'm with the delegation from Wuger, a Drazen open world. We recently had a bad experience with a contractor who brought in a crew of underage kids to sort mine tailings by hand. Nobody realized what was going on at first because the job site was at an abandoned mine on the other side of the continent from our community and we didn't have any direct oversight. When the Drazen authorities made us aware of the situation, we fired the contractor, but there was no justification to withhold payment for the work that was already done."

"Did your CoSHC representative report the incident?" Daniel asked. "It doesn't ring a bell and I'm sure I would have remembered."

"This just happened before the conference so I thought I'd report in person," Horm said. "A bunch of us forced our way onto the contractor's transport and talked to the kids to see if any of them wanted to stay behind, but they probably thought that the devil they knew was better than the devil they didn't know."

"Were you wearing your gloves?"

"These? I always wear them. Wait a minute. Do you think we scared the kids?"

"How old were they?"

"Late teens, mainly. Maybe a couple younger siblings mixed in. We all felt terrible about letting that transport lift off again, but we couldn't justify detaining the workers when they all insisted they wanted to stay together and leave."

"It's a tough situation," Daniel acknowledged. "Give us all of the documentation you have and we'll share it with EarthCent Intelligence. If you're willing to go on the record with the Galactic Free Press, it would help raise awareness about employing contractors offsite."

"Do we have a correspondent on your world?" Walter asked.

"A couple of our kids participate in the Children's News Network via their teacher bots, and I know we've had a few stories about local events make it into the Galactic Free Press through that channel."

"Why don't the two of you talk after the session?" Aabina suggested. "Where's the woman who approached me in the corridor with a question? Elizabeth?"

"Here," a middle-aged woman replied. "I'm from Jzeop, a Frunge open world where my group just completed a ten-year contract and has agreed to stay on to form our own community. We all came directly from Earth after signing up with a human who had a subcontract from the Frunge, but we didn't realize that he was acting as our agent."

"You mean all of the money went through him?" Blythe asked. "I'm afraid I know how this goes."

"Right. So our Frunge employers went beyond the letter of the contract in providing our housing and child support, and we received our salaries on time every week. But after we completed the contract and began negotiating directly to stay on Jzeop to work in the same jobs, it came out that our pension contributions had all been paid to the original human contractor."

"Who is no longer accepting your pings."

"There were just under eight thousand adults in our group working full time for ten years, and the Frunge were contributing ten percent of our salaries. It's not a small amount of money."

"And what actions have you taken so far?"

"Our situation is the same as the guy who just reported the child labor violation. We only found out a couple of weeks ago, so rather than throwing good money after bad on expensive Stryxnet calls to who knows where, we decided to wait until we were here."

"Were the Frunge able to tell you where they were sending the money?" Daniel asked.

"Yes, but the contractor was clearly preparing for this all along. He used to take all of the payments over the register network, but a few cycles ago, he had the Frunge start directing the payments to a Thark bank."

"Thark bookie."

"Most of us are still young and we have time to rebuild our retirement savings, plus we'll earn more now than we did the first ten years. But if there's anything we can do…"

"I'm afraid you're talking about a stern chase when the other ship is already over the horizon," Walter said. "If you're willing, the Galactic Free Press will send a correspondent to your world to do an in-depth series, and hopefully that will make other contract workers check with their employers about who is holding pension benefits and balloon payments. I'm sure that EarthCent Intelligence will contact ISPOA and do what they can, but that much money and that much of a head start will be a challenge. I can almost guarantee that he's no longer in Stryx space."

"So sad," Kelly subvoced to the Stryx librarian. "Is there anything you can do?"

"We have to draw the line somewhere, Ambassador, but I can offer you a bit of advice to pass on. Large sums of money often turn into a curse for white collar criminals because of the opportunity for legal operatives to make a big score. Tell the victims to offer a substantial reward for the recovery of their funds. Ten percent would come to millions of creds."

"Do you mean bounty hunters?"

"The advanced species don't prohibit their police forces from accepting rewards. They're very effective."

Fifteen

"Don't think of it as a tech-ban world," Samuel told the potential settler. "Think of it as a park or a nature reserve."

"With no holographic entertainment."

"Studies show that children learn better when they aren't distracted by technology."

"But we were counting on teacher bots subsidized by the Stryx for most of our schooling needs."

"And the Vergallian queens grant an exception for teacher bots as being part of humanity's cultural heritage since joining the tunnel network."

"You speak excellent English for a Vergallian."

"Thank you," Samuel said. He'd discovered through trial and error in two dozen similar conversations that it was best to accept the compliment and move on. "If I could just get your contact information…"

"Maybe I'll stop back after visiting the other booths," the woman said. "I heard that the Drazens are providing free housing for skilled equipment operators on the latest world they opened to immigration."

"I'll be here," Samuel called after her retreating back. He noticed that the tray of oversized chocolate chip cookies that helped attract passersby into the U-shaped booth was running low and busied himself refilling it. Not many people were helping themselves to the free wine, but it was still late morning so that wasn't too surprising. He took advantage of the extended lull to check the large cooler unit, which contained a dozen trays of pre-wrapped sandwiches and party platters prepared by Gem caterers, but decided against putting any of it out yet.

Aabina approached the booth and helped herself to a glass of red wine. "I'm done moderating panels for the day," she explained. "How's it going with you?"

"Not great," Samuel admitted. "People love our immersive dramas but they think that living on tech ban worlds means going back to the dark ages. Humans working on our worlds live longer and healthier lives than they would on Earth, and those statistics are based primarily on mercenaries and their families, so it could only improve for farmers and craftsmen."

"But our people have only had modern technology for a few hundred years," Aabina countered. "Why would we even consider going backwards, not to mention moving to worlds governed by queens?"

"Somebody has to be in charge, and you don't need to be a fan of Grenouthian documentaries to know how badly the governments on Earth were botching the job before the Stryx opened the planet."

"That's the problem with you advanced species," the Vergallian ambassador's daughter said. "You're always harping on humanity's failures and not giving us any credit for our successes. Just look around the trade show and you'll see what we can accomplish living under our own sovereign governments."

A man carrying a canvas bag stuffed with trade show swag stepped up next to Aabina and said, "You tell him, Miss," as he wrapped several cookies in a napkin. Then he looked at the Vergallian girl's face and his jaw dropped. "Aren't you on the wrong side of the argument?"

"I'm with the EarthCent embassy. Are you finding everything you need today?"

"Yes. Well, actually, I could use a replacement belt for an old Frunge conveyer but the vendors here all want to sell me new equipment."

"Try the booth in the far corner that has a windmill turbine on display," Aabina said. "They're from one of our communities that leases a Frunge recycling facility and they deal in used and remanufactured equipment. If you don't have any luck, the Eccentric Enterprises circuit ship will be arriving in a few days, and the Dollnick distributors on board stock millions of replacement parts for heavy equipment."

"That's great news. I know that the Dollys on Flower will have the parts because we've dealt with them before, but they skipped our world on the last circuit. Thanks for the cookies," he added, and then stepped around an approaching Verlock on his way out of the booth.

"Humans," Samuel complained to Aabina. "All you care about is the free stuff."

"Busy?" the Verlock inquired.

"Is that you, Wrylenth?" the EarthCent ambassador's son asked, peering at the photo ID the Verlock was wearing.

"Samuel McAllister," the bulky alien replied ponderously. "Why are you working in the Vergallian booth?"

"It's my co-op job. Did the Open University place you with one of the news services?"

"EarthCent Intelligence."

"I'm working for our embassy, Wrylenth, and I better check on the other booths before the lunch crowd shows up," Aabina said, offering the Verlock a human-style handshake. "If there's anything you need, just let me know. I'll see you later, Samuel."

"The Vergallian ambassador's daughter?" Wrylenth asked after she left.

"Yes," Samuel confirmed. "Aabina."

"Which embassy is her co-op job?"

"Ours. I mean, yours. I mean, EarthCent's. I used to take pronouns for granted but they're getting pretty confusing."

The Verlock took a minute to process this information and then fished a tab out of his large belt pouch. "Conducting survey," he said, minimizing his word count to save time.

"How long will it take? I'm the only one working the booth."

"Five hours?" Wrylenth suggested.

"Five minutes?" Samuel counter offered.

"We'll play it by ear," the Verlock ground out. "What are your strategic goals?"

"Do you mean for the Empire of a Hundred Worlds in general, or for our embassy's booth rental here today?"

"Trade show."

"We're trying to build a contact list of people who would be interested in attending events at our embassy promoting open worlds."

"The Vergallian embassy?"

"Yes."

"Vergallian open worlds?"

"Yes."

"There aren't any."

"No, but there are a number of forward-looking queens who are interested in—"

"Stop," Wrylenth cut him off. "We're under surveillance."

"What? Where?" Samuel demanded, looking around the crowded trade show floor. He thought he saw a figure ducking behind a Dollnick a few booths over but he couldn't be sure. "What species?"

"Can't talk now," the Verlock said. He put his tab back in its belt pouch. "Protocol. Must return to base."

"But we don't even know if they're watching you or me, I mean, the Vergallians or EarthCent—or the Verlocks," Samuel added in frustration as the other co-op student shuffled off. He spun back toward the booth where he'd spotted the possible agent earlier, and this time he saw Vivian tapping away on her student tab. Then she looked up again and blushed. A second later, he answered her incoming ping.

"Pretend you didn't see me," she said over his implant.

"Are you still mad about finding Aabina in my bedroom?" he subvoced in return.

"Yes, but that's not why I'm spying on you."

"You're spying on me?"

"Not you-you. I'm spying on the Vergallian booth."

"For EarthCent?"

"For the Drazens. Have you already forgotten who I work for?"

"But we're the good Vergallians," Samuel protested. "We're trying to help."

"That's for the analysts to say, I'm just carrying out surveillance."

"When do you get off work? We could grab dinner."

"I've got another ping. I'll talk to you later."

Samuel watched as his girlfriend broke off her surveillance to hurry in the direction Wrylenth had taken earlier.

He made a mental note to inform Vergallian embassy security that the Drazens were spying on the booth, and then ate another one of the cookies and started on an apple from the fruit bowl.

The noise on the trade show floor surged as the late morning sessions began letting out, and experienced convention attendees flooded the Nebulae room to see if they could manage a free lunch from the snacks on offer. Samuel hurried to put out a tray of pre-wrapped sandwich halves and one of the party platters. The booth was immediately mobbed as a result.

"Put your card in the fishbowl and win a free dinner for two at your choice of restaurant in the Little Apple," he repeated whenever a new face appeared. It was clear that the visitors were more intent on eating than talking, so he settled for playing the good host in the hope that they would remember the booth and come back to talk later.

"Do you have anything to drink other than wine?" a woman asked.

"Sorry, I forgot," Samuel said. He opened the cooler again and pulled out a bus pan packed with bottled juices and Union Station Springs water. "I have cups too if you prefer."

"No, this is fine," the woman said, grabbing two bottles of water. "One for later," she added apologetically.

"There's more where that came from. Just remember, the Vergallian embassy is here to serve."

"Serve who?"

"It's complicated."

"Do you have tuna fish?" a familiar voice asked.

"Mom! What are you doing here?"

"Trying to get a quick bite to eat. I've promised the Grenouthian network an interview and then I'm chairing a panel so I don't have time for a restaurant."

"Let me check the cooler," Samuel said.

"Bring the whole tray," his mother called. "These sandwiches are going fast."

"Are embassy outreach booths always this busy?" he asked his mother after he returned with the sandwiches. Kelly didn't answer because she was too intent on trying to find the edge of the plastic wrap on the triangular cut sandwich. "Here, let me get that before you smoosh it all together."

"Thank you, Sam. I can't even imagine what the Vergallian embassy's discretionary budget must be. Bakery cookies, sandwiches, bottled juice, and party platters? What you have on offer right now is more than we spend catering official events."

"Here," he said, giving his mother the unwrapped tuna sandwich. "I wouldn't have spent all this money myself but Aainda's embassy manager did the ordering. The Gem came and dropped off this cooler in the morning, and they said they'd be back to restock as soon as it fell to thirty percent of capacity. It must have sensors inside." He noted that his mother was wolfing down her food and unwrapped another half of a tuna sandwich for her. "I heard your keynote address was a huge success."

Kelly pointed at her mouth to indicate that she was too busy chewing to respond, so Samuel circulated with the fishbowl again, gathering another crop of business cards and holocubes. When he got back to the sandwich trays, his mother was gone. The feeding frenzy lasted throughout the lunch hour and two resupply missions from the Gem caterers, who didn't even bother putting the second delivery in the cooler since the sandwiches were going so fast. By the time the chimes announced the start of the afternoon sessions, the EarthCent ambassador's son felt like he had run a marathon.

"Bob Steelforth, Galactic Free Press," a tall, thin man announced himself.

"You don't have to introduce yourself, Bob. I was standing right in front of you at your wedding, if you've forgotten."

"Just following standard operating procedure," the reporter said. "I don't remember if Judith and I ever thanked you and Vivian for giving up your couples rings for us to use for the ceremony. I haven't taken mine off since."

"You can't, unless Judith uses hers to draw it off," Samuel reminded him. "It's Verlock memory metal."

"I forgot about that. Do you have time for an interview?"

"If you don't mind asking questions while I'm cleaning up."

"I'm in no hurry," the reporter said, snagging a broken cookie before Samuel could throw it away. "I'm on a panel later this afternoon and I don't want to go straight there from covering another session."

"Which panel are you doing?"

"Rumors. We've been hearing so many of them at the paper lately that Chastity is talking about starting a new desk to cover them. Hey, is it possible it's your people again?"

"My people?"

"The Vergallians. You're the ones who tried to manipulate us into voting to leave the tunnel network not too long ago. Don't you remember? Our managing editor originally came to Union Station as a political organizer who was unwittingly working for Vergallian Imperial Intelligence."

"I forgot about that," Samuel admitted. "I was only seven. Has the newspaper been around that long?"

"Chastity started it right afterwards. This latest rumor about the president of EarthCent quitting and your mom taking over has that same feel to it, and then there's the whole business with Gryph selling Union Station. The bigger the lie, the more likely people will believe it."

"I don't believe it, but if Vergallian Imperial Intelligence is involved, I wouldn't know anything about that. I'm working for the diplomatic service and my ambassador's world is in one of the anti-Imperial factions. You know how complicated their politics get."

"Not as complicated as the Open University's co-op program," Bob said. He peered at the label on the last unopened bottle of juice, which turned out to be papaya-cranberry. "Do you want this?"

"It's all yours. Does the Galactic Free Press hire co-op students?"

"Not yet, but I heard a rumor that we're going to start. When I tried to get an interview with Daniel this morning, he fobbed me off on a Vergallian girl who gave me enough material for two articles. She's brilliant."

"Aabina. She aced the EarthCent civil service exam. What did you want to ask me about?"

The reporter took a swallow of the papaya-cranberry juice and made a face. "Who comes up with these combinations?"

"Beats me." Samuel took a close look at the label on a juice container he was about to drop in the glass recycling bin. "Blended from the finest reconstituted molecules and bottled by Union Station Springs. I think it may be one of Libby's businesses."

"Then it's probably good for me," Bob said resignedly and took another swig. "So what can you tell me on the record about the Vergallian embassy's goal in coming to the trade show?"

"We want to improve our relations with the local humans and explore the possibility of acting as a waystation for homesteaders interested in setting up communities on Vergallian worlds."

"Sovereign communities?"

"We're working on that part, but some of the queens on the outlying worlds are willing to give it a try. You'd just be a drop in the bucket of our populations as there are over a trillion of us."

"So why bother with humans at all? There are plenty of Vergallians to go around."

"There's plenty of work to go around too. Do you have any idea how many available planets there are in the galaxy?"

"But how many of them are already occupied?"

"Fewer than you'd think. And you'd probably be surprised how many species automate everything and then end up dying out from lack of a reason to get out of bed in the morning. You can laugh at our use of manual labor and draft animals for farming, but the Empire of a Hundred Worlds has seen steady growth for over a million years."

"So what sized groups are you looking for?" Bob asked.

"If we could recruit a whole community coming off of a long-term labor contract on one of the alien ag worlds that would be great. We don't have a precise number in mind in terms of population, but the demographics would be important. The queens all plan for the long term, so they'll

189

want communities that are at least producing children at the replacement rate."

"Are you getting any takers?"

"No solid commitments if that's what you mean. My job was to gather contact information, and I'm getting plenty of that. The embassy has marketing people who will do a better job closing the deal than I ever could."

"What's the embassy's official position on—excuse me," the reporter cut himself off, pointing at his ear to indicate an incoming ping. "Sorry, I have to run. We'll talk later."

Samuel found the afternoon to be pretty much the same as the morning until the session on rumors in the Galaxy Room amphitheatre caused the trade show to empty out. He cleaned the booth again, doing a more thorough job than he had after lunch, and then used his student tab to start capturing images of the old-fashioned business cards collected in the fishbowl. A strange feeling that he was being watched intruded on his concentration, and he kept snapping his head around to see if he could catch Vivian in the act, but the room had gone unnaturally still. Then the Imperial Vergallian intelligence agent strode into the booth.

"Ajalah," Samuel greeted her cautiously with a slight head bow. "What brings you to our humble booth?"

"Don't talk smart with me, Human. I know that you're secretly working for EarthCent Intelligence against the empire. Just admit on the record that Aainda and Aabina are part of the plot and I'll let you slink back home with your tail between your legs."

"You're interfering in the lawful operations of the Vergallian embassy," Samuel replied, putting as much edge in his voice as he could muster. "It's obvious that you don't care about Ambassador Aainda's authority, but this badge means that I'm currently on the clock for my co-op job. I don't know what power you think you wield here, but I can assure you that the Open University administration is out of your league."

"I'm sorry," Ajalah said in a mocking voice. "Did I scare the little Human so much that he wants to run and hide behind the Stryx? I promise this won't hurt a bit."

Samuel stepped back and fell into the guard position of one of the mixed martial arts styles Thomas had tried to teach him, but he had always been more interested in sword fighting than hand-to-hand combat, and he had no doubt that Ajalah could wipe the floor with him. Then he noticed the odd look of concentration on her face and realized too late that she could simply dose him with pheromones and instruct him to make a false confession implicating the Vergallian ambassador and her daughter. His legs refused to answer his command to flee, and he found himself staring into the intelligence agent's beautiful eyes, waiting for her command.

"You will—ughh..." Ajalah gasped in pain and collapsed to her knees.

Baa stepped around the intelligence agent and snapped her fingers in front of Samuel's face. His mind cleared as if the upper caste Vergallian had never commenced chemical warfare and he found himself free to move. Ajalah continued to groan, her lovely features so contorted that it was hard to believe she was the same woman.

"Let her go, Baa," he said. "I'm okay now and there's no reason to make this into a big deal. It's just politics."

"Vergallian politics is a big deal," the Terragram mage retorted, but she grabbed Ajalah's upper arm and pulled her into a standing position. "Listen to me, little queen. You can hide behind the Stryx on the station, but if I ever

191

run into you out in space, we're going to have a talk that you really don't want to have." Then she glanced towards the ceiling and asked out loud, "Just this once?"

Ajalah intuited what was going on and turned to flee, but Baa must have gotten the answer she was hoping for because she performed an intricate casting. The Vergallian was suddenly transformed into a creature that looked like a large, hairless rat. It squealed piteously while fleeing the trade show floor.

"What did you do to her?" Samuel demanded. "If she goes missing on the station, my ambassador could get in trouble."

"Aainda would thank me for putting Ajalah permanently out of her misery, but the effect will wear off in a few hours. It's just a bit of holographic trickery, not that different from what happens in the LARPing studios with Non-Player Characters."

"You turned her into an NPC?"

"I meant it in the sense of binding a hologram to a physical form to give it substance. Your station librarian is using the holographic advertising system to maintain the illusion at this point. I can only do it when the target is in sight."

"Did Libby send you to help me?"

"I was already on my way to tell you that I finished enchanting your noodle weapons and Jeeves wants you and Vivian to practice with them at Mac's Bones after work. Apparently he doesn't trust me."

Sixteen

"What do two Frunge in the initial stages of courting do if they accidentally find themselves waiting for the same lift tube capsule?" Dorothy asked Kevin.

"Do you not know the answer or are you testing me?"

"It's in the quiz at the end of the chapter."

"One of them takes the stairs."

"There are no stairs on Union Station."

"So one of them waits for the next capsule."

"Correct," Dorothy said, making a little check mark in her freshly printed copy of *Frunge for Humans*. "Name three common foods from Earth that the Frunge won't eat."

"Bread, pasta and pizza crust."

"Isn't pizza crust just another kind of bread?"

"Not in my universe," Kevin replied indignantly.

"Huh, they have it as an answer," Dorothy said, making another note. "I wonder who wrote this book."

A heavyset man whose skin looked like it had been baked under a hot sun shuffled up to the table and addressed Dorothy.

"Need noodle weapons?"

"Yes. SBJ Fashions is seeking a wholesale relationship with a manufacturer because we're on the brink of creating an entirely new market, but we need a supplier aligned with the Grenouthians."

"Why?"

"The Grenouthians have a deal with the professional LARPing league that we need to respect."

"Fraction of the price," the man offered hopefully.

"You're from one of the Verlock open worlds?" Dorothy asked, and received a nod in return. "I really wish we could work with you on this, but it's more about the marketing potential than the cost. I'm sure that your noodle weapons are every bit as good as the ones made by the Grenouthians, but our contract has us locked up."

"Bunnies," the man grunted scornfully and shuffled off.

"If I was wearing a blindfold that guy could have passed as a Verlock," Kevin said. "It's funny how all of the humans living on open worlds end up going native."

"Why do you say that? Look at your own family and the Kasilians."

"Fair point. Oh, I think Marilla hooked somebody. Talk to you later."

Kevin crossed the interior space of the booth, which consisted of eight folding tables set up in a square at the start of a vendor row just inside the entrance to the Nebulae room. The booth could be accessed from three sides, one of which was taken by Dorothy for SBJ Fashions, another by Thomas and Chance recruiting for EarthCent Intelligence, and the third by Mac's Bones for the new spaceship rental business.

"We can sell you a modest number of ships, but you can also purchase your own, either used or new," Marilla answered a woman's question. "Each franchise buys its own ships, but you may not see them again for months at a time, depending on where one-way-trip customers drop them off."

"You mean I'm expected to make a huge investment in ships and then they'll just be sitting around some other franchisee's lot wasting space?"

"No, not at all. Every franchise must agree to FIFO scheduling, First In, First Out, and since all of the ships will be equipped with Stryx controllers, it's easy to monitor for compliance. When I worked at a Horten rental agency, we literally kept the ships in a line, like a taxi queue, so there was never any confusion about the order."

"But I'm responsible for cleaning every ship that comes into my franchise..."

"And handling regularly scheduled maintenance at a mutually agreed upon standard rate," Marilla said. "Of course, the other agency locations will be doing the same for your rental fleet, and it all tends to work out even in the end."

"My rental fleet," the woman repeated. "I like the sound of that. I'll talk it over with the rest of our delegation at dinner and get back to you."

"You're really good at this," Kevin said to the Horten girl after the woman left. "Are you sure you didn't study business at the Open University?"

"I can't believe I'm doing this at all. I'm usually really shy around strange aliens, but somehow it's different with Humans."

A man wearing a four-armed suit that marked him as a businessman from one of the Dollnick open worlds approached the booth. The extra set of arms were sewn to the sides of the jacket, with the sleeves terminating in the lower pockets, as if he had another pair of hands that were hidden from view.

"Hule," the man introduced himself. "I'm the mayor of Equipment."

"Is that a place?" Kevin asked.

"On Chianga," Hule replied. "We follow the Dollnick practice of naming towns after their functions. I've visited a number of worlds with CoSHC communities and I can't tell you how frustrating it is that they all name their cities 'Spring-something,' as if they were bouncy."

"I think it's an old Earth name. People were always happy to have a source of clean water."

"Then why didn't they build purification plants? But I'm going off subject. The delegates from our group who visited the trade show yesterday have been whistling in my ear about your plans to set up a rental network for small ships. Do I have the right place?"

"Tunnel Trips," Kevin confirmed. "The name is tentative until we can line up some potential business partners or franchisees to vote on it. Did you try one of our simulators in the lobby?"

"Yes. Makes me wish I could install Stryx controllers in all of the equipment we supply to the other communities on Chianga, but the Stryx don't produce them for ground-based navigation and operations."

"You supply equipment to the other Human communities and it gets lost?" Marilla asked.

"No, we have excellent tracking capabilities, but the controls are all manual, and some operators act like hydraulic pistons are indestructible. I'd like to bring them all up on charges of machine abuse."

"I spoke to a few delegates from Chianga yesterday. They said that space-liner service to your world is excellent, but only for connections to other Dollnick systems."

"That's right," Hule said. "Our delegation traveled here on a cargo ship that's on its way to deliver floater hardware to Earth and they'll pick us up on the way back. The local Dollnicks are able to bypass the Stryx stations on the vast majority of their liner routes thanks to their superior planning abilities. Practically all of their travel arrangements are nonstop."

"So that leaves your salespeople and field service engineers scrambling to make connections in order to reach Earth or the other sovereign human communities," Marilla said sympathetically. "It sounds like a perfect match for our Tunnel Trips business model."

"Almost too good to be true. The thing is, and please don't take this the wrong way, ma'am, I don't understand why we have to work with Hortens on this. If we're going to be dependent on another species in this business, doesn't it make more sense to stick with the Dollnicks?"

"Marilla is an Open University co-op student," Kevin explained. "She's working for my father-in-law's ship repair facility, and it happens that he and my brother-in-law have enough small craft available to dip a toe in the rental business. We can set up roundtrip rentals without any partners, but it's incredibly inefficient for all parties involved."

"I get it now," Hule said. "If your customers can't drop off the ship at the other end, you need to charge much more for the rental because your inventory is just sitting in orbit, or worse, docked at an elevator hub with expensive parking fees."

"Exactly. Right now we're just talking with people, but we've scheduled a meeting for the last day of the convention where we hope to iron out a basic deal with enough partners to launch a beta test this year."

"Will all of your partners or franchisees be required to buy ships from you?"

"We couldn't supply them all even if we wanted to. Since the ships we'll be committing are second-hand, we thought it would be best if everybody followed the same model for now, plus it will cut way down on capital expenses. As soon as we settle on the branding, we're going to find somebody to supply full-ship wraps."

"What are those?"

"You've seen the protective film the Sharf wrap around new ships to keep the paint jobs from getting scratched by micro-meteors and space dust?"

"Yes, but they always have Sharf advertising on them so everybody tears the film off as soon as—I get you."

"In addition to branding the rental agency, we can sell ad space on the wraps to help juice the profits."

"You've sold me," Hule said. "My only remaining question is whether I can see some of the actual rental units before the meeting."

"Just ask the lift tube to take you to Mac's Bones," Kevin told him. "I'll ping my father-in-law and tell him to expect you. And don't be put off by the fact it looks like a flea market. My mother-in-law is holding a multi-species tag sale after the convention and it's gotten a bit out of hand."

Three steps to Kevin's left, Chance was telling an artificial person who had asked about seeing the EarthCent Intelligence training camp, "—and ignore all of the junk. The ambassador is holding a multi-species tag sale, and some of the other diplomats have been taking advantage of her good nature."

"You allow aliens to wander in and out of your secure facility?" the prospective spy asked.

"It's not secure," Chance explained. "If you want a tour of EarthCent Intelligence's office space, that's different. There's not much to see at the training camp this week since there aren't any classes scheduled. I'll ping Judith and tell her that you're coming. She's down there playing with the holograms."

"Excuse me?"

"Thomas and I are the primary trainers, and while we're tied up at this trade show, Judith is taking advantage of the time to practice holographic design. Humans can have a lot of difficulty programming in 3D," Chance said, and continued in a lower voice. "Poor math skills."

Dorothy chose this moment to ask her fellow booth staffers, "Do any of you guys know what 'Discounted cash flow' means?"

"Traders use a discounted cargo value to reflect theft losses at port facilities, but it doesn't sound like the same thing," Kevin replied. "Why do you need to know?"

"It's part of the basic financial workup the Frunge matchmaker will expect from all of the immediate family members on both sides."

"Not just the parents?" Marilla asked. "That seems a little extreme."

"The way the author explains it, profligate siblings are both an early warning sign and a future liability."

"Let me see the context," Thomas said, coming over and taking the book from Dorothy. The artificial person studied the section pointed out by the girl. "In this case, the author is talking about the difference between the simple rate of return on an investment and the discount you have to allow for the time value of money and inflation."

"Do you think the matchmaker would include an accounting problem in my test?"

"Frunge kids study finance from childhood on, so I doubt she'll even think to ask anything so basic."

"Stick with what we need to know to chaperone a date," Kevin suggested. "That's probably what Mizpah will question us about."

"It's just harder than I thought it would be," Dorothy said. "How's recruiting going, Thomas?"

"I'm not sure whether the personality enhancement from QuickU that I'm testing is helping or hurting," the artificial person admitted.

"What was it supposed to make you do?" Kevin asked.

"Personality enhancements don't work that way. It's not like becoming somebody else, or only a deeply troubled AI would ever want to try one."

"Then what did you get?"

"The module changes the way I perceive external stimuli. So when I see somebody passing the booth, instead of assessing their potential threat level like an intelligence agent, I recognize them as possible customers. I've also noticed a difference in the way I read their body language and process vocal cues. The enhancement is intended to help artificial people who want to work as sales associates, but I'm not sure the same techniques are really applicable to recruiting."

"Can you undo it?"

"Of course, but it wouldn't be fair to QuickU to quit without giving it a serious test. Chance didn't load this enhancement so she's the control group and we'll see which one of us is more successful at bringing in new applicants." Thomas caught sight of a couple approaching his table and broke off the conversation with a terse, "I'm on."

Dorothy grabbed Kevin's wrist as he turned to go back to his side of the booth where Marilla was chatting with a couple of CoSHC members whose excessive make-up suggested that their community was located on a Horten open world. "Who will you sit across from when we go out to eat?"

"You're talking about double-dates?"

"Yes, but don't call them that in front of Mizpah. It's chaperoning duty as far as she's concerned."

"Give me a second," Kevin said. "The Frunge probably want to maximize the physical separation between the couple, so they can't sit next to each other, and probably not across from each other either. Diagonal?"

"If you've already read the book, just tell me and I'll stop asking questions," Dorothy said irritably.

"It was an educated guess. I spent ten years trading with aliens and you learn how to extrapolate from what you see. There's a Grenouthian standing in front of your table tapping his foot."

"When the bunnies tap their feet, it means they're impatient."

"I wasn't quizzing you."

Dorothy spun around to see a tough-looking bunny wearing a blue sash labeled "Visitor" glaring at her with his big black eyes.

"Can I help you?" she asked.

"First you made me wait and now you're trying to insult me? Perhaps standing on the business side of that folding table has gone to your head, but there's nothing any Human can possibly do to help me."

"Then why are you here?" Dorothy demanded.

"Because our ambassador strong-armed me into agreeing to attend a demonstration at this booth on the last day of the trade show."

"Do you manufacture noodle weapons? I'm Dorothy McAllister and—"

"I know who you are," the bunny interrupted. "Unlike some species, we do our research."

"So why are you here three days early?"

"Do you think I'm going to show up for your demonstration without laying the groundwork? That sales tactic might work on the Verlocks, but you'll have to get up earlier in the morning to pull the fur over my eyes."

"We're not keeping anything secret," Dorothy protested. "SBJ Fashions employs a Terragram mage to enchant some of our clothing and accessories for LARPing and we want to expand into noodle weapons. We wouldn't be talking to you at all if the professional league hadn't—"

"Given us an exclusive on providing noodle weapons for official league matches," the bunny interrupted again. "I should know, I helped write that contract."

"I still don't understand why you're here."

"Will you allow me to check your booth?"

"You mean, to come inside the tables? There's nothing in here other than the five of us and a few boxes with hand-out materials."

"I'll be the judge of that."

Dorothy hesitated a moment over whether to ping Jeeves, but she couldn't think of any grounds to refuse the request, other than the alien's rudeness. "Alright. Can you just duck under?"

The Grenouthian gave the ambassador's daughter a scornful look and then hopped over the table without even crouching first to gather himself. "Feel free to go back to whatever you were doing," he said, and then removed a device that looked like a hand-held medical scanner of some sort from his pouch and began examining the deck.

"Are you looking for anything in particular?" Dorothy couldn't help asking.

"The President of EarthCent. I heard a rumor that he abandoned his post. Now if you'll leave me to do my work, I'll be out of here that much quicker."

A saleswoman wearing a wreath of laurel leaves on her head arrived at the booth carrying an immense book of fabric samples. She set it on the table and opened it in front of Dorothy, whose jaw dropped at the iridescent threads used in the expensive micro-weave. Neither of the women even noticed when the rude bunny finished whatever he was doing and hopped back out of the booth.

"Order today and receive a ten-percent discount on quantities over one thousand," the saleswoman from the Frunge open world concluded her pitch.

"One thousand what?" Dorothy asked.

"SFU. Standard Factory Units. I'll just put you down for a starter order and we'll take it from there."

"I'm not supposed to spend any money," the EarthCent ambassador's daughter confessed. "I mean, we are looking for new suppliers and production facilities, but—" she gazed longingly at the shimmering fabric samples, "—how much is a starter order?"

"With the discount, ninety thousand creds, but you'll make back millions when your fashions hit the market. The cloth is produced with the latest Frunge process and our community is the first to be authorized to sell it to aliens."

"You mean humans?"

"Right, it gets confusing living on an open world. I'd offer you the designer pack, which only includes enough fabric to run up a hundred dresses for a fashion show, but I'd be doing you a disservice. As soon as your competition sees that you're using our cloth, they'll rush in their orders and you'll lose your head start."

"So you're saying you won't sell your fabric to anybody else on Union Station if I take the starter order for ninety thousand?"

"It's sort of all we've produced so far, and our delegation brought it along in the transport," the saleswoman admitted. "If you buy me out, there won't be any more of the new micro-weave on the open market for at least six cycles. It's incredibly time-consuming to manufacture."

"Oh, I want it so much but my boss would kill me. How much is the designer pack?"

"Two thousand creds."

"Can you bill us?" Dorothy asked in a whisper.

"Of course. We have an EarthCent Intelligence business subscription and I checked your credit rating before approaching the booth. Where would you like delivery?"

"I'd better take it at home. We don't have much room in the office these days with all of the enchanting work going on."

Seventeen

"Thank you for inviting me to participate in your meeting," the head of Drazen Intelligence greeted Kelly. "I hope you don't mind that I've brought my new assistant."

"Not at all, Herl," the EarthCent ambassador replied, and directed a smile at her son's girlfriend. "Hello, Vivian. I'm sorry to make you work after hours."

"I'm on the Drazen clock now and it's morning for us. Will Samuel be here?"

"Although our relationship with the Vergallian embassy is much improved, I don't think it would be appropriate for him to attend such a sensitive meeting."

Vivian looked past the ambassador's shoulder at Aabina and opened her mouth to speak, but recalling her own position as a co-op student working for Drazen intelligence, thought better of it. Her parents entered the EarthCent embassy conference room with Wrylenth in tow, and she felt a pang of sympathy for the young Verlock as he struggled to keep up with his employers.

"Everybody grab a seat," Kelly instructed the newcomers. "Don't be shy about taking Srythlan's chair, Wrylenth. As soon as Chastity gets here, Daniel will bring in our special—here she is."

"Sorry I'm barely on time," the publisher of the Galactic Free Press apologized, taking the seat next to her sister. "I got ambushed by the Grenouthian editor of their shipping news. He tracked me down to gloat about scooping us again."

"Anything important?" Blythe asked her sister.

"Apparently the president is here. Our president," Chastity clarified. "The bunnies are running with a story that he's on Union Station to abdicate his throne to Kelly."

"It sounds reasonable, except for the throne part," Herl observed. "I seem to recall that your last president fled office and had to be replaced."

"Did he arrive with Hildy Greuen?" Clive inquired.

"How did you guess?" Kelly asked.

"I knew that Hildy was coming to talk to CoSHC representatives about coordinating their public relations with the president's office. For the record, the president really should keep us in the loop about his travel plans. Maybe you could bring it up at the next steering committee meeting."

"You can tell him yourself in a minute. Libby? Could you inform Daniel that everybody is here?"

The associate ambassador and his surprise guests must have been waiting for the announcement, because a few seconds later, Daniel led Stephen Beyer and Hildy Greuen in through the large sliding doors separating the conference room from the embassy lobby. Aabina, Wrylenth, and Herl all stood and offered a polite round of applause, forcing the others to follow suit.

"Sit, sit," the president said. "I'm here unofficially so there's no need to stand on ceremony." He ran a hand over the conference room table's inlaid puzzle pieces and then gave his attention to the lacquer-on-copper scale model of Earth suspended from the ceiling. "Our holographic conferences don't do the globe justice."

"Dring made it," Kelly told him. "And I'm afraid I've just learned that the Grenouthians are running a story about your visit."

"How did they find out I'm here? We bought the tickets under Hildy's name and I traveled as Mr. Greuen."

"They probably have an agent on Earth watching your office by this point," Clive said. "The documentary tour business is turning into a big money maker for them and the Grenouthians are very proactive about protecting their investments."

"Pretty hard for bunnies to work undercover on Earth," the president observed.

"They probably have enough cameras installed around the neighborhood to keep an eye on you."

"The Grenouthians have floating mini-cameras that can follow a target from above," the Drazen intelligence head informed them. "The Dollnicks sell a version of their dragonfly counterespionage technology that can take down the cameras, but we rarely bother."

"You just let the Dollys spy on you?" Kelly asked.

"We use adaptive jamming, of course, but setting up that sort of system on Earth would cost you millions of creds," Herl said apologetically.

"Let them follow me if it makes them happy," the president said. "Now that I know about it, I'll find a way to use it to our advantage."

"Apparently the story goes beyond simply announcing your arrival," Kelly said. "Can you show us a feed of the Grenouthian's news report on the president, Libby?"

"The story is just going live," the station librarian reported. A hologram appeared at the end of the conference table where everybody could see it, and it opened with a scene of the president with his arm around Hildy entering the EarthCent embassy.

"Breaking news," the Grenouthian newsman announced. "The president of the Stryx-backed diplomatic organization for Humans has fled Earth with his lover and was spotted entering the EarthCent embassy on Union Station. Informed sources tell us that Stephen Beyer intends to resign his office in favor of Kelly McAllister, the current Union Station ambassador. In related news, the Conference of Sovereign Human Communities trade show at the Empire Convention Center will open for its third day at nine in the morning on the Human clock. Check with the station librarian for the actual time as it's become a moving target."

"If you want to make a statement to set the record straight, Mr. President, I can have it on the front page of the Galactic Free Press in minutes," Chastity offered.

"Can you hold off a while?" Hildy requested. "I know that it's your business to report the news as soon as you get confirmation, but this could really work well for me."

"Being identified as the president's lover?"

"The whole story about Stephen fleeing office. Do you think Earth would have made the headline news if we were here on an announced visit? And the Grenouthians probably wouldn't have mentioned the trade show at all if they weren't trying to fill out a thin story. It's a public relations dream."

"And we don't mind having our relations public," the president punned. "If I've learned one thing in my time with Hildy, it's that all publicity is good publicity, at least until the moment you're being led off to jail."

"So I can assure our diplomats that you aren't here fleeing your responsibilities as president," Herl surmised.

"I came along to carry suitcases of pamphlets for Hildy because we couldn't spare anybody else. My administration held an all-hands-onboard staff meeting last week to plan the trip, and it turns out that I'm the least important person working in EarthCent headquarters."

"No, you just have the most flexible schedule," Hildy corrected him. "Everybody else has a job to do, while your job is being available to meet important aliens and take midnight panic calls from ambassadors."

"Executive responsibility," Wrylenth pronounced slowly.

"May I ask if you took our EarthCent civil service exam?" the public relations expert asked the Verlock co-op student. "I was involved in creating the test."

"It was very entertaining. I recommended it to my friends."

"And you must be Aabina," Hildy continued, turning to the Vergallian ambassador's daughter. "I remember your perfect score. If you find yourself wishing for a change of scenery, we'd be happy to give you a job in the president's office."

"The paper has dibs on her," Chastity jumped in. "Besides, she's still a minor under Vergallian law so you'd have to get her mother's permission before taking her off the station."

"This is all very complimentary, but I don't recall seeing my future employment on the agenda I prepared for this meeting," Aabina announced in a firm voice. "First, is this conference room secure?"

"It was when we swept it this morning but you know how that goes," Clive replied. "Herl?"

The Drazen head of intelligence shook the sleeve back from his heavy bracelet and glanced at the glowing crystals. "It's clean of everything our technology is capable of detecting, but with those Gem caterers running in and out all the time, you never know if there are some nano-bugs around."

"My belief is that secrecy is overrated," the president said. "We've been doing without it ever since the Stryx opened Earth so why start worrying now? What's on the agenda?"

"As long as you're here, our main goal is to convince the Grenouthians to allow human settlements on some of their worlds that are open to immigration from the other advanced species," Aabina said. "We believe that the exponential growth of documentary tours to Earth gives you leverage in their entertainment community, and the Grenouthian diplomats will bend over backwards for their business leaders."

"And we've been picking up intelligence chatter that indicates the bunnies will be approaching us with a new proposition," Clive added. "Some of that has come from our Drazen allies."

"My new assistant is filling in for a vacationing analyst on our Earth desk," Herl said. "Vivian?"

"There's been a definite spike in communications traffic from Union Station-based Grenouthians the last three weeks, with much of it directed towards Earth," the girl said, looking down at her tab. "It's all encrypted beyond our ability to decode, but a source in the entertainment industry reports that the Grenouthians have been quietly lining up options on large numbers of background actors who are willing to temporarily relocate to a Tier-9 location with a space elevator and a tunnel connection."

"I'm not familiar with entertainment industry rank-ings," Kelly said. "What's the significance of Tier-9?"

"Tier-1 worlds are classified as highly civilized, and Tier-10s are worlds still undergoing the terraforming process. As far as anybody knows, Earth is the only Tier-9 planet on the tunnel network with a space elevator."

"The Grenouthians who negotiated with us for rights to our archival footage complained vociferously about the lack of video coverage from ancient wars," the president mused. "Could they be planning to shoot a major immersive on Earth? From what I understand, that could pump a lot of creds into the economy."

"I wonder if it has something to do with my daughter's latest project," Kelly said. "SBJ Fashions is trying to negotiate a deal with the Grenouthians to license some kind of toy manufacturing, and they even got Aisha involved."

"Noodle weapons, not toys," Daniel spoke up. "I didn't want to say anything about it, because as most of you know, my wife is the 'S' in SBJ Fashions."

"So what's the problem?" Herl asked. "It sounds to me like the ideal opportunity to work for your family and your species at the same time."

"But that would be nepotism," Kelly protested.

"Grenouthians take family seriously," Wrylenth contributed.

"I don't have any objections to double-dipping," the president said. "I've learned the hard way that when it comes to the bunnies, you can do things their way or not at all."

"If getting a toehold on Grenouthian open worlds is important to EarthCent, you should put all of these issues together in a package deal and have President Beyer handle the negotiations," Herl suggested. "Grenouthian businessmen always recruit the most senior diplomat available to represent them in contract talks, which in this case will be their ambassador."

"I'm happy to be of service while I'm here," Stephen said. "Somebody will have to brief me about these noodle weapons, though. I've never heard of them."

"The next item on the agenda is the presence of a senior Vergallian intelligence operative on Union Station," Aabina announced. "The ambassador tasked me to look into whether or not she may have been the source of the rumor about Gryph selling Union Station, possibly as a ploy to derail the CoSHC convention. I haven't been successful in running the source to ground, though forensic analysis has me convinced that the rumor did originate on Union Station. But the timeline doesn't work out for Ajalah to be fingered as the culprit."

"We've been keeping a close eye on the Vergallians since she arrived," Herl said. "My assistant participated in watching their embassy's booth at the trade show to see if they were recruiting undercover agents from the Human population. Vivian?"

"I was forced to break off surveillance of the, uh, subject after he was warned by an alien operative," she said, glancing across the table at the Verlock. "I didn't realize that Wrylenth was working for our allies in EarthCent Intelligence until I trailed him back to their headquarters. I later learned that the Vergallian embassy employee manning the booth was approached by Ajalah while I was away. The subject's meeting with the intelligence operative in question was interrupted by Baa, the Terragram mage who lives on Union Station and works for SBJ Fashions."

"I'm afraid I can't make heads or tails of what you're talking about," the president said. "Is this something I'll need to know for the negotiations?"

"The matter was on the agenda before I was aware you would be attending," Aabina told him apologetically. "Does anybody object if I move on to the next issue, and we can return to internal Vergallian politics later?"

"Please," Blythe said. "My sister shouldn't be getting this for free in any case."

"The third item is the expected arrival of Flower in time for the last day of the CoSHC convention," Aabina continued. "Many of the attendees have already visited the circuit ship when it stopped at their worlds, but Captain Woojin has requested that we announce the ship will be open for tours throughout its stay at Union Station."

"How do the people living on open worlds without space elevators get to visit the circuit ship?" Hildy asked.

"Flower has been deploying her shuttles, which are capable of ferrying a thousand passengers at a time up and down from the surface," Daniel said. "Apparently she's able to earn a profit even at a modest ticket price because some families make the trip to the circuit ship just for the amusement park."

"Do you want me to announce the open house on Flower in the Union Station edition of the paper?" Chastity asked.

"If you could," the Vergallian ambassador's daughter said. "There's no limit to the number of visitors they're willing to entertain, though anybody who fails to return home before the departure time is in for a long ride."

"I'd like to visit Flower again," Hildy said. "We took the elevator up from Earth when they were preparing for their first trip, but it was pretty chaotic."

"I'll be messaging all CoSHC attendees with a schedule for her shuttles as soon as Flower arrives, and I've already begun contacting the various taxi services that serve Union Station's near-space parking for larger ships to make them aware of the opportunity," Aabina said. "The final agenda item is the Galactic Free Press coverage of the conference sessions."

"What about it?" Chastity asked.

"We'd like to commission a conference proceedings book," Daniel told her. "Some of the delegates record the sessions they attend, but there's something to be said for preserving a written record for the ten billion people who couldn't be here."

"I'm not sure you're aware of how bulky it would be without editing." The publisher of the Galactic Free Press pulled a tab out of her purse and tapped and swiped her way through a number of menus. "You have eight tracks running simultaneously, with three sessions in the morning and four in the afternoon, plus evening events. We're only halfway through the conference and the paper has already published transcripts totaling over a million words in our special coverage section. By the end of the week, including those extra events, you'll be up to three million words easy."

"Is that a lot?"

"*Oliver Twist* was less than two hundred thousand words," Kelly volunteered. "I remember that from somewhere."

"How about *War and Peace*?"

"Libby?" Kelly asked.

"Less than six-hundred thousand words, though it seemed like more," the Stryx station librarian opined.

"How much would the paper charge for editing?" Daniel asked.

"A lot," Chastity replied.

"I can help," Wrylenth offered ponderously. "I read much quicker than I speak."

214

"Me too," Aabina volunteered. "I like English."

"I'm interested in what you can learn about this Gryph rumor, if like you say, the Vergallians aren't behind it," the president said. "It seems strange to me that the advanced species would be so quick to accept such a ludicrous proposition."

"Rumor-mongering is practically a sport with the Dollnicks and Grenouthians," the Drazen spy chief explained. "Apparently it goes back several million years to when the Stryx gave the Brupt an ultimatum to give up their military capabilities or leave the galaxy. Nobody believed the rumor until the Brupt actually left, by which time it was too late to collect any outstanding debts."

"What about all of the worlds they must have abandoned?" the president inquired.

"I remember this from when Libby showed me a planet catalog when I was shopping for a new home for the Kasilians," Kelly said. "The Brupt blew up one of their main worlds before leaving, and they booby-trapped the others with everything from orbital mines to metal-eating bacteria in the soil."

"But if the Stryx really did give the Brupt an ultimatum, it wasn't a rumor, it was a fact," Vivian pointed out.

"Hindsight is twenty-twenty," Chastity told her niece. "If Gryph does sell Union Station, or if Kelly does replace the president, those rumors will have become facts as well."

"It all happened long before we joined the tunnel network," Herl said. "I've read a little about the history from the Dollnick perspective and my understanding is that the Stryx didn't make a public announcement because they wanted to give the Brupt a chance to back down. Many warlike species have thin skin and will always react with force to protect their public image. Obviously, they rejected the offer in any case."

"So you're saying that a single event from over a million years ago is still influencing the behavior of the advanced species today?" Kelly asked.

"Rumors tend to come in waves with major changes on the tunnel network, and the timing for a new wave is about right, now that Humans have been members for a few generations. Take the rumor about you replacing the president. Keeping tabs on political movements and dynastic successions is one of the core missions for intelligence agencies, but due to Stryx involvement, the EarthCent process is completely opaque. It's that total lack of information that often gives rise to rumors."

"But like you just said, we've been tunnel network members for a few generations already. Why now?"

"I'm not sure how to put this exactly." Herl scratched his head with his tentacle while composing his thoughts. "Until recently, none of the advanced species cared about what EarthCent was doing one way or another. It's only since you've started growing your business footprint on the tunnel network that you've become worth talking about."

Eighteen

"What time is it now?" Dorothy asked Judith.

"Three minutes later than the last time you asked me," the EarthCent intelligence trainer replied. "And I still don't understand why you needed me when I don't even get to fight anybody."

"Somebody has to be in charge, and I'm going to be on the other side of the table in case the Grenouthian ambassador has any questions. All you have to do is read the script from your heads-up display and give the models their cues."

"And then they get to have all of the fun," Judith complained. "Why didn't you get Shaina or Brinda to do this part?"

"You're the best-qualified person to stay out of the way of the models while they're dueling, and we have to keep management in reserve to close the deal if the president can get the bunnies to agree to the broad outlines. Do you hear that? They're getting impatient."

Judith listened for a moment and realized that the soft thumping coming from two sides of the booth originated with the tightly packed Grenouthians tapping their furry feet on the deck. Then the thumb ring she wore on her left hand started to glow blue, and she turned slowly through three-hundred and sixty degrees, trying to locate the source.

"What are you doing?" Dorothy demanded.

"Somebody is jamming your booth. Blue indicates holographic suppression."

"Do you mean our competitors are trying to interfere with my demonstration?"

"That's exactly what I mean," Judith replied, puzzling over the fact that the intensity of the glow didn't vary with direction. Then she lowered and raised her hand, and the blue definitely brightened in the higher position. "What's that on the ceiling?"

"I can't see much squinting up into the lights. Where are you pointing?"

"Dead center over the booth. It looks like some sort of alien device. Have you let anybody else in here?"

"It's just a square of folding tables," the ambassador's daughter said. "Anybody could crawl under or hop—the bunny!"

"What bunny?"

"A Grenouthian came by a couple of days ago and asked permission to check the booth. He seemed to believe we were going to try to cheat him somehow, and I think that device might be the scanner he was using. He must have jumped up and stuck it on the ceiling when we all had our backs turned. Libby?"

"Yes, Dorothy," the station librarian replied over the girl's implant.

"There's an alien device attached to the ceiling above our booth and we're going to start as soon as the president and the Grenouthian ambassador arrive. Is there anything in your security footage?"

"Yes. The Grenouthian you let into the booth the other day jumped up and placed a magnetized Noho unit on the ceiling when you weren't looking."

"Noho?"

"That's what EarthCent Intelligence calls them. It's a multifunction device that can be used to scan for holographic projectors and to disrupt holograms before they can form."

"Should I ping Jeeves to come and take it down?"

"It won't have any impact on your demonstration since you aren't using holograms," Libby replied. "The Grenouthian was no doubt worried that you would employ holographic trickery, so the presence of an active jammer can only lend credence to your presentation."

"Thanks, I think." Dorothy turned back to Judith, who was studying the script on her heads-up display. "It's just a Noho. Libby says it's fine."

"I've heard of those, but they're really expensive and EarthCent Intelligence doesn't have room in the budget," Judith said. "Some of the rich aliens carry them all the time on the station just to save themselves from being bothered by interactive holographic ads."

"Here comes my mom and the president, and that's the Grenouthian ambassador with his posse. Libby is going to channel the audio from your subvoc pickup into the local public address system so you don't have to shout. Stick to the script," Dorothy added over her shoulder, as she crawled under one of the folding tables to get out of the booth.

Judith sighed and moved over to the pair of tables that formed the interior barrier with the adjacent booth. One of the tables had been replaced by a shorter version to make an opening into a space where dozens of musical instruments were on display. The saleswomen from the Drazen open world had agreed to allow SBJ Fashions to use their booth for the duration of the show in return for a pair of dancing shoes and a tube dress. Marilla was waiting first in line, though she carried nothing more than a small purse.

"Not sure I approve of all this magic business," the Grenouthian ambassador said to the EarthCent president as he bellied up to a table on the reserved side of the booth. "Bad precedent, letting Terragram mages run around the station enchanting things."

"I understand that Baa works exclusively for SBJ Fashions," the president replied smoothly. "She doesn't enchant objects willy-nilly. It's all done for money."

"Ah, that's different, then. Is this your daughter, Ambassador McAllister?"

"Dorothy," the fashion designer spoke up before her mother could reply. "Thank you for coming to our demonstration. We can start whenever you're ready."

The Grenouthian ambassador puffed out his chest and took his time staring down all of the other waiting bunnies to establish dominance. Then he said, "You may proceed."

Judith began reading from her script as soon as she received Dorothy's signal. "Welcome to our demonstration on reimagining the possible. SBJ Fashions is the leading provider of haute couture bags-of-holding for the rapidly growing role-playing market under our Baa's Bags brand, and we've identified a new opportunity in the area of custom noodle weapons with bespoke enchantments. We understand that important businessmen such as yourselves are unlikely to have the time to participate in LARPs, so we decided to bring the magic out into the real world to demonstrate it for you."

Marilla responded to the cue phrase by stalking out into the center of the square formed by the four pairs of long folding tables. She held up her unique six-feather bag pinched between her thumb and forefinger and turned slowly like a ring girl displaying the round-card at a cage fighting match. Then she reached in the purse and pulled out a long sword.

"Big deal," one of the Grenouthians commented immediately. "I've seen magicians swallow poleaxes."

"Could you assist?" the Horten girl asked Judith. The EarthCent intelligence trainer came over and held the small bag while Marilla plunged one of her arms in it up to the shoulder, eliciting a gasp from the audience. Then, with an obvious effort, she drew out a battle axe that couldn't have possibly fit inside. Using both hands, she brought it over to the table in front of the Grenouthian ambassador. He took it from her and his eyes went wide at the heavy weight.

"Folding space and reducing mass are the earmarks of Baa's Bags in LARPing," Judith read from her script, while Marilla stuffed the axe and her sword back into the little purse, which somehow made even more of an impression than pulling them out. "Baa's Bags also preserve the contents if the player is killed in the game, but a mage's true skill is measured by the enchantment of weapons, as our models will now demonstrate."

Marilla returned to the neighboring booth, and Samuel and Vivian came out, resplendent in their fashionable LARPing costumes. The two young people saluted each other with their swords.

"The male model is the new hire at the Vergallian embassy," the Grenouthian cultural attaché told his ambassador. "The female works for Drazen Intelligence. Something fishy is going on here."

"That's my son and his girlfriend," Kelly told them. "The Open University gave them co-op jobs with aliens."

"I knew that," the cultural attaché said immediately, but the Grenouthian ambassador gave him a scowl.

Judith stepped back into the corner of the booth to be out of the way. The young duelists circled each other for a minute, probing each other's defenses with feints before Vivian sprang to the attack. After trading a series of lightning thrusts and parries, the girl pretended to stumble, then took prompt advantage of Samuel's hesitation to slash his leg with the saber. The noodle weapon went soft the moment it made contact, and then re-formed as the two duelists separated.

"So what," one of the observers commented. "That's what all noodle weapons do."

Samuel retreated all the way to one corner of the booth while Vivian took the opposing corner. Then he brandished the sword and declared, "Winged Feet," and leapt toward the girl.

"Angel's Breath," Vivian cried in response as she jumped to meet his attack. They exchanged a flurry of strikes and counter-strikes as they floated past each other, hanging in the air like immersive actors suspended by invisible wires.

A number of the Grenouthians whipped out hand-held devices and began scanning the booth and the models for signs of magnetic fields or other technological means to explain the levitation, but their displays came back blank.

"Enchanted weapons can bestow on their wielders magical abilities," Judith read, and the duelists leapt into the air again, trading blows as they passed each other like knights at a joust. "The magic is invoked by non-mages through the use of voice commands, as we just saw with Vivian and Samuel."

The bunnies exploded in a round of belly patting as the two models landed lightly on their feet. Once again, they saluted each other with their swords, and then exited into the musical instruments booth.

"Pretty impressive, don't you think?" the EarthCent president prompted the Grenouthian ambassador. "I understand that there's a tremendous market opportunity for enchanted objects in role playing, but the prices demanded by your distributors for commodity noodle weapons are prohibitive."

"You overestimate my influence if you think I can say a few words and lower the pricing," the ambassador replied disingenuously. "Of course, I would be happy to make a few inquiries if it would help Ambassador McAllister's daughter and Associate Ambassador Cohan's wife."

"You've seen right through us, Ambassador," the president said, giving the Grenouthian cultural attaché a nod at the same time. "I'm sure that means you're also aware of the pressure I'm under to provide more employment opportunities for my people, especially in the entertainment field."

"Not very subtle, but I like a leader who knows how to talk business. What are you asking?"

"It seems to me that the simplest solution would be for the family that owns the Grenouthian manufacturing rights to the noodle molecule to license the process to a human group. However, it appears that there's a contract in place requiring that noodle weapons shown in professional LARPing broadcasts be manufactured on one of your planets."

"So you want us to allow Humans to move to one of our open worlds and establish a sovereign community." The Grenouthian ambassador regarded the president thoughtfully. "How much do you know about theme parks?"

"If I can have your attention," Judith announced. "Our next demonstration will illustrate the use of one of the more popular magical buffs used today in competitive LARPing. I give you Thomas and Chance."

The two artificial people strode through the opening into the booth, saluted with their swords, and then immediately attacked each other, moving faster than humanly possible. They were evenly matched and had practiced with each other so frequently that minutes went by without either of them penetrating the defenses of the other.

"Don't see what's so special about artificial people fighting each other," one of the bunnies muttered. "Sure, they're quick, but I'd be quick too if I was built from the latest technology."

Thomas and Chance disengaged and retreated to the corners of the make-shift dueling square. "That was just regular speed, folks," Judith announced. "Now let's see what enchanted weapons can do for our models."

"Faster," Thomas and Chance declared simultaneously, and then they were at each other in a blur of motion.

"How did Baa work an enchantment that could do this?" the Grenouthian ambassador demanded. "It can't be time dilation—the Stryx would never allow that."

"My understanding is that it's magic," the president of EarthCent replied. "Just like recreating Earth's history in theme parks on worlds hundreds of light years away. I understand your concerns with our limited facilities for hosting advanced species who visit our planet on your documentary tours, but I'm sure you know that 'Earth' is a registered trademark in tunnel network space. Of course,

I'm as open to entertaining your proposal as an open world is to immigration."

"I hear you loud and clear. So, we allow a Human community to set up manufacturing noodle weapons on one of our open worlds, either licensing the technology or supplying the molecular feedstock at wholesale, and you will authorize six Earth-branded theme parks on worlds of our choosing."

"Two theme parks, and they have to employ one hundred percent humans for reenactments."

"Four, and I'll go fifty percent. Where do you expect us to find enough Humans capable of staging an ancient battle with swords and axes? There are hordes of out-of-work Drazen and Horten actors just begging for that kind of work. With wigs and a little body paint, you'd never know they aren't the genuine article. Nobody is going to notice a few extra thumbs."

"Three worlds, and ninety percent humans, with a possible waiver for trained combatants, but no speaking parts."

"He got her!" a bunny shouted excitedly.

"They got each other," another said, staring down at a small screen. "I recorded it so I could replay in slow motion. See?"

Thomas and Chance exited the ring to enthusiastic applause and were replaced by Affie and Flazint while the EarthCent president and the Grenouthian ambassador continued to haggle over their newly defined RPoH, or Required Percentage of Humans. Just as they seemed to reach a compromise at seventy percent, the president threw a wrench in the works by insisting on a theme park hiatus if the volume of tourists taking documentary tours to Earth fell below the current level.

"He's good," Kelly whispered to her daughter. "I never would have thought of that."

"Did we get our noodle weapons supply?" Dorothy asked. "I lost track of the deal when they started bandying numbers back and forth."

"It sounded to me like everybody is getting what they wanted. Daniel will be happy to see humans allowed on a Grenouthian open world, you'll get your noodle stuff, and Hildy will get more publicity for Earth."

"It takes all types of players to raid a dungeon," Judith announced, drawing attention back to the ring where Affie and Flazint were now ready, "and not all of them duel with matching weapons."

Dorothy's two friends stood at opposite corners of the little square, Flazint with her bow and Affie with her rapier. At a sign from Judith, the Frunge girl nocked an arrow and drew the bowstring. The Vergallian girl displayed her lightning reactions by jumping to the side the moment the arrow was released, and Thomas leaned over the table from the musical instruments booth and snatched it out of the air. Flazint tried to deflect Affie's thrust with her belt dagger, but the noodle rapier slipped passed her guard and wilted like a thick strand of overcooked spaghetti when it made contact with her stomach.

"And that's the usual result when an archer misses an opponent at close range, but what happens if the weapons are enchanted?" Judith asked as the two models returned to their respective corners.

"Crystal Shield!" Affie cried as the Frunge girl nocked a fresh noodle arrow.

"Wise Bow," Flazint invoked, and let fly.

Again, the Vergallian girl leapt to the side, but this time the arrow curved in its flight like a guided missile to meet her. A golden bubble formed around Affie and absorbed the arrow without harm. The shield carried a two-second delay during which time the user couldn't move, and Flazint rushed to nock another arrow.

This time the archer intentionally aimed out over the crowd before firing and then turned back to meet Affie's charge. The arrow reversed course and returned to catch the Vergallian from behind just as she reached Flazint, again triggering the golden glow and giving the Frunge girl two seconds to duck out of the way and pull another arrow from her quiver.

"How are we going to split up our commission in these projects?" the Grenouthian ambassador asked the president. "Since there are three theme parks and only one noodle weapons factory, I'm thinking seventy-five, twenty-five."

"Seventy-five for me?"

"Very funny."

"The way I see it, the documentary tours to Earth offset the theme parks, so it's one-to-one, plus we have the open world community, so two-to-one."

"Two for me?"

"You should be on stage," the president replied.

"Sixty-forty, and I'm only offering that much because I like your style.

"Fifty-five, forty-five, and you start hiring human tour guides."

"But they don't speak any of the important languages," the Grenouthian protested.

The negotiation was interrupted by a deafening drumming sound as the other bunnies in attendance thumped their bellies in appreciation of the duel's conclusion. Affie and Flazint took their leave from the improvised ring, the Frunge girl carrying an empty quiver.

"Let me out there," Baa hissed at Judith, who was blocking the way into the booth. "Listen to that applause. They want me."

"I promised Dorothy to stick to the script, and everybody knows that the enchanter comes out last," the ringmaster said stubbornly. "Why are you always like this at our fashion shows?"

"Because I'm right."

"Excuse me, coming through," Jorb said, squeezing gingerly around the Terragram mage. "Let's go, Tzachan."

"I don't know why I'm playing a wizard," the Frunge complained. "I'm just an honest attorney."

Following the pattern of the models who had gone before them, the two men went to opposite corners while Judith found her place in the script.

"Enchanted weapons are one thing in role-playing, casting spells is another. What defense can a player mount against the magic of a hedge wizard?"

"Did Judith just make fun of Tzachan's hair vines?" Kelly asked her daughter.

"It's a role-playing term. It just means he never went to wizard academy or something."

Tzachan brandished a staff topped with a large glowing crystal, and he pointed one hand at the Drazen and began reciting a spell. Jorb immediately raised his axe and cried, "Peaceful Rest." All around the Drazen martial artist, everybody suddenly found themselves compelled to stretch out on the deck and go to sleep. The last thing Kelly remembered was making a pillow of one of the Grenouthian ambassador's furry legs. Jorb looked puzzled for a moment, yawned, and then collapsed himself.

A loud "Oops," was heard from the musical instruments booth. "Not my fault," Baa called in the general direction of the ceiling.

There was a popping noise as Jeeves terminated his supersonic flight and hovered above the booth. The Stryx spun three hundred and sixty degrees to survey the damage. "Knocked out everybody in the room," he commented. "Where were you with that trick a couple of days ago when Dorothy was spending all of my money?"

"If Gryph will let me tap into the grid, I can wake them all up," Baa offered. "It really was an honest mistake."

"Hold on," Jeeves said, swooping down to the booth directly across from the one taken by SBJ Fashions. "What do we have here?"

"You tell me. I can't see what you're doing."

"It's our friend Ajalah, the Vergallian secret agent. If I'm not mistaken, that's a very illegal piece of technology she's holding in her hand."

"Let me see," Baa said, leaping over a mound of slumbering bunnies. "I thought Alpha wave jammers were banned on Stryx stations. How much do you want to bet that she was trying to get the bunnies all riled up so they'd storm the booth and wreck any deal for new open worlds?"

"No bet. And while it's forbidden to use brainwave jammers, they can be imported in small quantities for legitimate research and development purposes," Jeeves said, taking the device in his pincer and crushing it.

"You know, you could have sold that for a lot more than whatever Dorothy could possibly have spent on fabric."

"Sometimes we all have to follow orders. Now I'm going to ship naughty Ajalah back to Vergallian space on a slow recycling barge. Go ahead and wake everybody up when I'm gone."

"So you owe me, right?"

"How do you figure that?"

"If my enchanted axe hadn't put everybody to sleep, the Vergallian would have blown your deal for noodle weapons, not to mention the political fallout."

"I suppose if you agreed to handle all of the complaints that are going to arise from everybody who was present, I could see my way—"

"Never mind," Baa interrupted. "Get out of here so I can start waking them up."

"Cleanup on aisle one," Jeeves declared cheerfully, and hoisting Ajalah, headed for the travel concourse.

Nineteen

The doorman at the Vergallian embassy looked Samuel up and down and shook his head in dismay. "Underdressed, as usual."

"What do you mean?" the co-op student demanded. "I'm going to clean out the back storeroom for the ambassador so she can pick out what else she wants to send to my mom's tag sale."

"Change of plans. Ball starts in twenty minutes."

Before Samuel could make up his mind whether to run home and change or to wear one of the embassy-supplied suits, Aabina came up behind him and pushed him through the doors.

"Get in there. I'm counting on you to give me a break from dancing with old men all night."

"Are you just getting off work?" Samuel asked the Vergallian ambassador's daughter. "I didn't realize it was that late on my mom's clock."

"That's because you've adjusted to my mom's clock, where every day is the same length," Aabina replied. Then she pointed at her ear before adding, "She wants you to stop in her office. I've got to get changed and do my hair so I'll see you on the dance floor."

Samuel bit back his reflexive response that her hair was already perfect and made his way to the ambassador's office. The doors slid open at his approach, and even though she was engaged in a holographic conference, Aainda waved him in.

"I triple checked with the Imperial College of Law and the regulations are absolutely clear on this point," an older woman in the hologram was saying. "Ambassadors have ten cycles to arrange for shipment of personal items from an embassy after the end of their term. Anything remaining behind after that time may be disposed of as the replacement ambassador sees fit."

"Thank you, Counselor," the ambassador said. "Give my best to my sister and her girls, and remind them I expect my planet to still be in one piece when I return."

"As you wish, Your Highness." The hologram winked out, and Aainda favored her co-op student with a brilliant smile.

"Are you planning on leaving Union Station?" Samuel asked.

"I just wanted to make sure about my legal position in selling the items left behind by prior ambassadors. As you heard, it turns out I can dispose of it all as I wish. I hope your mother won't feel like we're taking advantage."

"Don't worry. The Dollnicks and the Grenouthians have been dropping off more and more every day. My dad thinks it's funny, because the way he sees it, the whole point of holding a tag sale is to save having to move the stuff yourself."

"We all worry about rumors. Does a tag sale mean that an embassy is closing or that the ambassador has financial difficulties? Then you have to consider the practical aspects. Many of us live in our embassies and holding a sale on the premises isn't feasible. Your family's situation is somewhat unique. Ambassadors who live in private quarters have limited space and no 'outside' like your parents have managed by living in a ship parked in a hold."

"I hadn't thought of that. Ambassador Czeros has a yard, sort of, but it's not easy to find his house, and his ancestors are always complaining."

"Hurry up and get changed," Aainda said. "We're holding a celebration ball and the most influential Vergallians on Union Station will be here."

"What's the occasion?"

"I received a priority message from the Imperial Intelligence service requesting we get somebody to clean out Ajalah's quarters and send all of her things back to Vergallian space. It appears that she was suddenly recalled."

Samuel felt like a pile of second-hand furniture had been removed from his shoulders and he practically danced his way to the storage room that he'd been using as a walk-in closet. As he changed for the ball, there was a distinct 'ding' in his ear, and the name "Vivian" appeared on his heads-up display.

"Accept," he subvoced. "What's up?"

"Are you getting ready for bed?"

"I just got to work and it looks like a long one."

"Don't forget you have the Flower tour."

"I'm going straight to meet Jorb when I finish here. The trade show is over, so when I get back from Flower, I can sleep for a week."

"As long as you're keeping your priorities straight," the girl replied after a long pause. "I just had a thirteen-hour day with the Drazens so I'm off to bed."

"Talk to you later," Samuel said, pulling on the dress pants and tucking in the shirt before doing the magnetic seal on the waistband. Then he rushed through the bowtie, shrugged on the jacket with its long tails, and headed for the embassy ballroom.

The orchestra was already playing, and as usual, there were more upper-caste women than men in attendance. The co-op worked his way through the crowd until he caught the ambassador's eye, and she nodded him in the direction of an elderly Fleet diplomat who never missed a ball. Samuel squared his shoulders, approached the dowager, and requested her company for the first dance.

Four hours later, just as the orchestra struck up the traditional closing instrumental, Aabina rescued the EarthCent ambassador's son from a visiting Vergallian businesswoman who had already claimed four dances.

"I think I wore out another pair of shoes," Samuel groaned through his professional smile. "If it wasn't for the soft-armor toes, that visiting agricultural minister would have poked a hole in my foot with her heel."

"I heard her gushing to mom over what a wonderful dancer you are. Personally, I wish everybody danced with their spouses."

"She's married?"

"And her husband is handy, if you know what I mean."

"He groped you?"

"Nothing that would show on surveillance video—it's more about the intent of the hand than the location. A woman can tell. Your last partner was pushing the limits of good taste herself."

"I'm glad I didn't know," Samuel said. "Is your convention officially over? I closed our booth today."

"Yes, though most of the attendees are staying an extra day to visit Flower. There's even talk of her hosting the next CoSHC conference and trade show. She certainly has the available capacity."

"I've got to run and meet Jorb as soon as the orchestra stops playing. Did you know he wants to set up a dojo on Flower?"

"I heard he was chasing after a certain choir mistress."

"Maybe, but he needs a job as well. Vivian hooked him up with Drazen Intelligence so he can earn some steady income while he's building up the dojo."

"That makes sense. The Vergallian agent on Flower is actually a distant cousin of mine, and from what I can tell, she enjoys her cover job so much that she would stay there even if she wasn't double dipping."

"What does she do?"

"She's running a finishing school for young ladies. Poise, flower arrangement, hand-to-hand combat. Hey, maybe she can give Jorb some work."

"He's good at taking falls, but I imagine that playing the attacker and getting beaten up by teenage girls every day could get old after a while," Samuel said as the music came to the end. He and Aabina exchanged formal bows, and then the EarthCent ambassador's son was off to the storeroom to change back into his regular clothes to meet Jorb.

Samuel found the Drazen on the travel concourse, sitting on a large backpack with an axe strapped to the outside. The two immediately boarded one of Flower's giant shuttles, and luckily for them, it was almost at capacity and departed within minutes.

"Wake up," the Drazen said, poking Samuel with his tentacle after Flower's shuttle docked. "How can you fall asleep during a fifteen-minute trip?"

"Long day. Let me see if I can still reach the ship's AI over my implant. Flower?"

"Young McAllister. Are you here as a Human or a Vergallian?"

"You heard about that?"

"Technically, Lynx heard about it, but I may have been listening in."

"I'm off the clock so I'm here as me," Samuel subvoced. "I brought Jorb to see—"

"—about getting him space to open a dojo so he can woo my pretty Drazen choir mistress," Flower interrupted. "I've already picked out a room for him, but I'll let the captain show it to you so he can feel like he's involved. I understand that your friend has accepted a field internship with Drazen Intelligence, and Woojin makes a point of personally greeting all of the alien spies who come aboard. I alerted him to your presence on my shuttle when you left Union Station so he's waiting at the front ramp."

"Thanks," Samuel said out loud, and gave Jorb a thumbs up. "We're meeting the captain and he'll get you squared away. It sounds like he knows about your second job."

"I'm not sure what Drazen Intelligence really expects from me, but apparently the agent I'm replacing made so much money in his cover job selling women's clothes in Flower's bazaar that he quit to open a boutique."

"Well, I'm sure you'll get instructions. We probably shouldn't talk about it anyway since our people aren't on great terms."

"We cooperate on intelligence at the highest level," Jorb protested. "Vivian couldn't be working for us otherwise."

"I didn't mean me-me, I meant the Vergallian me. In fact, I may have already slipped and mentioned to Aabina that you were applying for an intelligence agent slot. I'm kind of sleep-deprived."

"Which is probably why you forgot that Aabina works for EarthCent, so it's all in the family," the Drazen reminded him. "Wow! What a cool uniform."

"Captain Pyun," the EarthCent ambassador's son formally greeted his father's oldest friend while performing a crisp salute. "Permission to come aboard."

"Permission granted," Woojin replied, returning the salute in the spirit in which it was offered. "I see Joe taught you our traditions from the mercenaries but we don't stand on formalities here. You know the only reason I wear the uniform is to get Flower to acknowledge my authority."

"If it was my uniform, I'd wear it all the time," the Drazen said.

"And you must be Jorb," Woojin said, offering a firm handshake. "I'm going to miss talking with your predecessor, and my wife did all of her clothes shopping with him. He was a great help to me in keeping all of the other alien spies in line."

"I'll do what I can, Captain, but I'm brand new to this, so I doubt they'll pay me much mind."

"Bring your axe to the meetings. That will get their attention."

"We have regular meetings with the other intelligence agents?"

"Most of the aliens on board have families, but the spies are on their own so they tend to eat in a small cafeteria Flower set aside for non-humans. I'll take you to your quarters and then bring you there. If you're willing to sit around and drink coffee for a day, you'll meet most of your colleagues."

"Will you be visiting Mac's Bones, Captain?" Samuel asked. "I'm taking the next shuttle back because I'm falling asleep on my feet, but I'm sure my dad is waiting to see you."

"Lynx is busy going through our quarters looking for things to bring to the tag sale as we speak. We'll be there in a few hours."

"Get back on the shuttle before it returns for another load, Sam," Jorb suggested. "You really do look tired. We'll catch up the next time Flower stops at Union Station."

"Take care of yourself, Jorb," Samuel said. "See you tomorrow, Captain." He went back aboard the shuttle and passed out in a seat.

Alerted by Flower that the EarthCent ambassador's son had slept through three round trips without disembarking from her shuttle, Libby dispatched Jeeves to claim him. The young Stryx used a suspensor field to carry Samuel home, by which time it was already six in the morning and Joe was up making coffee.

"Cleanup on aisle two," Jeeves announced, setting his load down on the couch.

"Where did you find him?" Joe asked.

"Riding back and forth to Flower on her shuttle. If it was anybody else, she would have charged him for three round trips."

"I'm tempted to wake him up to ask how it—Dring! Welcome back."

"And glad to be back," the Maker said, showing his blunt teeth. "Thank you for holding my space while I was gone."

"Gryph would evict me if I didn't. How was the trip?"

"You know what they say about gravity wave surfing. It always gets you where you want to go if you can just live long enough. I started back five months ago."

"Ugh!" Samuel cried, sitting bolt upright on the couch. "Stop that, Beowulf."

"You know the rules," Joe said. "You sleep on his couch, he gets to lick you awake."

"I must have been sleepwalking when I came home because I don't remember anything. Welcome back, Dring."

"And it's a pleasure to see you again, young McAllister. It's strange to think that being away for six months I missed two and a half percent of your life to date. Speaking of which, isn't this the big night?"

"It's morning," Samuel said, reflexively checking his implant. "Mom is planning a party for after the tag sale, but she's going to change it to a welcome home party as soon as she sees you."

"I meant your proposal to Vivian. Did I get the date wrong? I normally have an excellent memory for calendars, and I made a mental note of the date when you told me your plans."

"That's right," Joe said. "What did she think of your grandmother's ring?"

Samuel's face turned pale. "I am so dead."

"You forgot to propose? I better loan you my old body armor."

"I don't understand," Dring said. "You have another hour. Are all of your clocks running fast?"

Samuel stared at the Maker, uncomprehending.

"Dring's right," Joe exclaimed when the solution dawned on him. "Technically, it's still last night on Union Station. Universal Human Time doesn't officially take effect for another hour. That's the reason your mom is giving out for throwing a party after the tag sale, to celebrate the days returning to normal."

"Still last night?" Samuel repeated, groggy from lack of sleep.

"I know you read all of my old Jules Verne novels when you were a kid. It's like 'Around the World in Eighty Days,' and you've crossed the international date line, except this one is only good for seven hours. You've got fifty minutes until we make the jump from midnight to seven o'clock in the morning, but you better take a shower and change first. Besides, Vivian's family may still be sleeping."

"Shower," the young man repeated, and ran for the bathroom.

"Why didn't you tell him?" Dring asked Jeeves.

"I was going to wait another half an hour so he could drink a coffee. He's going to need his wits about him."

"Let me whip you up a vegetable smoothie," Joe offered the Maker. "Mike and Fenna have been harvesting your garden and sharing the produce around. It will just take me a few minutes."

By the time Samuel rushed out of the ice harvester, clutching a small box in one hand, Paul had arrived and was bringing Dring up to date on the rental business. The tardy lover sprinted out of Mac's Bones to the nearest lift tube, practically shouted, "Vivian's", and slid into the corner when the capsule took off with unusually strong acceleration. When the doors opened less than a minute later, he cursed himself for not taking his mother's advice and writing something down beforehand, and then he ran all the way to the Oxford's apartment. The door opened just as he arrived.

"Morning, Sam," Vivian's twin brother said. "I'm taking the dog for a walk if you want to come along. You don't want to go in there."

"I do. I have to. Is she mad?"

"Let's just say when I told her 'Happy Birthday' this morning, she tried to decapitate me with her noodle sword."

"It's not your birthday for another twenty minutes. We haven't switched to UHT yet."

"If you say so. Good luck convincing her of that."

Samuel shook hands with Jonah and received a pat on the shoulder from the soon-to-be eighteen-year-old before entering the apartment. Blythe and Clive were seated at the breakfast table, and both looked up in surprise when the EarthCent ambassador's son entered.

"This might not be a great time," Clive told him. "Viv's not in the best mood."

"It's a mistake," Samuel insisted. "I still have nineteen minutes. Can I just talk to her?"

"I told her she was being silly getting so excited about the exact date to start with, but you know how Vivian is," Blythe said. "She must know you've been working crazy hours for the Vergallians because the Drazens had her watching you enough times. Just knock before you go in."

Samuel started briskly for Vivian's room, though his steps grew slower as he approached her door. He almost subvoced Libby for help on proposals, but then all of his years of dancing, dueling, and going to school with the girl flashed before his eyes, and he felt a surge of confidence. It lasted for exactly seven seconds, which was the amount of time it took Vivian to open the door and glare at him. He dropped to one knee, still in the hall, and held up the jeweler's box.

"What's that?" she growled.

"My grandmother's engagement ring. She wanted you to have it."

"You're proposing for your grandmother?"

"No. I'm proposing for me. I know that I almost messed up, but Dring pointed out that it's still the day before your birthday, or it will be for another eleven minutes. I don't know why you care about that anyway, but I ran all of the way here because if you do care about something, I have to care about it too."

"And?"

"And I've known you since you were a baby, and we danced together for almost ten thousand hours—"

"You were counting?" Vivian demanded, her voice rising.

"Not like that. It's an estimate. I look forward to seeing you every day, even when you have me under surveillance for the Drazens, and you've always said that we'd end up together and—what?" Samuel broke off, seeing that her face was just getting scarier.

"You tell me."

"I don't know what to tell you, Vivian. I don't even know how I got home from Flower. I don't believe that you're really angry at me about dancing with Aabina, and, uh, Ailia, or for that time I was lying next to Marilla to get her sleeve unstuck. I've been thinking about this moment ever since you said you wanted a proposal the day before your eighteenth birthday, but I ignored my mom when she said I should write out what I was going to say beforehand, and I'm sleep deprived, and I love you—"

"You love me?" she interrupted.

"Yes, I love you," Samuel half-shouted, feeling that he had finally hit on the magic formula. "I love you, I love you, I love you. Take the ring."

"You didn't have to shout," Vivian said, accepting the box. To her suitor's surprise, her next words came out in a sob. "Do you know how long I've been waiting to hear you say that you love me out loud? Was it really that hard?"

"If it's so easy, how come you never said it to me?"

"I didn't want to put any more pressure on you. It's not like you didn't know I've always loved you."

"Oh," Samuel said, realizing that was true. "Sorry. Can I come in now?"

After the door closed behind the young lovers, Clive commented to his wife, "It's a good thing Jonah took the dog for a walk or that scene might have put him off of marriage forever."

Twenty

"How much is this vase?" a young woman asked Kelly.

"Is there a sticker on the bottom?"

"Yes, but I can't make out the amount."

"That looks like Dollnick script to me. Libby?" Kelly subvoced, flipping the vase upside down and inadvertently dumping ashes all over the deck. "Can you see the price on this vase through your security imaging?"

"It's an urn, and the tag reads, 'Please hold for Ambassador Brule's family.' The ambassador served on Union Station approximately forty thousand years ago."

"So it's too late to send it back. Does ten creds sound— Hey, where are you going?" Kelly called after the woman, who was making her way rapidly towards the exit from Mac's Bones. "Oh, well. Maybe I can use it for dried flowers."

"Or you could scrape up the ashes and return the urn to Ambassador Crute," Libby offered an alternative. "He just entered the hold, along with the Horten and Grenouthian ambassadors."

"Cleanup on aisle three," Jeeves muttered, gently pushing Kelly out of the way. He took the urn in his pincer and employed some sort of field manipulation to scoop up the ashes and dump them back in the glazed ceramic container. "A little ionization in the right quantity works miracles with dust."

"Is that really all that remains of Ambassador Brule?" Kelly asked.

"His last feast," the young Stryx explained. "The Dollnicks traditionally celebrate funerals with a banquet and then they burn all of the leftovers to feed the departed soul while it waits for reincarnation. I wrote a detailed section about this practice in the second edition of *Dollnicks For Humans*. I thought it was on the required reading list for EarthCent diplomats."

"I'll pick up a copy," Kelly promised. "Dorothy is really enjoying your book about the Frunge."

"I've watched her read and she's skimming," Jeeves said dismissively, handing the urn back to the ambassador. "Did my old games sell?"

"A collector paid five hundred creds for the lot. Paul said that it was an excellent price."

"Enough to cover a quarter of your daughter's latest fabric purchase. I'll be selling my accessory limbs by the time she's through."

"But I thought that SBJ Fashions just landed a monopoly on the enchanted noodle business. I know that after we all woke up on the trade show floor, the president closed a deal with the bunnies to allow our first sovereign community on one of the Grenouthian open worlds."

"Thanks for reminding me," Jeeves said, turning towards the ice harvester. "I need to pick up Samuel's sword and have Baa remove the enchantment."

"Don't tell him I had anything to do with that," Kelly called after the Stryx. "Samuel loved being able to fly. And feel free to wake him up if he's in there. I haven't seen him all day."

"Ambassador," Crute greeted her. "How did my items sell?"

"You did very well, but I'm returning this," she said, handing the urn to the Dollnick ambassador. "Don't turn it upside down!"

"I have a hand under the mouth. Did you think my lower set of arms is just for show?" He squinted at the tag. "Oops. I wonder how a funeral urn got mixed up in the tag sale lot."

"Probably the same way my staff accidentally dropped off all of the contents of our embassy's paint closet," Ortha said. "Did any of it sell? I don't see much left on the tables in our section."

"I think Joe found a few cans of enamel he could use," Kelly told the Horten ambassador. "Libby has been keeping a running total for everybody and you only owe her twenty creds."

"I owe the Stryx librarian? How did that happen?"

"Some of the larger cans from your paint closet turned out to be hazardous waste and she had to send a couple of maintenance bots to take them for incineration. Still, you came out way ahead of where you'd be if you hadn't sold everything else to cover the costs."

"Did you decide to hold onto that sink after all?" Crute asked, pointing at the object that had originally inspired the tag sale.

"Nobody was interested. I told Joe to leave it there and I'll use it as a planter."

"Begonias would be nice," the Vergallian ambassador announced her presence. "Happy Universal Human Time."

"Is that today?" Ortha asked. "What a relief. Mornich has been driving us crazy with creeping schedule changes ever since his girlfriend started working for Joe, I mean, doing primitive outreach work for our Peace Force. I don't understand why you didn't just move your clock forward in one chunk and get it over with."

"All's well that ends well," Kelly said. "I hope the four of you are staying for the picnic. Joe is going to start the grill at any time now."

"I suppose it will give me a chance to see my son for more than two minutes, assuming that his girlfriend is here somewhere," the Horten ambassador grumbled.

"Marilla insisted on coming in on her day off to finish up work on the first restored rental ship. It looks like that business is really going to happen."

"It's five o'clock," the station librarian alerted Kelly over her implant.

"That's it," the EarthCent ambassador declared, clapping her hands. "Can you put me over the public address system, Libby?" She paused a second, and then placing her hands over her ears to block feedback, subvoced. "Attention all shoppers. The tag sale is officially closed. If you see anything left on the tables that you want, the price has dropped to free, but you have to take it with you as you leave."

"Free?" Crute demanded.

"Would you rather pay for disposal?"

"I'll be back in a minute," the Grenouthian ambassador said, hopping off between the tables.

"It's just that you could have tried fifty percent off first," the Dollnick grumbled. "How much did I make?"

"Libby kept track of who gets what and Donna collected all of the money," Kelly told him. "She's around here somewhere."

"I see her," Aainda said. "Why is your embassy manager pulling a Frunge wagon?"

"And why is her husband pushing?" the EarthCent ambassador added. "What's wrong, Stanley? Are the wheels frozen?"

"It's just heavy," Donna replied for her husband. "Next time you have a tag sale, borrow your son-in-law's mini-register so you can accept programmable creds. I swear that the highest value coin I've seen all day was five creds, and at least half of these coins are denominated in centees."

"I suspect your shoppers were taking advantage of the opportunity to clean out their spare-change jars," Aainda observed. "I suppose it's a form of poetic justice since we were all cleaning out our closets."

The Grenouthian ambassador returned with a distended belly, causing Kelly to do a double-take before she remembered that he had a pouch.

"Did you find something you needed?" she asked the giant bunny.

"Free is free," the ambassador replied complacently. "If I can't find a use for these things, I can always bring them to your next tag sale."

"Grill's heating up," Joe announced as he passed the ambassadors on his way to the ice harvester. "Can I take any drink orders?"

"Beer," the four alien ambassadors replied at the same time.

"I'll come with you and help," Stanley offered. "No sense in making two trips."

"Speaking of trips, Dring's back, and he'll be eating with us this evening," Kelly told the ambassadors triumphantly. "Are you finally ready to accept that the whole business about Gryph selling Union Station was just a rumor?"

"We always knew it was a rumor," Crute said. "We just didn't know if there was any substance behind it."

"Our intelligence gave it zero credibility," the Grenouthian ambassador added.

"But when you came to the pre-convention meeting in my embassy, you claimed to know the auction date!" Kelly protested.

"That's after my cultural attaché informed me that you were planning a tag sale," the bunny replied. "I wanted to make sure you'd let me participate."

"Why didn't you just ask?"

"The intelligence assessment suggested that if I approached you about participating in your tag sale without using the rumor to provide cover, you would have tried to extract a diplomatic advantage. It wouldn't have looked good if I let you manipulate me into allowing Humans onto one of our open worlds in return for cleaning the junk out of my embassy."

"But you agreed to that anyway!"

"In return for the right to establish three Human theme parks, with a point of ownership in each going to yours truly for negotiating the deal," the Grenouthian replied. "If you add that income stream to my point in 'Let's Make Friends', I'm going to be the wealthiest ambassador on the tunnel network. As a matter of fact, why don't you donate my share of the tag sale proceeds to your charity for underage contract runaways?"

"I was going to suggest you do the same with my receipts," the Dollnick ambassador chimed in. "I recently found out that I'm in line for the highest business commendation from the Princely Council in return for my surprising discovery that there's money to be made in doing business with Humans. It's a pity there aren't more of you."

"Now it's going to sound like I'm just playing copycat, but of course, you're welcome to donate whatever was earned from my embassy's unclaimed goods," Aainda said. "And I'm thankful for all of the real-world experience you've been giving my daughter. Even if our embassy should host an event as large as your CoSHC convention, Aabina's youth would make it impossible for me to give her the level of responsibility that you and your associate ambassador entrusted to her."

The three alien ambassadors all turned to Ortha, who shrugged. "Your charity is welcome to take responsibility for the twenty creds I owe the station librarian."

"Chastity just pinged me," Donna told Kelly. "The Galactic Free Press is running a front-page article about the source of the Gryph rumor, with a map showing how it spread."

"Dorothy," the EarthCent ambassador called to her daughter, who had appeared to browse the picked-over remains of the tag sale for free treasures. "You can take whatever you want before your father recycles the rest. Can you help me bring a few things out for the picnic and then fetch your tab so we can all read the paper?"

"It's time to feed Margie," the girl replied, beating a hasty retreat. "I'll be back in twenty minutes."

"Why don't you all grab some carbon fiber chairs and make yourselves comfortable," Kelly suggested to the alien ambassadors. "I need to start bringing out the salads and side dishes."

"I can help," Aainda volunteered. "I find Human kitchens strangely fascinating. So many interesting gadgets."

250

"You can make Dring's smoothie if you'd like. As soon as I heard he was back, I chopped up plenty of vegetables. All you have to do is put them in the blender and add fruit juice. And if the three of you want something to keep you busy while you're waiting for your beers," she addressed the other ambassadors, "you could clean off a couple of those folding tables for our guests."

By the time Dorothy fed the baby and returned with her tab, Marilla had finished detailing the first reconditioned rental ship with the help of the Horten ambassador's son. Together with Kevin, the young people appropriated one of the now-cleared tables for their own. The whole Oxford clan showed up next, along with Samuel, who had slept the entire day at their apartment. Aisha led her family over from Baa's former habitat, accompanied by Daniel and Shaina, who had brought Mike and Grace to play with Fenna.

"Where are Thomas and Chance?" Kelly asked Joe after she finished putting out all of the prepared food. "Did you forget to invite them?"

"I told them I would light the grill at five o'clock so they'll probably show up around six," her husband replied. "You know they don't eat unless they're under-cover and passing as humans. Woojin and Lynx are hosting the president and Hildy on Flower, but they'll all stop by for drinks in a few hours. Did you invite Bob and Judith?"

"They should be here anytime. I think I told the other ambassadors to come at five-thirty because I thought we'd have to clean up, but there's hardly anything left to move."

Joe turned down the flames on the grill and gestured at where the Grenouthian, Dollnick, Horten, and Vergallian ambassadors were drinking beer together and laughing at somebody's joke. "Do you remember dragging me around visiting all of their embassies twenty-odd years ago when they finally invited you? They used to call themselves the Natural League or something like that, and they looked down on humans for not developing our own interstellar drive. Even ten years ago they would have been embarrassed to be seen socializing with us. You've done a good job for EarthCent, Kel."

"You make it sound like I'm retiring," the ambassador said. "Are those Vergallian vegan burgers you're going to broil?"

"Samuel brought a case of them back from the trade show because the Empire Convention Center wouldn't let him set up a grill in the booth. I want to use them up on the aliens so they don't sit in the freezer, and they aren't terrible after a few minutes on the fire if you add enough condiments."

"Oh, here come Bob and Judith. I'll see if he knows anything about the Gryph rumor."

"Bork and Czeros just came in as well, so Srythlan is probably shuffling along behind them," Joe said. "You go ahead and socialize and I'll bring over a platter of these burgers as soon as there's enough to go around."

Kelly wasn't surprised to find that the Galactic Free Press reporter was taking advantage of the presence of the alien ambassadors to lobby for future interviews. She stopped by the bar cart on her way over to pick up a bottle of wine for Czeros, and smiled to herself when she realized that the ambassadors had arranged themselves around the folding tables in the same order as they sat in her embassy's conference room.

"So what can you tell us about the Gryph rumor, Bob?" Kelly asked at the first opportunity.

"You haven't seen the article?"

"I'm getting too old to read anything off of my heads-up display."

"Then to make a long story short, the reporter who was covering my beat while I was on special assignment to the CoSHC conference ran the rumor to ground. It started when a dishwasher at the Italian place in the Little Apple asked his boss for a raise. She said something like, 'When Gryph sells Union Station,' and it took off from there."

"How? I don't understand."

"Apparently the dishwasher had a habit of finishing off the glasses of wine and beer that came back in bus pans, so he mistook his boss's meaning and pinged a group of friends to go out and celebrate his raise after work. As soon as he told them what the manager said, they all figured out that she had rejected him, but kids being kids, they turned it into a sort of a meme. For the next few days, the whole bunch of them kept referring to Gryph selling Union Station in every conversation, and since one of them worked as a porter at the travel concourse, it spread across all of the species in less than a week."

"Sounds reasonable to me," the Grenouthian ambassador said. "Does anybody remember the rumor that the Stryx were pulling twenty-cred coins from circulation, and if you didn't bring them all to an official money changer by the end of the day, they'd be valueless?"

"And you believed it?" Kelly asked incredulously.

"Better safe than sorry," Crute told her. "If I recall, it turned out that the rumor was started by a money changer who was short on twenty-cred coins."

"How about the one just a few cycles ago where the Verlocks were developing an inter-galactic wormhole and the Stryx asked them to put it on hold?" Ortha added with a chuckle. "A broker tried to sell me distressed bonds in the supposed project, saying that the hold-up was just temporary."

"That wasn't a rumor," Srythlan informed them, lowering his bulk into a carbon-fiber chair. "The Stryx hinted that we should check the math again. The last I heard, the developers were bringing in a team of Cayl consultants."

"Vergallian vegan burgers," Joe announced, arriving with a large platter. "Get them while they're hot."

"Just like home," Aainda declared, though Kelly noticed that she didn't make any move to take one of the burgers, which were famous for being high in fiber and low in taste. "Would it be considered prying to ask if your son succeeded in his wooing?"

"That's what Donna tells me," Kelly said, squinting across at the table where the young people were sitting. "I'm always the last to hear about anything. She's definitely wearing my mother's engagement ring."

"How many for you, Kel?" Joe asked, holding the platter with one hand and the tongs in the other.

"You know, maybe you should serve the youngsters first. There's some cold quiche in the fridge that I've been meaning to finish off."

"Quiche sounds lovely," the Drazen ambassador said. "Don't forget the hot sauce."

When Kelly got to the top of the ice harvester ramp, she spotted Donna sitting on the couch with a glass of wine, busily rubbing Beowulf's belly.

"He ambushed me," the embassy manager explained. "If I had to live my life over again, the one thing I would change is I would have adopted a dog."

"You would have needed a bigger apartment."

"That's what the park decks are for. You know, it's just sinking in that my granddaughter is engaged to your son. I feel old."

"That's only because you and Blythe both married in your teens and had children right away. I was forty-two when I had Samuel," Kelly said.

"Just imagine if the girls hadn't given you that gift subscription to Eema's dating service all those years ago. It feels like we're closing the circle."

"You know, the more I see Libby operate, the more I'm convinced that she would have stuck me and Joe together one way or another. Jeeves," Kelly addressed the young Stryx who had just emerged from her son's bedroom with a sword. "Have you been in there all this time?"

"I had a minor calibration to do on Samuel's toy robot to keep the multiverse in balance. And congratulations on a successful convention."

"You used to be a troubleshooter for Libby's dating service," Donna said. "Would she have found a way to put Kelly and Joe together if my girls hadn't bought that subscription?"

"Where do you think a ten-year-old and a twelve-year-old heard about Eema's to start with?" Jeeves replied. "If it hadn't panned out, I was ready with a backup plan to—sorry, I can't say."

"Can't say what?" Kelly demanded.

"I've been reminded that my confidentiality agreement with Eema's is still in effect, but if you'd like to place a little wager on who Margie will be marrying—"

"That's enough, Jeeves," Libby interrupted. "Ambassador, your colleagues are asking for you. They've arranged a little surprise."

Kelly headed back outside and did a double-take when she saw all of the alien ambassadors standing like a chorus, the shorter diplomats in the front. Czeros stood a little to the side, holding a spoon as if it was a conductor's baton, and as soon as Kelly appeared, he let out a creaking hum. The seven ambassadors began to sing to the tune of the 'Let's Make Friends' theme song:

You ran Kasil's auction, and gave up the money,
You'll never be rich, but you'll always have friends.
When Baa overdid it, you slept on a bunny,
And sold all our junk, so we'll always be friends.

"I take it they didn't ask for your help with the lyrics," Jeeves commented to his parent.

"No, but I think it's an impressive collaborative effort given the two minutes they invested in composition. Kelly never realized what an impression she made on the advanced species by running that auction for the High Priest and giving up the trillions of creds to resettle the Kasilians. And now that I've stopped watching you every minute, are you going to tell me how you manipulated that restaurant manager into coining a phrase about Gryph selling Union Station?" Libby asked.

"That was easy. I used the holographic advertising system to pose as a customer with a complaint about the takeout, and I shouted at the manager, 'I'll order from here again when Gryph sells Union Station.' Then I sent a hologram of a union organizer into the kitchen to tell the dishwasher he was underpaid. The trick with Humans is that their minds are last-in, first-out queues. It all comes down to putting them together immediately after planting a suggestion."

"There's still a troubleshooting job waiting for you in my dating service if you have free time," the station librarian told her offspring.

"I'll see how my finances are doing at the end of the month," Jeeves replied. "I couldn't afford another employee like Dorothy."

From the Author

The next EarthCent book is a spin-off which takes place on the circuit ship Flower. I started it almost two years ago and kept moving up the time frame so it will fit after the most recent Union Station release. Ideally it will be readable by people who haven't discovered the series. I hope to revisit Union Station soon after (despite the current **Last Night** title) because I'm addicted to the characters, but it's difficult to find new readers for an aging series. Your reviews on early books in the series may help with visibility on Amazon. And if you haven't tried my new AI Diaries series, the first book is **Turing Test**.

About the Author

E. M. Foner lives in Northampton, MA with an imaginary German Shepherd who's been trained to bite bankers. The author welcomes reader comments at e_foner@yahoo.com.

Other books by the author:

Meghan's Dragon

Turing Test

EarthCent Ambassador Series:

Date Night on Union Station

Alien Night on Union Station

High Priest on Union Station

Spy Night on Union Station

Carnival on Union Station

Wanderers on Union Station

Vacation on Union Station

Guest Night on Union Station

Word Night on Union Station

Party Night on Union Station

Review Night on Union Station

Family Night on Union Station

Book Night on Union Station

LARP Night on Union Station